WRITTEN IN RUBERAH

Age of Jeweled Intelligence

P. CHRISTINA GREENAWAY

for you

'Don't be satisfied with stories, how things have gone with others. Unfold your own myth.'

–Rumi

PART ONE
PROMISES MADE

CHAPTER ONE

The Age of Jeweled Intelligence
The Ending

The quake rumbles beneath the palace gardens, and the earth splits in zigzags like forks of lightning. Princess Li'ram leaps onto a thick block of gold still standing solid beneath the sundial. The weight of guilt lies heavy in her heart. She clutches the ruby pendant at her throat and presses it hard against her skin. "I am so sorry, Beloved." She shields her eyes against dust and debris swirling in the air, and gazes at the palace gates.

Da'krah strides into view, his black hair flying in the wind, a crown of emeralds sitting low on his brow. To be loved by Da'krah is the dream Li'ram has harbored since she first laid eyes on him, when he presented her with an emerald birdcage containing two small white birds. "They're lovebirds," he said. "One cannot live without the other."

Da'krah stalks into the gardens and leaps over gouges in the land like an animal roaming its natural habitat. Li'ram's heart lightens a little. Command is Da'krah's nature. He will not mourn the moment; he will take action and lead the people.

Landing on the sundial beside her, Da'krah crushes Li'ram in an exuberant embrace, brushing his cheek against hers. "We have little time. Are you ready to begin the ceremony?"

Li'ram touches her fingers to his brow. "We thought we were doing the right thing for our people, didn't we?"

"We did what they insisted upon. Everyone wanted us to use Rube Force to try and ignite the energies of emeralds. Everyone wanted the riches of the Emerald Kingdom."

"Not everyone. My father—"

"Your father was ill and barely cognizant when I discussed the matter with him. Do not torture yourself over what is done. *The Ending* is here. We must move forward. Plans to save as many people as possible are in effect. We will lead them to a new land and a new life."

Positivity radiates off Da'krah, heady and vibrant like the shimmer in the big emeralds encircling his head. "Make haste, Li'ram. Ask the Goddess for the mating rings."

Da'krah's certainty gives rise to Li'ram's courage, and she lowers her eyes and stills her thoughts, seeking her jeweled vision.

When its soft pink glow shades her world, she glances at her astral disk shimmering on the palm of her hand like a second skin. She taps the disk. Icons flash into view. She touches the symbol for Astral Command and asks to speak to the Goddess of the Ruby Sphere. A wisp of pink mist floats across her palm. She is connected.

"Beloved Goddess ... I ... I ..." Sorrow overshadows her cause, and she stutters and stumbles, feeling regret for having caused the disaster that befalls Ruberah. I—"

"Speak your request, Princess Li'ram."

The directness of the Goddess daunts Li'ram, as it always does, but doubly so today as she longs to seek her forgiveness. Li'ram steels her emotions, knowing the Goddess will grant her but a few moments of her time. "Da'krah, Prince of the Emerald Kingdom, and I wish to be mated for life. Will you grant us the most precious gift of the rings of the Ruby Sphere?"

"It is so."

Tears well in Li'ram's eyes, but she quickly pulls herself together as Da'krah warns her that to weep as they join souls is to weep forever.

His dark, close-set eyes glow as if lit from behind by the moon. Li'ram chokes back sorrow and envisions the children they will have, the beautiful little souls she will cherish and adore.

A swirl of pale pink stars twinkles over the palace, and jeweled circles begin dropping down from the astral sphere of the Ruby Kingdom, thousands of them, whirling in and out of each other like hoops of fire, falling over Li'ram and her lover.

Li'ram speaks her vow. "I, Li'ram, join my life with Da'krah. I pledge to live in love and harmony with him, and to hold kindness in my heart for all who cross my path. So help me, Beloved of the Jeweled Spheres." She slips a band of rubies on Da'krah's finger.

Da'krah pledges the same vow, and places a ring of emeralds on Li'ram's finger. She falls into his arms, wishing they could stay forever, safe inside the fire of rubies. But the jewels retreat to their cosmic home, and a savage wind blows in.

Red-hot lava rolls up to the palace steps, and the marble pillars surrounding the palace crumble. Da'krah grasps Li'ram's hand and they flee, jumping over flames and craters in the earth, running all the way to the harbor. Huge waves crest and flood the quay. Da'krah sweeps Li'ram into his arms and carries her onto the gangplank leading to the royal ship, the *Silver Serpent*. The wooden slats creak and sway beneath his feet.

Da'krah lowers Li'ram onto the deck. "We'll leave soon."

"No! We cannot go until my mother and sister join the ship."

"I'll ready the crew for departure." Da'krah kisses her

cheek and heads toward the bow.

His kiss lingers on Li'ram's skin and seeps into her body like liquid fire. She dismisses shame. She understands the laws of the universe. In one way or another, be it a moment from now or the next life or a thousand lives later, she will meet the consequences of her actions. She draws in a deep breath. She will not wait for the repercussion of the law. She will set her punishment now. Li'ram looks into the tunnels of time through the light of her ruby vision. "For my hand in the destruction of Ruberah, I shall bear guilt and sorrow through many ages and lifetimes to come, and the suffering of all who perish today shall live in my heart." Li'ram calls upon her soul guide to seal this destiny. "River Spirit!"

The winding and slightly rose-tinted waters of the River of Life sweep alongside Li'ram. River Spirit swims up to her, a maiden with golden tresses as long as the river itself. Her huge aqua eyes shine clear as ever, absent of fear or blame. "Do you seek my counsel, beloved princess?"

"I know many are calling upon you today. I will not keep you long."

"This is your time with me, Li'ram."

"I have in every way placed my love for Da'krah above my duties as princess of the realm and High Priestess of Sound. I enticed my darling sister Sol'aria to use her Sun Master gifts to

5

assist Da'krah and myself in our experiment to capture the power of emeralds. My father warned that the human family was not ready to harmonize their consciousness with emeralds. He said it could result in a power beyond our control. I turned a deaf ear to him. The ruin of Ruberah rests on my soul, and I have cast a heavy debt on myself for this."

River Spirit speaks, and her voice rings soft and carries a faint echo like a wind chime. "Your father was the sole dissenter in the matter of this experiment, and yes, his was the voice of wisdom, but all others are complicit in this disaster. You could better serve the human family by healing your troubled heart, as they must heal theirs, rather than inflict a long sentence of suffering upon yourself."

"The only way I dare to love Da'krah now is to know I will suffer for it tomorrow. Do not try to convince me otherwise. My mind is made up."

"Then what do you ask of me?"

"Will you, one day, many ages from now, when I am strong enough to face my guilt and regret, guide me on a sacred future in which I might redeem myself?"

"What task shall you perform to free yourself from suffering?"

Li'ram thinks of the many who will drown today, drown and be taken prisoner in the Black Heart of Dark Master's empire.

"I will enter the Black Heart and rescue someone for the benefit of another. I will take the first step into the underworld alone. Once inside, I will call your name and seek your guidance."

"Do you understand the risk of such a mission?"

"Yes."

"If you smite yourself this way, without compassion, you will lose your ability to think and see with your jeweled intelligence. This will make it very hard for you to believe in me many ages from now when your sacred future comes due."

"I deserve no less. My mind is made up. I seek no further guidance."

"So be it, Li'ram. Your sacred future is written on my river."

River Spirit's image fades away, and Li'ram meets again with the horrors sweeping through the city of Az'Rayelle.

A broiling vortex of flames scatters across the skies. The suffocating smells of ash and sulfur sicken her. Smoke burns her eyes. She blinks and scans the docks for sight of Sol'aria and her mother. Another rumble groans beneath the land, and marble buildings crumble as if made of sand and paste. Li'ram shields her ears against the screams of those being crushed to death beneath the heavy stone.

She looks to the high plains above the city where Mt. Rube

towers into the sky. The land suddenly rips open beneath it, and plumes of crimson light shoot up from its jeweled peak. The mountain sinks at an alarming speed. This tells Li'ram her mother and sister have successfully completed the program to save Rube. Now it will descend straight to the ocean bed where it will rest unharmed, waiting for another time—for a race of people more highly evolved than they. Or for a High Priestess who would not wield her power for her lover's gain.

Li'ram wonders if Sol'aria managed to hide the Scrolls of Knowledge—a written account of how to operate Rube Force. The Scrolls should be entombed in a golden casket inside the mountain. This would be a treacherous task. Sol'aria would have little time to get in and out of the mountain between quakes. All being well, her mother and Sol'aria should arrive at the docks any moment now.

She lowers her eyes to the city. In yet another volcanic eruption, the ruby light paths—their crystal transport system— explode. Splinters of red light shoot into the sky. The Crystal Temple of Science shatters inward, crashing into mounds of gold, glass and marble.

Black dust billows over land and sea. Li'ram squints and searches the tangled mass of bodies racing toward the docks. Some jump onto ships waiting to carry them to other lands. Others stumble, trodden to death by the crowd surging behind them.

The captain of the *Silver Serpent* shouts orders, instructing the sailors to push the ship away from the dock.

"No—stop. My mother … the queen, my sister …" Li'ram runs to the gangway. "Let me off!"

A sailor points out to sea where the golden galleon *Mercy* cuts through the angry waters, her sails full with wind, heading for a distant land. "Queen Leah and Princess Sol'aria will most likely be on her," he says.

Li'ram folds her arms across her aching heart, telling herself that must be true. The golden galleon always came for the brave.

Oarsmen heave. The *Silver Serpent* edges forth, dodging debris and the oars of other ships. Li'ram strains her eyes to the harbor and catches sight of her sister's unmistakable flame-colored hair streaking through the smoke. She screams Sol'aria's name across the water. The girl runs onto the docks, her arms loaded with rolls of parchment tied with ruby ribbons: the Scrolls of Knowledge.

Li'ram's heart sinks. "Dear Goddess, please keep the scrolls safe from the Black Heart." She ruminates on the fate of her fellow citizens should the sacred documents fall into the hands of Dark Master. The ruler of the underworld would forever hunt them, no matter who they might become in the future. Rube is the strongest force on the planet and Dark Master lusts after its power. Though few had assumed the duties of High Priestesses and Sun Masters of Rube, the sound vibrations and light forms needed to activate Rube abide in the soul of everyone born in the Ruby

Kingdom. Her mother said it was but a decision to hear and see them.

Li'ram cups her hands to her mouth and shouts at the top of her voice. "Sol'aria, toss the scrolls in the fire. Burn them!" She yells it over and over, but her words drown in the sounds of wind, sea, and the pain of the dying.

Sol'aria staggers toward a ship still moored to the dock. Li'ram prays to the Goddess with the full force of her soul for her sister to reach safety, but the Goddess does not answer. The ground erupts again, and the cliffs around the harbor crack and crumble and roll down to the docks on a flow of crimson lava.

The oily, dark waters of the underworld spin to the surface of the sea. Small boats crowded with those trying to escape overturn. Li'ram covers her ears against the gasping sounds of the drowning.

The *Silver Serpent* pitches from side to side. Li'ram hugs a mast, wondering where her mother might be. As Queen of the Ruby Isle and devoted servant of the Goddess, she surely escaped on the golden galleon. Scanning the harbor again, Li'ram catches sight of Sol'aria, swimming in the sea. She rounds up those who've jumped off the quay to escape the fire. Then, waving the Scrolls of Knowledge above her head, Sol'aria directs the survivors to form circles around her. She cloaks them with her courage and leads them in a chant to the Goddess.

As Li'ram aches to possess an ounce of her younger sister's valor, Sol'aria's attention falls on the *Silver Serpent*. Li'ram lets go of the mast and crawls across the deck for a closer view of her sister. Clutching a rope, she steadies herself against the waves crashing over the ship. She meets Sol'aria's eyes and together they float outside of time in a soft pink haze. A foreknowledge of their future shimmers in the ether. They sit astride a black horse, galloping across a field that borders a rocky coast.

Sol'aria waves the Scrolls of Knowledge at Li'ram, gesturing for her to join in their song. As Li'ram sings, the chant carries her into the stillness at the core of her being. In that peace, she hears Sol'aria praying to the Goddess. Her sister asks for all who have died to pass quietly into the light of their souls, and for those on the ships leaving the harbor to settle safely in other lands. Sol'aria's prayer awakens the Deva Chorus of the jeweled mountain, and ten thousand voices rise in song. Their sound activates Rube and its dazzling red force spirals up from beneath the ocean and floods the sky.

The dead walk into its glow—thousands upon thousands of them—radiant and happy—led by Leah, their beloved queen. Li'ram weeps as her darling sister Sol'aria takes up the rear, helping those with the greatest needs, all the while smiling back at her.

CHAPTER TWO

Eons later in Ancient Kernow

Tamara follows her father up the stone steps leading to the moor. She guides her bare feet onto the exact places where he trod before her. The energy of his understanding, which he says rests on the soles of his feet, tingles on hers. She senses the beat of his heart, and imagines the light of his soul overlaying hers.

Cool night air cloaks the moor, and the stars sparkle behind low-flying clouds. They step inside a circle of stones, collected and placed by her father. They kneel and kiss the earth, grateful for their place upon its soil. The wind whispers and the aromas of grass, heather, and sea envelop them. They sit crossed-legged and look into the night skies. Tamara follows the beam of her father's gaze, just as she followed his footsteps. Her sight pares into space in the wake of his, beyond the stars and the moon and into the deepest, darkest realms of the universe: into the Cycles of Time.

The history of everything that has ever happened on Earth resides in the Cycles of Time. Shaped like the symbol of infinity, the loops of the past and the future glitter and flow in constant movement. She follows her father's gaze into the present, the black dot where the past crosses over the future.

Her father whispers, offering his service to the universe. Then he speaks to Time, the keeper of the Cycles, asking to be shown what he needs to know to lead his people to their highest destiny.

The ley lines beneath Kernow light up in the Cycles— an intricate pattern of energy fields that twist and swirl with the life force of the planet. A red glow radiates in the line beneath the cliffs where Ruberah was once joined to the earth. Gusts of blue-black vapors from Dark Master's kingdom gather around the area, as they always do, ever watchful for any sign of contact with the lost kingdom. Her father suddenly withdraws his gaze from the Cycles.

"What is it?" Tamara asks. "I did not see or hear anything unusual."

"We are blessed that you will marry soon."

Tamara moves through the crowd in the gathering hall of the cavern where she lives with her parents. Today is her fifteenth birthday and the formal announcement of her betrothal to Prince Ulen of the Northern Isles. Men converse excitedly of how the alliance will strengthen Kernow's hold in the maritime world.

Tamara is congratulated and admired by one and all. Being the fairest nymph in the land, she is, according to her mother, obliged to be grateful for compliments. Tamara yawns, bored to the bone. She'd rather be with her father, absorbing his wisdom. Avoiding a surge of guests bounding down the steps from the moor, she hoists up the silken skirts of her party dress and heads toward her father.

He dominates an area in the center of the hall. His stance is ramrod straight, and a thick braid of chestnut hair dangles between the sharp blades of his shoulders. Young warriors surround him, their heads bent in deference, their hearts eager to emulate his bravery. Tamara quickens her step, holding her gaze high to avoid the eyes of others.

The grip of her mother's hand lands hard on Tamara's arm. "Mingle with our people, Tamara. Conduct yourself as befits a future princess." Her mother's dumpling cheeks flush the color of beets. Her eyes scour Tamara's.

Tamara shakes herself free of her mother's grasp. "I am a woman now. I'll do as I please."

Her mother's pupils widen into big black pools of curiosity. "And what could that be other than to greet your guests?"

Tamara regrets evoking her mother's curiosity, as she plans to escape their cave unseen around midnight. She proffers a fond smile and quickly swoops into a group of women from the village.

Blessings of fertility are showered upon Tamara. She gives gracious responses, although she fails to share in the tittering excitement. Her future mate is not present. An attack upon his territories preempted his visit. Tamara has never met him. Her father arranged their union upon her birth. As Lord Defender of Kernow, her father can, with one breath, repel an armada of enemy ships. She adores him. In recent battles, she has taken her mother's place by his side. Her father requires a field of feminine energy to balance his warrior might. While her mother's energy grows weak, Tamara's increases with the rise of every moon.

Tamara smiles and nods at the women as if intrigued by their conversation, but her thoughts wander. This is the time of night when she usually accompanies her father up to the moor to consult the Cycles of Time. Knowledge redeemed by him comes to Tamara too, by osmosis, but it didn't last night. When she asked him about it, he said if she didn't intuit the knowledge then she was not meant to know it. He spoke with finality, and Tamara knew better than to pursue the matter further. Upon marriage, she will assist Prince Ulen as he consults the Cycles of Time. It is her dowry—the worth her father has invested in her. But for this duty, she might refuse to wed Ulen. Tamara is in every way better suited to be a warrior leader than a princess consort.

"Tamara!"

Fingers snap before her, and Mawden Trelisk, her mother's closest friend, thrusts her face up close to Tamara's.

"Imagine … a nymph living above ground in a castle. I wouldn't say no to Prince Ulen myself. You must be ever so enchanted by it all."

Mawden's eyes search Tamara's. Tamara emits her most enthusiastic smile—spreading her cheeks so wide they almost scrape her ear lobes. Mawden takes a step back but Tamara keeps beaming. Mawden is a tricky old woman, and should Tamara look anything less than exuberant about her wedding, she will report it to her mother, spinning it into a tale worthy of a drama at the annual Festival of Words and Warriors.

"Aye, 'tis right grand," chimes in Gretchen Smythe. "Don't 'e be 'appy, Tamara?"

Gretchen Smythe, mistress of needle arts, beams at

Tamara, which is quite a feat, as her overbite all but obscures her bottom lip. As a child Tamara used to mimic Gretchen. She ground her teeth over her lower lip until she drew blood. Then she parted her mouth to its narrowest opening, flicked her tongue out, quick as a snake, and licked the blood. The iron-like taste lingered in her gullet, telling her about a wonderful strength that slept inside her, curled up like a river. Tamara never had much time to speculate on that, as her mother invariably caught her grinding and licking, and would clout her about the ears, warning her to stop lest the wind change and she be stuck forever looking like a lunatic. Oh, how she begged the wind to catch her. No man would wed a woman with self-inflicted facial deformities, and she would be left alone to claim her own great strength.

Gretchen releases the tortured smile. "You be thinking about pleasing your prince and not them cosmic wanderings your father speaks of. They won't keep your man warm at night."

The women chuckle and speak in hushed tones about the marriage bed. Tamara ponders her midnight plan. She has arranged to meet the giant brothers Tavy and Tawridge. It is forbidden to mingle with the giants. Lore has it that centuries ago, the giants ruled the moors until Raging Storm ravaged the land, killing man and beast alike—all but Tavy and Tawridge. People claim they survived by clinging to a rugged headland and looking the other way while everyone else perished. Tamara doesn't believe it. She never has. She knows in the deepest region of her heart, where truth speaks to her, the giants have been falsely accused. As a child, she promised to set this record straight. Now she has but a few days left to keep that vow before leaving Kernow to wed Ulen.

Wind swishes down tunnels furrowed into the earth and whips around the great hall. Torches flicker. Some are extinguished by the gusts. The guests begin to leave, climbing the rough-hewn steps leading to the moor.

Tamara's father appears at her side. His weathered skin rests taut on his high-boned cheeks. His eyes—sunk far back in his head—move from side to side as if reading from the core of his knowledge. A zigzag of scars lines his neck. Their pallor shines in testament to the strength of his jugular.

"You are the light in my eyes, the wisdom in my heart, beloved child. You will lead our people when I depart this life. Your marriage will seal that destiny. You must not leave our cave without a chaperone until you are wed."

Tamara swallows hard. Bile surges up from her gut. Her mission with the giants runs riot in her thoughts. She lowers her eyes for fear her father might discern her angst. He can usually sense when she's preoccupied with thoughts of Tavy and Tawridge. She's been pleading with him since she was a small child to look into the record of Raging Storm in the Cycles of Time to see what truly happened. His eyes always harden as he tells her he consults the Cycles only on matters of leading their people.

He tilts Tamara's chin. "What disturbs your heart?"

Oh, dearest father, if you would but give Tavy and Tawridge a chance to tell their side of the story. She gazes up at her father, her eyes dripping with distress, a look she's seen women use to sway men to their advantage.

It doesn't work for her. Her father tightens his mouth into a grimace. Tamara feels an iron-hard wedge settle between them, and her heart hurts as if pierced by a poison arrow. She heaves her shoulders back, musters courage, and tries to alleviate the tension between them.

"I shall be wed in a gown of woven silver and with daisies and clover threaded through my hair," she declares, placing her hands on her hips and twirling around. Nervous laughter escapes her, and her high-pitched giggles echo around the gathering hall— becoming louder and louder and bouncing off the walls. A scene from the future shines on her mind's eye, rather like events from history that flash open for her father when he searches the Cycles of Time. She sees herself in a far distant time. She traverses oceans, mountain ranges, deserts, and cities stacked with tall glass towers. She laughs the same laugh that spills from her now. Children and all manner of people run after her. The sound of their happiness bounces from one land to another, ringing around the globe.

She wants that future.

"Lower the tone of your merriment, Tamara. Prince Ulen expects a dignified princess."

Her father departs, and he does not kiss her on the forehead, as is his habit at night.

Tamara sweeps back the heavy curtains to her sleeping room and dashes to her dressing table. She picks up a looking glass and scours her face, searching for signs of deception her father might have perceived. Her usually pale aqua irises bear a deeper hue—the mark of buried secrets. Tamara drops the mirror and rips off the crown of wild flowers encircling her head. She bends over and trails her hands through her tresses, removing combs and ribbons dyed flaxen to match her hair.

Stepping from her shoes, she hauls off her party dress and flings it on the bed. She presses her feet to the floor—cool plates of sandstone cut from sedimentary rock, polished and laid by loving hands for her, the hope of their people. Guilt strikes. She dismisses it, and peers through the curtains. The gathering hall lies dark and empty. She pulls on a thick wool tunic, tiptoes into the hall, and eases her body close to the walls. Her parents sleep in an alcove to the right of the stone steps. She waits until their breathing becomes noisy with the grunts and stutters of sleep, and then dashes up to the moor.

Midnight on Goon Stones

The smell of damp earth permeates the air. Tamara inhales deeply, stretches her arms up to the stars, and runs to the far side of the moor.

Goon Stones glisten in the moonlight—two monolithic hunks of granite—stark but regal on the barren land. Tamara climbs to the top of the tallest stone. A short distance ahead, the rough moorland gives way to a quilt of green fields that slope down to the cliffs. Tamara settles her gaze on Trellan Point, the great headland beneath which the giants live. She cups her hands to her mouth, "Tavy, Tawridge!"

Rose light pulses on the horizon like breath rising from the ocean. Tamara trembles from her scalp to the soles of her feet, certain the light emanates from the sunken lost kingdom of Ruberah. She longs to run back to their cave and tell her father. Even he has never seen the light of Ruberah rise over the earth. Legend says he who does will soon meet the master plan in his soul. A cluster of pink stars shine directly above her. *I'm ready, soul.*

Wind bangs in her ears, and her father's voice echoes in her thoughts. "A heart divided cannot pry wisdom from the Cycles of Time." The reality of having disobeyed him hits Tamara for the first time, but she quickly justifies her act. She cannot bring a pure heart to her union with Ulen without first clearing the giants of the suspicion surrounding them. She breathes slowly and evenly until fear fades and a feeling of being right with the world settles over her.

"Tavy, Tawridge!" A gust of wind picks up her voice and carries it out to sea. "It's me … Tamara. I want to help you. Trust me. Please!"

A subsonic tremble rumbles beneath the moors. Is it a cosmic realignment? Is Mt. Rube about to rise from its ocean grave? According to knowledge intuited by her father from the Cycles of Time, that will not happen for many an age to come. But her father also says that time bears no static markers. Time can run backward and forward and turn itself inside out at any moment, because all moments carry all time. It's about how far human consciousness can probe the moment.

Tamara focuses hard on the moment, diving deep and long toward a soft rose light. "Come back, Ruberah. Come back to me."

Ruby flames blaze on the horizon. Tamara's skin quivers over her bones. She calls the giants again and again, as if driven by an unstoppable inner force. She calls them until her voice runs hoarse. Then looming in the distance, she observes two massive men standing on the sands of Trellan Bay.

"Tavy, Tawridge. Over here." Tamara gestures wildly,

throwing the whole weight of her body into the act. "Over here!"

The giants stride to the base of the cliffs, then reach their arms up to the land and slap their hands onto moor. They haul themselves up, and within a couple of paces, they stand at arm's length from Tamara. Their broad identical faces break into wide-open smiles, and kindness cloaks Tamara like an invisible veil. She is exactly where she's meant to be. She holds no inkling of what she should do. She just is, and that's enough.

Tamara can't utter a word. She simply stares at the huge men in their baggy trousers and shirts of rumpled sackcloth. Their hair grows back from the middle of their scalps and flows about them like fine-spun silver. Their skin crinkles, bearing the story of lives lived with joy. Their amber irises glow like the gold of sunset, conveying the measure of their longing for human companionship.

Greetings spin in Tamara's mind, but she is unable to select one. She giggles, the same silly giggle that overtook her earlier in the evening when she envisioned her distant future. The giants thrust back their shoulders and release roars of rich, belly-deep laughter.

Soul speaks: *You are destined with the giants.*

Tamara's mood swings between relief and fright—fright of her father's reaction should she not marry Prince Ulen and relief that she might not have to. But why should it be one or the other? If she introduces the giants to the people of Kernow, they will quickly realize their fear is misplaced. She will wed Ulen and they can all live happily together.

Still, no words pass between her and the giants. They are familiar with each other, as if their lives have picked up from where they left off in another age. The giants scoop Tamara into their arms and they sweep across the wild terrain, dancing to the music of the night wind.

Warm air, thick with the scent of almonds, blows up from a southern sea. Happiness swirls off them—floating on the air like the afterlife of dandelions—dusting the planet with joy. This is Tamara's work—their work. This is her great strength.

In a lilting stride, the giants dip Tamara backward. Her hair trails among the heather. Laughter chortles in the curve of her throat, until in her upside-down vision, she sees her father striding onto the moor.

"T A M A R A!"

Her father snatches her from the arms of the giants and casts a sleeping spell on them. They plunge to the ground. Their massive bodies sprawl inert beside Goon Stones.

"No! Stop!" Tamara pleads. "Please don't hurt—"

Her father shakes her by the shoulders. "Your false gaiety did not deceive me. Return to our cave at once and never make mention of your liaison with the giants."

"But Father, I have seen the pink light and the flames of Ruberah, and my soul has—"

"You are mistaken, Tamara. The rose light has lain dormant in the Cycles of Time for uncounted centuries. If it moved, the earth would tremble, and I would know."

Tamara wants to insist that the earth did tremble, but her father's jaw stiffens, and he widens his stance and draws his elbow to his sides, closing his energies as he does before battle.

Tamara glances at the giants asleep at her feet, their mouths parted in the suggestion of a smile. She looks to her father. "Tavy and Tawridge would harm no one. They are kind and they seek friendship with us. Please, do not ask me to abandon them."

"You have no choice."

No choice!

His words scald her senses. Where has her beloved father gone? Where is the man of compassion and wisdom? Tamara digs her heels into the heather. "The rumors about Tavy and Tawridge are false. They love people, and they would never just watch as Raging Storm swept them out to sea. I will not be parted from them."

The pitch of her will against her father's breeds an eerie

stillness. Time stretches into all the moments of her eternity, inflicting them with the sorrow swelling in her father's heart, and in her own at the thought of losing him. Most blessedly, the euphoria of joy touches her at the same time, and her surroundings grow vague. A haze of pearly light diffuses her worldly sight. Hundreds of white pillars spring up and form a circle around her.

They glow like candles nestled in beeswax, and seem to have no beginning and no end—all except one, which glimmers on a lower beam. A scroll wrapped with white ribbon rolls to her feet. Tamara unties the bow. The document unfolds.

> *One,*
> *You stand in the counsel of your soul.*
> *You are the column of lesser light.*
> *You have chosen to illuminate its*
> *presence.*
> *One*

Tamara's heart tells her she wrote this message many ages ago before her first birth into the human family. A sense of previous lives floats around her—hundreds of lives, their joys and sorrows crowding into her soul. The pillars vanish as quickly as they appeared, and her father comes back into focus.

"Do not disobey me, Tamara. The prince expects a bride well-schooled and obedient to the rules of our society."

"There is no harm in my friendship with the giants, and I will not wed a man who would think otherwise."

Tamara's father sweeps an icy gaze over her and inhales his fighting breath. The winds gust in from all directions and streamnto his body. With no female energy committed to his cause, he emits a staggering field of warrior might. Tamara sways on her feet. The moor spins around her and the seas meet the heavens. Voices whisper to her father, but Tamara can't hear what they say. What could he find so unforgiveable about her wish to help Tavy and Tawridge? The whole community considers her father the most just of men. He never ruled on an offense without a fair hearing for the accused. She begs him to explain himself, but the winds roar and break up her voice.

Her father's chest expands, and his cheeks puff out like clouds heavy with rain. He exhales, and the winds fly from his mouth and rip across the peninsula, tearing it up at his bidding. The earth beneath Tamara cracks, then splits in two. Her father stands on one side of a gaping new gash in the land. She stands on the other.

"You will be a river," her father says, "A river made of your own tears, and you will fill this divide for all time to be."

The unbending force of her father's will settles on Tamara. She recalls the many warriors she has seen fall to their deaths, trying to resist his resolve. She stares him down, willing the might of her existence into her feet, holding her ground. "Why?"

Her father blinks, and the anguished cast of pain contort

his face. Her hopes soar as she senses him reconsidering. He lowers his eyes as he does when he communes with his inner knowing. His chest caves in, and he nods, bowing deeply as if accepting an awful but inevitable command.

"Father, please!" She shouts across the divide, "Please let me stay with you."

Her father hauls his energy field back under his control, and a cold, gray cast settles in his eyes—in the place where his love for her once shone.

Her heart begins to swell as all the sorrows of the world flood into it forming an ocean. The waters burst the boundaries of her chest and back up to her eyes. Pressure pounds against her temples and tears pour forth, melting her down, spilling her soul into the earth.

She trickles into the ground and washes over rock, granite, silt and slate. Her tears multiply, and treasured memories of her father haunt her. Riding into battle by his side, hearing him say, "Grant me the wisdom of your feminine powers, Tamara." The sheer ecstasy of sharing her spirit with his. The touch of his hand on hers, "You are the reason for my life, beloved child." Where did his love go? She has lost it all, and she did not save Tavy and Tawridge from the loneliness of their cast-out lives.

Between sobs, she hears the soft hum of the planet's

spin. It forms a hollow—a hushed and sacred space wherein the murmurings of the subterranean kingdom become audible to her.

"The planet constantly changes," the minerals whisper. "We erupted into life hundreds of millions of years ago—in an age when Kernow lay south of the equator—when the earth's crust buckled under the strain of another set of opposing wills, not unlike that of yours and your father's today. You are not separate from us, Tamara. We are all streams of ever-evolving consciousness—connecting and interconnecting to serve the humanity. You are still a vital part of the whole. The universe needs you to complete yourself."

The words of the minerals sound similar to those of her father's teachings. "Give yourself to the great source, Tamara, and you shall fulfill your right destiny." Despite her father's heartless treatment of her, his guidance rings true. "I'm just tears flowing into the earth. What can I do?" she asks the minerals.

"Accept what you are and the rest will follow."

Tamara rallies herself to do as the minerals suggest, and her heartache eases a little as the great strength inside her stirs. The hum of the planet grows softer, and a golden glow filters into her vision. It emanates from deep in the earth, issuing numerous streams of light, creating an ever-expanding sphere of radiance.

A whisper-soft voice drifts around Tamara, "I am Gold,

the earth's heart. Your love for Tavy and Tawridge resonates with the true nature of mankind. Thus, I invite you to be a guide for the human family—for those ready to awaken to the truth in their own consciousness. This is the calling of your soul. Do you accept it?"

"Yes," Tamara answers, quite swept away by the invitation. "What must I do?"

"You will soon form a river with your tears. Ages ago as Ruberah sank, many Ruberians wrote sacred futures—promises seeking to redeem themselves from the mistakes that led to that disaster. Some live on the planet today, and their sacred futures will come to rest in you. As they come due, those souls will find their way to your river. If a former Ruberian's face reflects on your waters, you'll see a number of possible futures for that person. One will be sacred, and if realized, will heal them of their suffering. You may serve as a guide while they fulfill that destiny."

"How will I know what to do?"

"The mists of Ruberah will gather around you and show you. You will receive many powers, but there is one thing you must not do."

"Oh!" Tamara's rebellious streak breaks loose. "What's that?"

"If the person rejects his sacred destiny, you must not

use your influence to cause a change of heart."

"Why not?"

"People change when they are ready. If you interfere, you will die to your life of service. You will be reborn in the human race in a position of bondage to others. And your soul pillar will grow dark."

Tamara whips up her tears in a fit of horror. She cannot imagine she would be even remotely tempted to force her will on anyone—not she, who has suffered at the effect of her father's volition.

Tamara bows to Gold, accepting the mandate.

Gold directs a beam of light into Tamara's head. "I open your spirit vision. You are now a guide for mankind."

All at once, Tamara's sight expands, and she scopes the world, the stars, and the whole universe. A white luminescence floats behind the stars, dotted with tiny pinpoints of silver. The dots seem identical, and yet her eye rests on one. Her whole being trembles with anticipation.

"Gold, are you there?"

"I am."

"What am I seeing?"

"You are looking into the atmosphere of the brilliance,

and the dot in the line of your vision is your orbit. It holds the sounds, lights, and laws of creation for our universe. As you stand ready to serve the human family, your orbit will bring you whatever knowledge you need. One day, with the touch of your finger, your orbit will expand into a great sphere, and you will find yourself inside it."

"And then what?" Tamara's asks, nearly breathless with wonder.

"You may use the laws of creation as you choose. You may form a new star, or planet, or even a new universe, should you so wish. I now invest you with your own dedicated ray into the earth's heart through which you may seek my guidance. Farewell, Tamara. Foretune to travel well."

"Wait!" Tamara can barely contain herself, she has so many questions to ask, but one rides above all others. "What about Tavy and Tawridge? My soul said I was destined to be with the giants!"

"You are. You wrote that destiny many ages ago, as did Tavy and Tawridge. Thus, when they awakened from your father's spell and realized what had happened to you, they asked me to transform them into rivers so they might forever flow alongside you. You will find them waiting for you."

The golden presence folds back into the earth. Tamara feels numb with wonder, and even numb to the loss of her father. Eager to begin her new life, she directs her tears back up to the earth's surface. They erupt on a high, boggy scrap of land not far from the north shore of Kernow. As they fountain into the air, Tamara transforms again and finds herself in her astral body—a glittering body of light identical to her young nymph form. She runs her fingers through the long tresses of her sparkling hair, then stretches her arms forward and dives into the great gash in the land created by her father.

Her tears cascade behind her, forming a fusion of lucent waters that roll back through time, all the way back until they flow into the lightly tinted, rose-colored waters of Ruberah. The mists of the Ruby Kingdom swirl around Tamara, whispering, "Welcome home."

"Who speaks to me?"

"We, the mists, the collective consciousness of the wisdom of Ruberah. You know us well, for you lived among us during the Age of Jeweled Intelligence. You were River Spirit, the guide for all Ruberians."

Memories of Ruberah rush into Tamara's mind—so many and so fast that she cannot comprehend them. "Help me to remember, please," she says to the mists. The soft pink vapors envelop her and lift her up from her tears. Scenes from *The Ending* come into clear view. Tamara feels her presence as River Spirit, flowing through the crumbling city of Az'Rayelle, opening her heart to all. She remembers her own heartbreak as the dying masses wrote sacred futures and tossed them into her river.

"Why didn't I stop the tragedy that caused *The Ending?*" Tamara asks the mists.

"You could not. Man is his own master. He is as wise as any of us; he's just working in the physical world, trying to remember. You must travel on now, dear friend. Once you find your new life, we will be ever with you."

The soft pink vapors begin to evaporate, and Tamara wants to beg them to stay with her, but she knows she must earn their company. She falls back into the grief and confusion of losing her father. Time swings her tears around and thrusts her river forward. Centuries fly by. She glimpses herself living as a young girl among a tribe on the moors, but it all passes so quickly that she can grasp no details. The whiz and whirl of landscape skims past her, but then, through the turbulence of her tears, a glorious sphere of golden light appears. She remembers her meeting with Gold, which brings her a sense of time and place. She is at the beginning of her new life as a river, serving once again as a guide for the human family.

She courses through the gash in the earth created by her father, forming the River Tamar. Ruberians start to reincarnate on Earth at the beginning of the Paleolithic age. Hundreds of them find her river. With great joy in her heart, Tamara guides them to fulfill the acts of atonement written in their sacred futures.

Kernow shifts and changes, forming new valleys, coves, and fields golden with wheat. Villages and towns spring up, their close-clustered buildings bustling with people. Moons come and go. Fashion gives way to tailored suits, gowns of silk and linen, and skimpy attire for bathing in the sea. Steamships traverse the oceans and dock in ports along the coast, puffing smoke from bright-colored funnels. Spices, tin, china clay—all manner of merchandise changes hands.

The twentieth century rolls into the twenty-first, and time slows to the present, to the long warm days of August 2010. Her river streams under ancient Roman viaducts, through rich farmlands, beneath low-hanging forests, high cliffs, and meadows. She laps against derelict mining areas, once rich with copper and tin. Bridges span her river, some wooden and narrow and some wide with roadways and arcs of steel.

Kernow is now called Cornwall, and Tamara is legend.

PART TWO
PROMISES DUE

CHAPTER THREE

Crossing the Tamar
Cornwall, UK.

A pale pink current wends in from the Atlantic and flows into Tamara's river, releasing a message.

Another Ruberian will cross your river soon. Guide her well, beloved friend.

Written in the language of rubies, the missive shimmers in jeweled facets, waves, dots, suns, and stars. Pink mists rise over the runes, investing Tamara with knowledge of her charge to be. She glances to a bend near the far end of her river, to a well of calm waters where promises from Ruberah lie sleeping. She touches the surface. History stirs. Tamara whispers, "Come forth, you who are ready."

A little red hatchback rolls onto the Tamar Bridge, an elegant suspension bridge over which cars stream back and forth.

The hatchback approaches from the Devonshire side of the Tamar, a county of lush meadows and pretty upmarket villages. A man drives. He taps his forefinger against the wheel, idly, as if bored. Tamara spots the rose glow of Ruberah in the aura of the woman in the passenger seat. The woman's nose twitches as if sniffing danger. She darts anxious glances at the man. He appears oblivious to her. The car rides under the arch in the middle of the bridge. The man and the woman enter Cornwall.

The woman presses her forehead against the window and stares down. Tamara surfaces in her sparkling light body, and waves to the woman. The woman's gaze widens, and her mouth freezes in an open gasp. Tamara's hears her inner talk. *Stop the car! Turn around! I want to go home!* These commands lie mute in her mind. Fear clamps her vocal chords closed.

A reflection of the woman's frightened face lingers on the river, and Tamara sees two possible futures for her. In one, she attains her strongest desire—lifelong love with a man— hopefully, the one she's traveling with. In the other, she undertakes a journey to search for someone who has vanished from the face of the earth. This is her sacred future, the vow she made eons ago as Ruberah split from the earth and sank into the depths of the ocean, the promise she's ready to meet.

Tamara dives back beneath her river, but keeps the woman clearly in her view. She watches her regain control of her facial muscles. The woman closes her eyes, but the glowing image of Tamara's light body remains for an instant on the back of her lids. The woman's heart palpitates, and she grips the man's wrist, which causes him to tug down hard on the steering wheel. The car swerves into another lane and almost collides with a large van. The man corrects his course.

"What the hell is the matter with you, Mir? You almost caused an accident."

"I saw something strange in the river … something shiny … brilliant … oh god, it looked like a girl with masses of hair—dazzling bright hair—flowing everywhere, up over the banks of the river and onto the land. *Everywhere*. Oh, I can't describe it. You look. *Please*."

"You're not making any sense, Mir. Get a hold of yourself."

"I'm telling you, I saw a girl, maybe a teenager. Her body was made of light, and her eyes …" Miriam gulps. "Her eyes were big and shiny and sort of aqua colored. Look, for God's sake. Just look into the river."

The man sighs and does as asked. "I don't see anything there."

Glancing up from her riverbed, Tamara is surprised to see the man's face reflecting on her river. The current from Ruberah spoke of only one woman, one sacred future, but a possible future begins to form over the man's image. A golden sail blazes on the surface of the Tamar. Tamara recognizes the sail at once. Tall and buoyant with wind made of prayers from the human heart, it belongs to the golden galleon *Mercy*, a vessel that sank with Ruberah. But she is not alone in recognition of the sail.

A sudden squall thrashes upon the ocean, and a violent wind whips across the peninsula. Blue-black waves crash onto the shore. Dark Master, ruler of the underworld, surges up from their midst. His massive shoulders fill the sky, and his shadow falls heavy on the land, stirring the fears of mankind. He furls and unfurls his great cape—countless panels of black fabric— glistening like wet cobra skin. Tamara feels the spirit of the human family collapse under the dread of being touched by the darkness. The golden sail falls slack.

Dark Master swoops low over the Tamar, thrusting his black-hooded head forward, blinding Tamara to any further sight of the possible destiny of the man in the little red hatchback.

Tamara raises an arm and draws on the fireball of energy at the center of the sun, readying to strike the dreaded ruler. Before she can reach him, he whips his cape back and forth over the golden sail and batters it back down to its ocean grave. Then, slick as rain in a gale-force wind, he plasters the cape to his sides and sluices back into the ocean.

The wind drops. The sea resumes its normal rhythm. The storm registers as a blip on the measure of linear time—a blink of the human eye. The man and the woman in the little red car retain no conscious memory of the event. However, it leaves them with a heightened sense of something dangerous hovering about them.

Indeed.

CHAPTER FOUR

En route to *Penrose Hall*
Cornwall, UK.

Those about to embark on a sacred future usually stay at *Penrose Hall*, an inn several miles down the coast. Tamara glances in that direction and scans the reservation book. Two guests are expected today: Mitch Devere and Miriam Lewis, both from New York. Tamara smiles. She does so enjoy Americans. They venture into Cornwall ready to be charmed by one and all, although this sometimes makes them a bit of a handful. Cornwall is rife with Piskies—little faerie folk who like to play tricks on the unsuspecting visitor—and locals who like to spin tales of ghosts and witches.

The red car rolls off the Tamar Bridge and onto Cornish soil. Tamara rises from her river in her light body and slips into the car through an open window. Neither Miriam nor Mitch sees or feels her presence. Miriam's spirit vision, which flashed open to allow her to glimpse Tamara as she crossed the Tamar, has fallen asleep.

Tamara drifts around Miriam, familiarizing herself with her characteristics. The year of her birth shines inside a star at the top of her head. She's just celebrated her fortieth birthday. Celebrated might be the wrong word. Miriam met forty as she would the horrors of a nuclear holocaust. She believes she must nab a mate before time etches deeper into her skin and casts her into the crush of aging women, alone and desperate.

What a grim outlook. However, it does not play upon her countenance. Her lively blue-green eyes dart around, observing the sights and measuring them against her expectations. She has short, frosty blonde hair that flops onto her cheekbones in a diagonal cut. Her skin glows as if cared for with rich, youth-enhancing creams. She's painted her lips hot pink. Her fingernails and toenails have been varnished to match. She's a real estate broker. Her mind flips between the details of the sale of an apartment in New York and her reason for coming on this trip.

Miriam reflects on the latter. She pictures herself wearing her new black lingerie in a cozy room, lying on a four-poster bed with Mitch, broaching the subject of taking their relationship to the next level—moving in together with an eye toward marriage.

"Brr!" Mitch closes his window. "I hope you brought

your flannel pajamas. There's no central heating at *Penrose Hall.*"

"What? It's August, for God's sake!"

"This is England, Mir. It's wet and cold."

Tamara considers that a bit of an exaggeration. Granted, light rain sprinkles on the busy Port of Plymouth, but it's far from cold. Sunbeams light up the golden tropical grasses that fringe the rocky coast. Of course, a few miles inland showers fall like liquid mercury. Such is the nature of the Cornish climate.

Miriam digs into a large canvas tote. There's a mesh pocket on the outside of the bag, a place for the inevitable bottle of water tourists carry everywhere. A piece of paper sticks out behind Miriam's bottle. Tamara peers inside the folds—an exercise schedule, which tells her that Miriam has recently been to a health spa. Tamara looks further into Miriam's tote. Low-carb protein bars, chips, and bitter chocolate have been crammed into an inner pocket. Miriam's fingers pass over them and land on a packet of cigarettes. She craves a smoke. Mitch detests the habit. Since Miriam is forty, and according to hearsay, more likely to be killed by a terrorist than find another man, she resists the urge. Miriam rummages up a protein bar, breaks off a small piece, devours it, and tucks the rest back in the bag. Seconds later, she fishes the bar out again and measures off another piece. She does this again and again until she gobbles down the last bit.

Miriam slaps her hands on her thighs. "This will be fun,"

she says, as if determined to make it so.

Mitch yawns. "I doubt it. Tom Reilly's the only writer I know who's good at this road-less-traveled stuff. Crazy guy, breaking his leg hiking in Tibet, sticking me with this assignment."

"To say nothing of doing me out of five days in Tahiti."

"Sorry about that, Mir. You know I didn't have any choice."

Miriam rubs his shoulder. "Yes, but you promised we'll go there one day." Miriam has already exacted that promise from Mitch, but she'd like to hear him confirm it again. He doesn't.

World Over, a glossy travel magazine, lies open on the back seat. A photograph of Mitch heads a column titled *Style & Glitz.* An old nymph giggle tickles Tamara's spirit. Mitch will find no terraces trailing exotic vines at *Penrose Hall,* no turquoise pool or ocean warm enough to idle away the hours while sipping tall drinks, rich with rum.

She judges Mitch to be about the same age as Miriam. He's of average height, with dark hair that straggles over his collar. He wears jeans and a blue checked shirt with the sleeves rolled up to his elbows. His skin is deeply tanned and lined by the sun. His close-set brown eyes give him the look of someone good at ferreting out information.

The car spins along, and Mitch enjoys shifting gears and mastering the challenge of driving on the left side of the road. He boasts to Miriam of daredevil road trips in Mexico, Turkey, and Kathmandu. Miriam listens, nodding in the manner of one who has heard these stories enough times to tune them out, but still nod or murmur where comment seems necessary. Her thoughts switch to her daughter, and a shiver of fragility creeps over her.

Elaine. Miriam questions her decision to leave home while Elaine remains in rehab. What if she runs away again? Miriam closes her eyes. Her daughter's face floats before her. Platinum bleached hair frames her thin face, and bright blue bangs flop over her brows. Her morose and fidgety gaze frightens Miriam. The urge to call Elaine strikes. Miriam grabs Mitch's cell phone.

"Sorry, Mir. The battery's dead. I forgot to charge it last night."

"I'm worried about Elaine."

"She'll be all right."

Contradictions pile up inside Mitch, but he dismisses them. He's well practiced at denial. He constantly strives to push back painful memories of his childhood. To let one loose might be to free them all, a terrifying thought.

Miriam reaches back into her canvas tote, yanks up a packet of low-carb chips, and munches on them, salivating as the taste of salt seeps into her mouth. She determines to eat only half of the chips. This will amount to fifty calories. That, plus the protein bar she consumed earlier, add up to three hundred and thirty calories. Forty-five minutes on a treadmill, a machine Miriam assumes she will find at *Penrose Hall*, and she'll work those off in time to enjoy dinner.

"Keep a look out," Mitch says. "We should be close to the road leading to Trellan Bay."

They approach a roundabout, and Mitch downshifts and guides the car into the traffic whizzing around the concrete circle. He misses his turn. Damning the British for their silly traffic system, he circles back and veers onto the correct road. After a few yards of paved surface, the road becomes little more than a dirt lane. Mitch eases the hatchback between hedgerows overgrown with long, lacy weeds that flop against the windows. Ancient elms tower above, darkening the day.

"Jesus!" Miriam eyes the narrow lane. "What happens if we meet a car coming in the other direction?"

"Let's hope we don't." Mitch tightens his grip on the wheel and steers the car around a sharp bend. The road plunges downhill at a terrifying angle. He navigates the twists and turns, passing perilously close to the edge where the land falls sharply away.

A waterfall gushes through a ravine in the cliffs. Sunlight

plays in mist rising off the water. A rainbow spans the sky. Mitch rounds another turn in the road. The shining body of the Atlantic spreads before him, heaving and rolling to shore like a carpet of diamonds. Waves crash against the sharp-serrated cliffs, carving a savage face on the land. The sky swells with yellow and pewter clouds.

Miriam's breath catches in her throat. This sudden proximity to nature makes her feel vulnerable. She longs to be back in the concrete safety of her New York apartment.

A dark green Range Rover approaches. The general rule on these roads is that the person traveling uphill has the right-of-way. Mitch is lucky the driver of the Range Rover is Lance Penrose, owner of the inn.

Lance tips his fingers to his tweed cap and reverses. The hatchback and the Range Rover travel downhill, radiator to radiator.

"This is the craziest thing I've ever seen," Miriam says. "How can you have a hotel in a place where you have to take your life in your hands to get to it?"

Mitch laughs. "Tom Reilly told me that local lore claims no one is the same after a stay at *Penrose Hall.*"

"I believe it."

The road levels and widens a little. Lance Penrose pulls

off to the side to let Mitch and Miriam pass. The brim of his cap shadows his face, but Miriam catches a cast of sadness in his eyes. His misery touches her. Her neck hairs prickle. She looks quickly beyond him to a spread of rich, green fields that sweep down to the edge of the cliffs. A herd of Guernsey cattle huddle together, grazing, while sheep nibble under a sprawl of large oak trees.

"Look at that girl," Mitch says, pointing his finger in front of Miriam.

Miriam's glance falls on a girl riding a black horse, galloping flat out, heading toward the inn. Her flaming red hair trails behind her like a river of fire. She leans forward on the beast, her face nuzzled in his mane. A sense of déjà vu sweeps over Miriam—a sense of something lost.

"This is fantastic," Mitch says. "That must be Kate Penrose, daughter of the owners." He bangs a fist on the steering wheel. "I'll be darned. Tom Reilly said that as you near *Penrose Hall*, you'll see a girl with long, red hair riding a black stallion." Mitch lowers his window and sniffs the salty air. Words spin in his mind. He'll pour them into his computer as soon as he's settled in.

Thoughts of Tom Reilly and the metaphysical junk he writes about increases Miriam's anxiety about the place. She rifles the cigarettes from her bag.

Mitch snatches the packet from her and stuffs it in his jeans pocket. You quit, remember?"

"Goddammit, Mitch. Don't tell me what to do. Give them back to me."

"I'm trying to help you, Mir." Mitch guides the hatchback onto a gravel pathway. "You just spent a fortune to quit smoking and lose twenty pounds."

"Yeah, well it was my fortune."

Mitch bites his lip. They ride in contentious silence.

Penrose Hall comes into view. True to its brochure, the ancient house stands on the cliffs above Trellan Bay. Long, mullioned windows front on the driveway, and a portico overhangs them, supported by twelve pillars that form an impressive colonnade. A swathe of pink mist clings to the turrets of a small, round tower rising above the west wing of the hall. Sun sparkles in the quartz-rich granite, lending the house a fairy-tale quality of belonging to the sky.

Mitch stops the car and hauls up the parking brake. He fumbles for the keys, knocking the windshield wipers on as he searches for the ignition. "Damn!"

Miriam yanks the keys from the lock and slaps them in his hand. She opens the door, puts one foot on the driveway, and then draws it back. "I don't know."

Mitch eases himself from the driver's seat and struts over to Miriam's side. "Mir … listen … Elaine told me she's going to get clean and stay clean this time."

"She said that the last time."

"Not to me."

Mitch and Elaine. Miriam cannot fathom their relationship. Something passed between them upon first sight of one another. Miriam felt it slip through air—a slender recognition of something shared. They sit next to each other on the sofa like a storybook version of a father and daughter watching TV. They view whatever program the other selects and laugh at the same things, usually in contrary amusement. They seldom speak, but when one does, the other listens as if privy to top-secret information. Miriam searches Mitch's expression. "Elaine really said that to you?"

"Yeah."

Miriam swings her feet onto the gravel path and stretches her arms above her head. She must convince Mitch that it's time to move in together. Mitch may be a little vague, as if separate from the everyday nuances of life, but he has endearing qualities too. He often brings her flowers—usually three or five carefully chosen blossoms nestled in a piece of exotic greenery. When he gives them to her, she feels like the most loved person in the whole world, and her nerves fuse as if she's hardwired to be with him. She loves him. Elaine loves him, and Elaine needs the comfort of family life.

Gulls swoop and wail. The eternal thud of the sea pounds against the land, and a bank of clouds block the sun. The thundering of horse's hooves draws near. The great black stallion sails over a hedge and lands on the driveway, clouding the air with dust.

Kate dismounts. Despair shadows her expression—a grief that pains Tamara. Kate, Tamara's earthly helper, was born with her spirit vision open. Tamara communes telepathically with Kate. She has since her birth. Tamara catches the girl's glance and knows at once that Kate has perceived Miriam could resolve the sadness she's carried for nearly a month now.

The girl narrows her eyes—pools of deep green, like ancient jade. She studies Miriam and then looks back at Tamara. "She's the one to bring her home, isn't she?"

"Maybe, Kate. But don't bank on it. I saw two possible futures for Miriam. We'll have to wait and see which one she chooses."

"What's the other one?"

"She finds lifelong love with a man."

Kate glances at Mitch and sniffs and wrinkles her nose in disgust. She beckons to a young man from the village who does odd jobs around the inn. He runs toward Kate, his sturdy legs bringing him briskly to her side. Kate strokes the sweating stallion between his ears and hands the reins to the youth. "Take Firebrand back to the stables, please."

Mitch saunters over to Kate. "I'm from *World Over*. I'm filling in for Tom Reilly, who broke his leg hiking in Tibet."

"You were always expected," Kate says with the aplomb of a prophet. Her certainty makes Tamara wonder whether she's intuited information about Mitch, or if it's just bravado, a trait she's not short on.

"Really?" An amused smile wavers on Mitch's lips.

Kate ignores him, latches onto Miriam's arm, and leads her toward the house. Mitch clips along beside them.

"Your room is next to mine," Kate says to Miriam. "It's small, but it faces the sea and has a little balcony."

Miriam stops in her tracks. "There must be some mistake. Mitch and I are staying in the Tower Suite."

Kate drags Miriam on toward the house. "That bedroom is tiny. It only sleeps one. *World Over* booked that for Mitch."

The three of them pause by the front door. "Mitch!" Miriam glares at him, squaring her shoulders and shoving her face up close to his. "Solve this."

Mitch lowers his voice to a polished, patient tone—the kind learned by every experienced traveler. "Honey." He squeezes Kate's shoulder. "You can fix this, can't you?" His eyes glow with the expectation of a positive response.

Kate flicks his hand off her shoulder. "No. We're fully booked." She leans on the heavy wooden door to the inn. A scale of eerie notes shiver on the air as it opens.

"Whoa!" Mitch laughs. "That sounds scarier than any haunted house I've ever been in."

Kate rolls her eyes, then walks toward the reception desk. Mitch ushers Miriam inside. "I'll work things out. Just leave it to me."

Sunlight streams through the heavy, leaded windows of the reception hall, reflecting their diamond-shaped panes on the oak-paneled walls. A grandfather clock ticks noisily. Outside, the gaping blue mouth of the Atlantic opens to a choppy sea.

Kate lifts two large keys from hooks behind the reception counter and dangles them in front of Mitch and Miriam.

"Look honey." Mitch leans an elbow on the counter. "I'm here to write an article about the area and your inn. Not giving us a room big enough to share isn't a good start. I want to speak with your mother or father."

"My father's out. You passed him in the Range Rover on your way here."

"Then we want to speak with your mother," Miriam says.

Kate tenses her shoulders and glances up the main staircase to a portrait of her mother hanging on the landing. Lara Penrose gazes back at the world through pale blue eyes laced with a dreamy, far-away look. Long, wheat-colored hair frames her face. Her lips part in a slight smile, an expression caught somewhere between mirth and solemnity.

Tamara speaks telepathically to Kate, repeating the words her mother said to her on her last birthday:

"Now that you're fourteen, the River is strong in you and you may awaken to the ruby fire in your aura. Promise me, my darling you will not use it without seeking Tamara's guidance, as you cannot yet see the many shades of right and wrong."

Kate pouts. "If I'd known she was going to disappear the next day, I'd never have made that promise."

"But you did make it."

"Who's that woman?" Mitch interrupts their silent communication. He points to the portrait.

"My mother," Kate says. "She's missing. She's been gone for almost a month."

Kate's cold delivery of such devastating news confuses Mitch and Miriam. Tamara chastises the girl, not that it does much good. Kate is a Leo, a fire sign. Tamara is all water. The pink mists of Ruberah that cling to the turrets of the west tower sometimes grow stormy from the clash of Kate's will against Tamara's wisdom. Since Mitch will occupy the Tower Suite, Tamara looks into his thoughts to see if he feels the effects of this.

He does not. Mitch smells a story. He wants to ask Kate when her mother went missing and how and where and why. He wonders if the girl's father, that morose-looking man they saw in the Range Rover, killed his wife and hid her body. Perhaps it's right here, rotting beneath the floorboards. His nose twitches. He sniffs—three short sniffs—imitating Jed Flyer, the erudite detective of his many unpublished books. Mitch senses a novel forming—a bestseller for sure.

"Your keys," Kate lays them on the reception counter, opens the guest book and hands Mitch a ballpoint pen. "Sign your name and then initial the date of your departure, which is Tuesday."

Mitch cools his interrogative fervor, mumbles his regrets about Kate's mother and signs as instructed. Kate retrieves an ornate fountain pen from beneath the desk and lays it in front of Miriam. She smiles, "You use this pen because you're special."

Touched by Kate's sweetness, Miriam grips the ruby red,

gold-trimmed instrument. She scrawls her name and laughs as it appears in pink ink. "I've never seen that color ink before."

Kate points to the departure date. "Initial here, please."

Miriam does as she's told without question. Kate's loss of her mother disturbs Miriam deeply. She can't help but imagine Elaine alone, without Miriam to fend for her. She moves to lay a comforting hand on Kate's shoulder, but the girl backs away beyond her reach.

Miriam's eyes tear up, and Tamara reaches back into her river and gathers a strong current of golden light from the earth's heart. She whirls the waves around Miriam, directing them into her heart. Euphoria replaces Miriam's sorrow, and her feelings expand, unlocking a seemingly never-ending supply of love. *Where does it come from?*

"From me," Tamara whispers in her ear. "I am your guide while you're in Cornwall. Your sacred future has come due. You are to find Kate's mother and bring her home. Do this, and you will live forever in the abundance of that love."

Miriam does not hear Tamara, and her senses cloud over with the troubles of her life. Bliss fades. She drags her mouth down at the corners.

Kate bangs her fist on a brass bell on the reception desk. The chime reverberates on one clear note that travels in ever-expanding circles, passing over time as measured by the ticking of the grandfather clock, sailing through the tall windows, slipping onto the winds of summer—echoing the world over.

The double doors leading to the kitchen swing open, and nineteen-year-old buxom and beauteous Gwenellen Tremont bursts into the reception area. She claps a hand to her mouth, stifling some amusement she's been sharing with the staff.

"Gwenellen, this is Mr. Devere." Kate nods at Mitch. "Show him to the Tower Suite."

Blue-black vapors from Dark Master's kingdom float in from the terrace and swirl around Mitch. He gapes at Gwenellen, dropping his jaw and sticking his neck out like a star-struck turtle. His attraction to her palpitates on the air.

"Mitch!" Miriam tugs on his arm. Her eyes bulge with indignation.

"Look, Mir." Mitch shifts his weight from one foot to the other. "The magazine made my reservation. This is work for me."

Gone are Miriam's memories of boundless love and worries about Elaine. Gwenellen dominates her thoughts. Gwenellen, whose bosom strains at the seams of her black sweater, Gwenellen, who with a toss of her golden curls, bats her eyes at Mitch and says, "Follow me."

CHAPTER FIVE

Penrose Hall

"This is not acceptable." Miriam glares at Kate. The image of Mitch traipsing off with that young maid sticks at the forefront of her mind. "If I'm not in a room with Mitch by tonight, I'll see to it that his article reflects the shoddy management of your inn."

Kate shrugs. "Our guests don't care about that sort of thing."

Tamara sweeps in close to Kate and reminds her that Miriam is their best hope for her mother's safe return. Quick as a fox, Kate drops her lethargic attitude. Her eyes shine like polished gems, and she parts her pouty lips into a radiant, megawatt smile.

"Things will work out." She picks up Miriam's suitcase. "We'll just put your luggage in the room next to mine until then. Follow me."

"Okay, but that had better be just for now." Miriam trudges behind Kate up three flights of stairs, calculating the caloric burn of each stride. "Where's the workout room? I need to use a treadmill or an elliptical before dinner."

"The workout room?" Kate giggles. "It's outside. I'll take you riding, if you like. Or sailing or hiking. And of course you can always go for a swim."

"Yeah, thanks a lot, but I don't do any of that." Miriam climbs the last stair. Light filters in through a row of narrow windows sunk deep into the thick walls. She leans against the cool granite. Her heart bangs in her chest. "It's musty up here."

"This used to be the servants' quarters, years ago when our mine was working."

"What kind of mine was it?"

"Tin. We operated Wheal Penrose. You can still go into the tunnels. Some run under the ocean." She lowers her voice to a whisper. "There's a ley line beneath the mine ... a living field of energy that runs all the way back to Ruberah. It's the only link on the planet to the lost Ruby Kingdom." She smiles. "I'll take you there sometime."

"Yeah? That sounds fascinating, but I'll pass. I prefer to stay above ground."

"Oh, but it's fab beneath the sea." Kate glances back at Miriam, trailing her spirit vision through the pale pink light in Miriam's aura. "Super! Rubies are your favorite gemstones. Rubies generate tremendous creative energy. I'll show you how that works."

Miriam laughs. The girl irks her a bit, but there's also something irresistible about her. "You sure are a different kind of kid."

"I know." Kate points to a door on her right. "This is your room. Mine's the next one down. My brother's is at the end of the hall, but he's in France for the summer. Another guest is using it. His name is Harry Treadwell." Kate flips her hair over one shoulder. If she could get rid of Mitch, Miriam would choose to follow her sacred future. A new romance might do the trick. "Harry's just divorced." Kate grins and widens her eyes.

Tamara whispers in Kate's head, telling her to stop manipulating Miriam, but Kate pretends not to hear her. Rules be darned, getting her mother back comes first.

The girl cocks her head to the side and smiles at Miriam. "Harry's really nice. So you never know, do you?"

Miriam barges past Kate, ignoring her innuendo. The small room with its white walls, single bed, and sisal carpeting feels like a monk's cell. An antique walnut wardrobe stands on an angle in one corner. The door hangs open, revealing four shelves and a rod wide enough to hang a couple of items. "I could never stay here. There's not enough room for my things."

Kate opens a set of French doors, steps onto a small balcony and flings her arms open in a wide gesture, "You've got all the room in the world." A changing wind tosses her hair across her face. Kate laughs. Fire sparks off her aura. "Mummy, can you hear me? We're coming to get you."

Tamara warns the girl to stop it. She's frightening Miriam, but Kate ignores her and whirls around and around like a triumphant ballerina. Tamara reaches to the sky and touches a cloud. Sheets of rain drench down. Kate stops spinning.

"Why did you do that?" the girl asks.

"What the hell is going on?" Miriam stares at Kate. "Who are you talking to? Why is your hair wet?"

"Oh, it's just weather." Kate saunters back into the room, flicking water from her hair. "They're serving tea on the Atlantic Terrace. Are you hungry?"

"Starving. Where's the phone?"

"Downstairs at reception."

"What!" Horror registers in Miriam's eyes. "I've got to be in touch with my office. I must have a phone nearby."

"Haven't you got a mobile?"

"Mine doesn't work over here. I'm using Mitch's. So you'd better hurry up and put another bed in the Tower Suite or get us another room. Where's my bathroom?"

"Down the hall. We share it with Harry."

Miriam's mouth drops open. She glares at Kate. "Tell me you're kidding."

Tamara leaves Kate to handle the irate Miriam and drifts down from the balcony of her room to the Atlantic Terrace. She perches her light body on an iron leaf, a decorative piece in the filigree frame surrounding the semicircular porch. Rose arches meander down from the house to the cliff path, where palm trees sway in a breeze warmed by the Gulf Stream.

Mitch stands by a trolley laden with tiny sandwiches and iced cupcakes. Tamara flows over his shoulder. Fragrance wafts off his cheeks, a sophisticated blend of cypress and cedar. He's changed into a cream safari jacket and tan slacks. He circles the teacart, fancying himself Jed Flyer, the detective of his creation. Assuming Jed's persona brings him a feeling of power—not that it would stand up to close scrutiny, and not that Mitch is unaware of that. He moves quickly among the guests, speaking of his assignment to write an article about the area. He chats and charms, although he's not interested in these people. Mitch has met them all before. A group of sturdy women gathered for a walking holiday. The red-cheeked man in a tweed jacket, eating the foods he is directed to eat by his wife. The young couple ogling each other out of honeymoon eyes. Elderly ladies rocking in wicker chairs, sipping tea, marking time.

Munching on a cucumber sandwich, Mitch glances at his watch, then at the entrance to the veranda. Gwenellen, the gorgeous girl who escorted him to the Tower Suite appears, nods at him, and vanishes. Excusing himself from his doting audience, Mitch leaps off the porch into the garden. At the same time, Kate propels Miriam onto the terrace.

"Mitch." Miriam breaks away from Kate and runs after her fleeing lover. "Where are you going?"

Mitch stops midstride. He watches Gwenellen disappear around a bend in the rose arches. He looks back at Miriam. "Hey!" He slaps Miriam on the shoulder in a jovial way, as if meeting an old school chum. "Are you settled in?"

"Settled in!" Suspicion blazes in Miriam's eyes. Has something already happened between him and that maid?

Mitch huffs a nervous laugh. "Calm down, Mir."

"Calm down! I'm in the servants' quarters. I've got no phone, no bathroom of my own, and I absolutely can't share one. And there's some other man staying up there, too. You've got to fix this."

"Yeah, I'll straighten everything out. But right now I've got to explore the area."

"I'll come with you."

"Nah, I work best alone." Mitch swings an arm around Miriam's waist, guides her to the tea trolley and thrusts her into the company of the ladies on a hiking holiday. "Have some tea. I'll be back in fifteen minutes."

Mitch dashes off, and Tamara senses she needs to follow him and know what he's up to in order help Miriam. She approaches Kate, thinking a little responsibility might evoke her better nature. "Miriam's very upset, Kate, and she needs looking after. I'd like you to stay here and be kind and helpful to her." The girls nods, and Tamara enfolds her in her sparkling arms, the way she did when Kate was a small child and fearful of the dark. "Who is the darling of my heart?" she whispers.

"I am."

Tamara leans her cheek against Kate's. "Remember the things your mother taught you. Introduce Miriam to the other guests. Since she's American, ask her if she would prefer coffee to tea. And make certain Miriam meets Harry. It would be uncomfortable for her if she ran into him coming out of the bathroom without having met him. And please don't do anything to embarrass either of them."

"Of course not," the girl says, as if such a thought would

enter her mind.

"I'm trusting you, then." Tamara gives Kate a last hug and sweeps off the terrace. She flies through the rose arches, looking for Mitch. She finds him just as he reaches the cliff path. He turns his head sharply to the left, then right. "Gwenellen, where are you?"

Something rustles in a huge, flowering rhododendron bush. "Boo!" The boisterous young woman leaps from the plant, scattering the air with bright pink petals. "Did I scare you?"

Laughing, Mitch holds his hands up like a man at gunpoint. Gwenellen scares him all right. She's like a whirl of pink cotton candy, and he wants to lick her all over and suck up her sugary youth.

Tamara glances to the west tower. The mists surrounding its turrets hold a record of all that happens inside those rooms. She peers into them, looking back to when Gwenellen led Mitch up to the Tower Suite.

Mitch followed her up a winding iron staircase to his bedroom, his gaze transfixed on her buttocks. Gwenellen patted the pillow on his bed. "Some people don't sleep well here, but I've a notion you will." Her soft, West Country brogue lilted with invitation. Desire soared through Mitch, but Miriam crossed his mind. He felt comfortable in his relationship with her. She seldom traveled with him, so he had a life of his own and he looked forward to being with her when he returned from a trip. He steeled himself against Gwenellen's flirtation. "What happened to Lara Penrose?" he asked.

"Meet me on the cliff path at four-thirty, and I'll tell you."

So here Mitch is, gazing at the voluptuous maid. His heart hammers in his chest.

"Come on then." Gwenellen links her arm through Mitch's. They stroll along the path. She chuckles, a deep throaty chuckle, and looks at Mitch out of eyes that shift in shades of blue as variable as the sea. "Tell me something about you that you've never told anyone else."

Mitch laughs. "You were going to tell me what happened to Lara Penrose."

"I will, after you trust me with something secret about you."

"I could probably find out about Lara from the local newspaper."

"Yes, but I was the last person to see her. I could tell you things I didn't tell the police."

Mitch stops. "You didn't tell them everything?"

Gwenellen rolls the tip of her tongue over her lip.

"Maybe I was waiting for you."

Mitch stares into her eyes and brushes a golden curl off her forehead. As he touches her skin, a cold wind intercepts the summer breeze. It bears a warning for Mitch. Tamara speaks it to him, "Be careful of her." He hears her not.

Gwenellen withdraws her arm from Mitch's and skips along the path, trailing a peal of laughter.

Mitch sprints after her, breathing in the sound of her mirth. The fire of his youth burns in his groin. He aches to kiss this girl, to feel her firm flesh against his. Panting, he catches up to her. "Okay, I'll tell you something about me I've never told anyone else."

Gwenellen rubs her hands together like a child suddenly granted a wish. "I love secrets." She leads Mitch to a wooden bench. They sit. She nestles close to him. "What is it?"

"I ... well ..." Mitch sucks in air between his front his teeth. He hates sharing intimacies, mostly because he really doesn't have any. "This is just between you and me, right?"

She nods, lowering her eyes, imparting her promise.

"I like the place between places. You know, being on trains, ships, and planes. I never want to get anywhere." He stops. "This is silly."

"No it's not. Go on."

He fingers the ends of his hair, twisting them. "I've always felt that one day I'll sail into a special place, my own Shangri-La, I suppose. I don't know. It's a blur in my mind, sort of like a Polaroid photo coming into focus." He wrings his hands together, gazing out to sea. His fantasy began as a child. He had been shuffled back and forth between his divorced parents. Mitch hated leaving his mother. The sight of her slender, fine-boned fingers pressing against her temples, and the weight of her angst as she searched for words to ease his nervousness about spending time with his father. Words she never found—that never could be found. But on the plane—in the place between places—he dreamed of being hijacked and flown to an unknown island—a place where no one would ever find him.

"I can feel the place." Mitch draws his fantasy to mind. "The climate is warm and tranquil. There's no sense of time passing. No one knows I'm there. I busy myself with fishing for food and maintaining a hut I built with my own hands." He laughs nervously and glances at Gwenellen. "That's it."

Gwenellen looks to the sky, squinting, saying nothing. The interminable sighing of the sea fills the silence. Mitch fears it might have been a mistake to speak of something so fanciful to someone so young. Does she think him an old fool? Should he say he was just kidding and make up a story—one she would like—perhaps a story of love lost?

The glitter of victory shines in Gwenellen's eyes. Mitch

mistakes it for interest in him. His lips part, and he pants like a puppy in desperate need of petting.

"Mrs. Penrose went missing on the second day of August, the day after Kate turned fourteen," Gwenellen says.

At the sound of her voice, Mitch breathes a sigh of relief. "What happened?"

"It was evening. I was walking from the village to the inn. I worked the late shift that night. I'd just crossed over Devil's Neck." She points to a craggy strip of land leading to a promontory reaching into the sea. "Then I saw her—Mrs. Penrose. She was wearing a pale pink sweater and a matching chiffon scarf. She was gazing at the sky. She looked beautiful, all radiant like. I stopped and glanced up, expecting to see something fantastic like a comet or a falling star. I couldn't have looked for more than a second, because there wasn't anything to see. The night was cloudy. When I glanced back at Mrs. Penrose, she wasn't there."

"Wasn't there?" Mitch's voice trembles. "You mean there was no trace of her?"

"There was a trace of her." Gwenellen gets up and walks to the cliff edge. Mitch follows. Gwenellen kneels and pats the ground next to her. "This is where Mrs. Penrose was standing when I last saw her."

Mitch falls to his knees. The thrill of the story and the

closeness of the girl cause his hands to tremble. He flattens his palms to the earth. "What happened?"

Gwenellen leans over the cliff. "After she vanished, I saw her scarf. It was caught on that thicket of gorse." She points to a rocky ledge a couple of feet below.

Mitch peers over the edge of the cliffs. He imagines the body of Lara Penrose hurtling past the rugged rocks, scraping against them, bleeding, plunging into the sea.

Waves thrash against the land, one after the other, creating plumes of foam that shoot into the air, then vanish on the wind. Mesmerized, Mitch stares into the ocean. Whirlpools of angry, blue-black waters spin before him. As if in a mirage, he sees himself on a never-ending journey with Gwenellen. He can taste the sweetness of her kisses and feel the gentle caress of her hand on his forehead. His whole body aches to be with her.

The angry waters fall placid as a lake. Pale blue eyes gaze back at Mitch.

CHAPTER SIX

On the cliff path

"You look as if you've seen a ghost." Gwenellen stands, offering her hand to Mitch.

He grabs it, hauls himself onto his feet and stammers as he tries to speak. "I … I saw eyes in the sea."

"Everyone does."

The wind whips Gwenellen's hair across her face, blinding Mitch to her expression. He considers asking her more about the eyes in the ocean, but decides to let it go. He trains his mind to his sleuth, Jed Flyer, and slaps his hand against his waist to the place where the detective packs his gun. He assumes Jed's interrogative manner. "Did you see someone with Lara Penrose before she vanished?"

"Mrs. Penrose heard the chorister singing."

"Huh? What does that mean?"

"You're here to write about Cornwall, and you don't know about the Mermaid of Zennor and the chorister?"

"I'm filling in for someone else. Help me out. What should I know?"

"'Twas her, the Mermaid of Zennor, that passed me by quick as a blink right after Mrs. Penrose vanished. She took her, she did. Mrs. Penrose heard the chorister singing. That's why she looked so happy, so radiant, and that mermaid, well ... the chorister belongs to her." Gwenellen digs her fingers into Mitch's arm. "That mermaid is a shape-shifter. She can grow legs and come up on the land. They say young Matthew Trewhella had the sweetest voice God ever put in a boy. One Sunday, the Mermaid of Zennor heard him singing in the church choir, and she walked up out of the ocean, appearing to Matthew as a beautiful girl. Then she lured him back into the sea with her. Now he sings for her—and only for her—and God help you if you hear him."

Mitch laughs, thinking Gwenellen is spinning him a yarn, having fun with him.

"What's funny?" Gwenellen frowns.

Mitch kicks his heels into the rocky path. In his travels

he hears many a tale about deities and mythological beings. He usually responds with a well-practiced smile and appropriate murmurings of interest. He employs that tone with Gwenellen. "That's fascinating. I'd like to hear more about this mermaid, but right now I need to know if there was any hard evidence showing that Lara was here."

"What's hard evidence?"

"Like Lara's scarf. You gave that to the police, right?"

"I did."

Gwenellen blinks and looks away. Mitch senses she knows more. "Was there a shoe, a handkerchief, a handbag?"

"No."

"A note?"

Gwenellen licks her teeth with the tip of her tongue. "Maybe."

"A note? What did it say?"

"Tell me more about your Shangri-La. Could Miriam be there with you?"

"Miriam?" Mitch shakes his head. "Nah, I'm there alone. Well ... maybe there's someone with me."

"And who could that be?"

Gwenellen wriggles her shoulders and scrunches her breasts together, while chuckling her deep, throaty laugh. Biting back lust, Mitch sticks his hands in his pockets to stop himself from grabbing her. Murky vapors spew up from Dark Master's kingdom beneath the sea, and seep into his thoughts. Mitch reaches out for Gwenellen, but she runs off down the cliff path. She pauses briefly and blows Mitch a kiss.

Mitch rocks back and forth on the balls of his feet, his hopes for a life with her soaring like a bird caught in an updraft.

Tamara rises above Mitch, bathing her light body in sparkling atoms made of sunlight and water, cleansing herself of the long-reaching tentacles of the Black Heart.

CHAPTER SEVEN

Tea on the Atlantic Terrace

"Would you like some tea?" Kate asks Miriam.

"Never touch the stuff." Miriam flicks her hand in a dismissive gesture. "Get me a drink ... vodka ... make it a double."

"Sorry, the bar's not open yet. How about some coffee?"

"Listen to me, kid, I've had all I can take. I need a drink. Bring it in a teacup if you have to."

"I could do that, but first I've got to introduce you to Harry, you know, the man staying in the servants' quarters with us."

"I don't want to meet Harry or anyone else." Miriam

hustles Kate over to the door leading into the house. "Go to the bar and bring me a drink, and while you're at it, get me a pack of cigarettes."

"There's no smoking at the inn."

"I'm not in the inn. I'm out here on the terrace."

"Same rule, but I've got some fags in my room. We can smoke there later. I'll also bring you a teapot full of vodka, if you'll just come over and meet Harry."

Miriam frowns. "Why?"

"Because ... since Mummy isn't here, I'm supposed to introduce you to the other guests."

Miriam's heart softens. "That's great, honey, but don't bother about being polite with me. Just be yourself."

"Well, actually the river wants me to look after you."

"What?"

"The River Tamar, you crossed it as you entered Cornwall. Tamara, the spirit of the river, will be your guide while you're in Cornwall."

Miriam shakes her head. The girl is beyond comprehension, but perhaps it's a result of her mother's disappearance while taking a walk along the cliffs. What a terrible thing! "Okay, I'll meet Harry, but you'd better be working on my room situation, or both of you will be sorry you ever met me. Got that?"

"Got it." Kate ushers Miriam across the terrace toward Harry. "Dump Mitch," she whispers. "Harry's a better catch."

"Excuse me." Miriam stops and glares at the girl.

"What?" Kate says. "Harry's nice. I want him to meet someone special."

Miriam keeps a firm gaze on the girl. "I don't know what you're up to, but I'm here with Mitch, and you know it."

"Okay," Kate sighs, then grips Miriam's arm. "You have to meet Harry anyway. He's sort of our roommate." The girl steers Miriam to the end of the terrace where Harry sits by himself. "Harry, this is Miriam. She's staying upstairs with us."

Harry Treadwell stands, sweeps a thatch of light brown hair off his forehead, and shakes Miriam's hand. "I'm delighted to meet you."

Miriam takes in the broad slope of Harry's shoulders, his wide, strong jaw, and the melting look of kindness in his light brown eyes. Her annoyance with Kate fizzles.

"I'll fetch your tea." Kate scampers into the house.

Certain Mitch is off somewhere with that young maid, Miriam decides to give him a dose of his own medicine. She'll flirt with Harry. See how Mitch likes it when he returns and finds her gazing starry-eyed at another man. Miriam flops in a chair. "So, where are you from, Harry?"

Harry clears his throat and shifts uncomfortably in his chair. "London."

"Great. I love London. What brings you here?"

"I'm just divorced." Harry raises a tentative brow as if confessing to a shameful disease.

Miriam cringes, thinking of the men she's nursed back from the ravages of divorce. After months of loaning them a sympathetic ear, they had recovered, then marched off and married the next crafty bitch that came their way.

"Tea." Kate rolls a trolley up to the table between Miriam and Harry. She lifts off a tray, places it in front of Miriam, and points to a teapot. "I made white tea for you. Iced, because Americans like everything cold." She rattles a tall glass filled with ice and sets it beside the teapot. "I rustled up some food too." She unloads the trolley, filling the table with tiny cucumber sandwiches, fresh-baked scones, homemade jams, a bowl of thick clotted cream, and little iced cakes covered with silver sprinkles.

"And these are fresh-baked pasties, a Cornish specialty." Kate lifts a dish from the bottom layer of the trolley. "They're made of chopped beef, potato, and onion, wrapped in pastry, and baked till golden brown. You've got to try one."

The aroma of hot pastry drifts up Miriam's nose, and her stomach growls.

Kate bends and whispers in Miriam's ear, "That's vodka in the teapot. I've got to leave now, but meet me later in my room. We've got to talk."

Miriam grabs the teapot and sloshes vodka into the glass of ice. She gulps a mouthful, lets out a long sigh, and leans back in her chair. She glances toward the cliff path. No sign of Mitch. She looks at Harry. He squirms in his chair and wriggles his forehead as if at a loss for words. The horrors of the dating life return. Miriam shudders and asks Harry the question newly divorced men seemed to like the most: "What was your ex like?"

As if injected with adrenaline, Harry sits upright in his chair. "Pammy." His voice quavers with emotion. "Pammy had a life-long dream to sail around the world. I wrote her a poem for a wedding present, promising her we would do that in our golden years." He blinks back a tear. "We honeymooned here. I read the poem to her on this terrace each night before we went to bed."

Miriam swigs her drink, numbing herself to the sound of Harry speaking the words of his love-struck youth. She eyes the sandwiches, little triangles of thin white bread with cucumber slices. About thirty calories apiece, she figures. She takes one and works her tongue between the bread, licking the butter, relishing the forbidden food.

Harry finishes reciting his poem and stares out to sea. A pained look fills his eyes.

Miriam glances over her shoulder, searching for Mitch. The walking ladies stride through the rose arches, arms swinging, jolly voices trilling on the air. Part of Miriam wishes she could be like them, and part of her is terrified that she will be.

Miriam looks back at Harry. "Sounds like you and Pammy had a great honeymoon. I bet you came back here to celebrate your anniversaries."

"Oh, we did." The pained expression fades from Harry's eyes, and he smiles at Miriam, thinking what an unusually perceptive woman. Encouraged, he talks about the early years of his marriage and the births of his two wonderful daughters.

Miriam refills her glass with vodka and slurps it down, warding off memories of her very un-wonderful early marriage, and of her daughter, Elaine, harboring some terrible unknown hurt, an agony she defuses with cocaine rather than her mother's open arms. To console herself, Miriam eats another sandwich— another thirty calories—what the heck.

Harry explains how he and Pammy built their business—Treadfast—some sort of innovative marketing system.

The stress of feigning interest in Harry's life, coupled

with worrying about Elaine and now Mitch, provokes a raging hunger in Miriam. She reaches her hand over the platter of pasties and crumbles a piece off the ruffled crust along the top of one. The crunchy taste of butter and flour lifts her spirits. Her fingers travel back and forth, picking off the rest of the crust, bit by tiny bit. So tiny they don't register on her inner calorie counter.

Harry talks about how Treadfast became a brilliant success. Miriam probes inside the pasty and eases out chunks of beef. She consumes them one by one, sucking the juices off her fingers.

Harry shifts from his business life to the pleasures of sailing. As he covers the acquisition of his first, then five subsequent boats, Miriam delves deeper into the pasty, easing out the potato cubes, then sweet, soft onions. Finally, she breaks the pastry shell into small pieces and devours them, mopping up the juices from the beef.

Harry's voice drones on. Miriam checks her watch. Mitch has been gone for forty minutes. *Is he back in the Tower Suite having sex with that maid? She scoffs a cynical laugh. What would a beautiful young woman want with a middle-aged, barely solvent, rather disappointed man?* It's different for Miriam. Mitch needs her. He's told her so dozens of times. He admires the way she chases down a deal. Her aggression absorbs his lack of it—it's their comfort zone. Mitch wouldn't check out of that, would he? She tunes back to Harry.

He talks about his holidays with Pammy, how they sailed the oceans of the world, gazing at each other beneath the exotic sunsets of Capetown, Baja, and Bombay. Miriam picks up a scone, breaks it apart and spreads a thin layer of jam on each side. She avoids the clotted cream. It's made from fat-rich milk simmered over a low flame until the fat surfaces and forms a solid crust. She absolutely will not touch it. Not even a teeny-weeny taste. She's not even having butter on her scone, and butter is her favorite food. When Harry begins a discourse on the merits of coastal and celestial navigation, she considers adding just the thinnest layer of butter to the scone. If anything could be less interesting than Pammy, navigation might be it. Then again, there may be a greater challenge ahead. She decides to hold the butter in reserve.

Her eye falls on the cakes. They're about one inch square and coated with icing of various colors. She pops a pink one into her mouth. The sugar in the icing meets the sugar in the vodka. She enjoys a burst of new energy. Miriam nods and smiles in response to Harry's occasional inquiry as to whether she understands the coastal-celestial navigation thing.

Harry goes on to describe the differences between sloops, ketches, and yawls. Miriam eats another teacake. Then another. She glances frequently to the cliff path. A terrible emptiness gnaws at her gut. She's been dating Mitch for almost two years. Her girlfriends don't think he's a good marriage prospect because Mitch has never married. Miriam has always considered that a plus. Mitch has no bitter memories, no alimony, and no child support or custody battles. Having flitted away most of her thirties on men lumbered with this kind of baggage, Mitch came as a pleasant relief. She hasn't yet figured out his resistance to commitment, but senses it stems from an unhappy childhood. They'd fallen into an easygoing relationship, meeting for dinner, movies, and sex two or three times a week. Up until he laid eyes on Gwenellen, she'd never suspected him of being interested in other women. Mitch spent his spare time holed up in his dingy studio apartment writing detective novels that no publisher wanted.

She grabs the teapot and shakes it over her glass, eking out the last drops of vodka. Harry rambles on about the recent sale of his company. He says that while he took care of that, Pammy, an in-her-own-right dynamic businesswoman, charity worker, world's best mother, daughter, and wife, went looking for the right sailing instructor for their round-the-world venture.

Miriam slugs down her drink. She's heard this story a dozen times. Pammy found Mr. Right-Sailing-Instructor in the form of a twenty-two-year-old Norwegian and fell in love with him. What does surprise Miriam, and what wipes everything from her mind, even her suspicions about Mitch and that tramp of a maid, is the way Harry speaks about Pammy and her lover.

Harry lowers his voice. "Pammy, wonderful, sweet Pammy, really tried not to fall in love with this young man." Tears slip from Harry's eyes. "I ... oh ... I felt her pain. She hated hurting me. She wept when she told me of their affair." He withdraws a white cotton handkerchief from his pocket and blows his nose. "It was so awful for her. She told me all this two days before our twenty-fifth wedding anniversary. Then she had to ask me for a divorce. Oh ... it was frightful! I thought she might suffer a nervous breakdown."

Oh, my God! Miriam grips the arms of her chair. *What denial!* Her head swims with images of the adored Pammy—no doubt thin, with girlish blonde hair and peachy skin. She probably eats enough to feed a whale and never gains an ounce, and when the young Norwegian dumps her for the next bored bitch, she'll run back to Harry—and he'll welcome her with open arms. *Why am I listening to this shit?*

Miriam swipes a scone off the plate and slathers it with butter—soft, yellow, fresh-off-the-farm butter. She bites into the pastry and moans as the creamy rich flavors sink into her taste buds. "Umm ... umm ... umm!"

Dear God, thank you for butter.

Miriam writhes in her chair, helping herself freely to everything on the table. The inner critic falls silent. She floats in a place where pain and ecstasy rub against one another—where reason says it's impossible to have one without the other, so enjoy. She eats without conscience, basking in unfettered delight, until she hears Harry calling her name. "Go easy, Miriam! You could get sick."

Conscience flies back into action. Horror flares through Miriam as she finds herself clutching the bowl of clotted cream to her breast, whipping a spoon around the edges, scraping off the last of the crusty substance.

Goddamn!

She slams the dish on the table. Ten gazillion fat grams sink like the Titanic into her stomach. Her head swims in a haze of booze, sugar, and fat. Mitch still isn't back, and Harry's looking at her as if expecting an explanation.

A button pops off the waistband of her slacks. "Shit!"

"Is something wrong?" Harry furrows his brow.

Angry responses spin in Miriam's thoughts: *Why the hell do you call a grown woman Pammy? Why do you sing her praises when she broke your heart?* Before she can express them, Harry leans closer to her.

"I'm so sorry you're upset, Miriam. Is there anything I can do to help you?"

Miriam shifts her glance to the cliffs. This is all Mitch's fault. He's started an affair with that young maid. She can feel it in her bones.

Mitch turns onto the path beneath the rose arches. Catching sight of Miriam on the terrace, he feels relieved. He knows his attraction to Gwenellen is foolish, but she makes him feel so alive and young. He just wants to flirt with her. There's no reason why Miriam should ever find out.

Mitch plucks a pink rose from an arch and strides forth, waving the flower at Miriam. He prances up the steps to the terrace. With his head full of Gwenellen, he doesn't notice Miriam's agitated state. He introduces himself to Harry, then embarks on a travelogue about his expedition into the area. He twists the rose between his fingers and speaks a little too quickly and with much too much gusto—describing rocks he has not climbed over, coves he has not seen, and the feel of foam cresting off a sea he has not felt. All of which is obvious to Miriam.

Accusations roil in Miriam's head, and just as she prepares to unleash her fury on Mitch, Harry senses her intention. He rests a firm hand on her arm, imparting a gentle warning. His touch sends shockwaves through Miriam, shockwaves of kindness. They penetrate her heart, feeling like rays of warm light, melting her rage. The man—who minutes ago had seemed pathetic in his love for his wife—becomes desirable.

"Mir." Mitch frowns at the sight of Miriam staring at Harry, her mouth parting in a sensuous smile. "Mir." He waves the rose in front of her. "This is for you."

CHAPTER EIGHT

Friday evening, ocean dancing

Dusk mottles the sky in shades of purple and amber, and the magnetic draw of the moon tugs on the ocean. The smaller rivers of the region begin emptying into the basin of the Tamar. Tamara floats on their swells in her light body, waiting for Tavy and Tawridge to join her on their evening journey into the sea.

Tavy comes first, moving his light body in a fast-paced crawl. On the night the giants were transformed into rivers, Tavy preceded Tawridge. Tavy, precise and cautious in his ways, found Tamara's river immediately and gushed alongside her, following her path into the sea. Tawridge, excitable and impulsive by nature, spun his waters around and around, delighting in the agility of his new light body so much that he lost his sense of direction and found himself flowing away from Tamara. Hence,

Tawridge flows toward the north coast. He'll meet with Tamara and Tavy shortly as he bounds around the peninsula, coursing his own unique current.

Fishing boats and merchant vessels chart their courses for night, while smaller craft slip into harbors and drop anchor. The warm wash of the Gulf Stream carries the faint echo of steel drums playing in the Caribbean. Tavy and Tamara lock their light bodies in a dancer's embrace and sway to the beat of the calypso as they glide into the Atlantic. The cooler drift of the Canary Current melds into Tamara's river, followed by icy streams from the Arctic Ocean. She welcomes the glacial flow, as it sluices her innermost waters and cleanses a residue of sorrow—painful last memories of her father—stirred up by her recent skirmish with Dark Master.

"Taw! Over here." Tavy waves his arms, beckoning his brother to join them. Tawridge plows through the North Sea, tossing fish high in the air in the wake of his exuberance. As they meet, they twine their rivers and light bodies together and dance as they once danced on the moors, but their stride is longer now and made more fluid by being one with the purpose of their lives.

They sweep from ocean to ocean around the globe, lapping onto every shore, showering hope and love onto the beaches and into the cities of the world. In the sparkling blue Pacific, they slither over the black lava rock of the Big Island in

Hawaii and pause for a little river talk. Tamara tells the giants about Miriam and the two possible futures she foresaw for her, and the golden sail that appeared as Mitch glanced upon her river. She describes how Dark Master swung his great cape over that sail and blinded her to a future that might have belonged to Mitch.

Tawridge gasps a noisy breath. "A golden sail? It must belong to *Mercy*. Do you think the great galleon could be ready to rise up from the ocean bed?"

"Not yet. The time doesn't feel right."

"Let's get back to Miriam and her sacred future," Tavy says, pressing a finger against his right cheek, a mannerism he employs when he intends to get to the bottom of things. "You said Miriam's strongest desire is to marry Mitch, but Mitch appears unaware of this."

"I wouldn't say he's unaware; I think he's just not ready to make such a commitment."

"Does he love her?" Tawridge asks.

"I suspect Mitch hasn't asked himself that."

"That doesn't sound promising for Miriam," Tavy says, scratching his chin. "Have you told Miriam her sacred future is to rescue Lara Penrose?"

"Yes, but Miriam does not hear me yet. Her sacred

destiny sleeps in her subconscious, buried beneath layers of guilt and fear."

"Oh, dear," Tawridge sighs, "that means she'll be very resistant to meet it."

Tamara fills them in on Mitch's obsession with Gwenellen. "It's obviously orchestrated by Dark Master, as the blue-black vapors of the Black Heart follow Mitch whenever she's around."

Tavy's brows shoot up. "If Mitch leaves Miriam for Gwenellen, Miriam's likely to be so upset that she'll hear you, Tamara. Once a cherished dream is lost, even our most unwilling charges have been glad to discover they have a sacred future."

Tawridge laughs. "Miriam won't give up on Mitch easily. She's a tenacious woman. I picked up on that the moment you mentioned her, Tamara."

"But she's no match for Dark Master," Tavy says.

"Shush!" Tawridge commands, swirling around in his river and bending his ear to the ocean floor. Minutes pass. Neither Tamara nor Tavy disturb him. Tawridge can hear around the bend in the wind and to the other side of the sun. He whispers, "We've got to go," then thrusts Tamara and Tavy in the direction of their native shore, giving them no time to question his order.

They flow as one river, zooming through the creatures of the sea, paring the waters with their spirits. "What is it?" Tamara asks, separating her river from the giants' as they roll into Trellan Bay, a little horseshoe cove beneath *Penrose Hall*.

"I heard the Deva Chorus singing," Tawridge says, the great bell tone of his own voice reverberating through the ocean. "They were chanting inside Mt. Rube."

"But that's impossible," Tavy says. "The Deva Chorus has not been heard since Ruberah sank."

"Well ... they have now," Tawridge says. "It was as if no time had passed since we all lived on Ruberah. I understood the language of rubies, and I was not mistaken in what was said. The Devas told me Mitch is destined to be the next prisoner in the Black Heart."

A crease of disbelief gouges Tavy's brow, and Tamara cuts in before he disputes Tawridge and they engage in a long argument. The brothers love to disagree; it comes from having been alone with each other for so long. "Let's consider why Dark Master would want to capture Mitch," Tamara says.

Tavy's frown fades. "Did you see the rose glow of Ruberah in Mitch's aura? Is there a chance he's an old Ruberian?"

"As Mitch is not under my guardianship, I've not felt sufficient cause to look deeply into his aura."

"Wait!" Tawridge flips his eyes upward, and an enraptured smile shivers over his countenance. "I'm receiving an impression about Mitch." He shifts his eyes from side to side as if scouring the landscape of his memory. "I see the tracings of his spirit in the Time of Ruberah, but I cannot locate him." He blinks. "How strange; it's like he's neither there nor here."

"Maybe you misunderstood the Deva Chorus," Tavy says.

"I did not. They distinctly said Mitch would be the next prisoner of the Black Heart."

To quell a rivalry about to flare up between the brothers, Tamara makes them an offer neither will refuse. "I think we should look back to Ruberah through my spirit vision. Perhaps we'll discover whether Mitch lived at that time, and if so, what kind of relationship he had with Miriam."

CHAPTER NINE

Illumined vision

Tavy and Tawridge press their heads close to Tamara's and stare through the beam of her spirit sight as it cuts through the Atlantic. The giants' hearts pound with excitement, reminding Tamara of how she felt when she followed her father's gaze into the Cycles of Time. The pain of losing him stabs her in the heart, raw as ever.

Tawridge points into the ocean. "There it is ... the pink light of Ruberah."

The rose luminosity wafts into the underbelly of the Atlantic, spiraling up in long tendrils that flare out like fireworks and fall back down over the lost kingdom. Debris from the once glorious capital city of Az'Rayelle scatters far and wide, mounding on the ocean bed like an artist's rendering for a futuristic society. Mt. Rube, the great ruby mountain, towers above the rubble, unscarred by the violence that ripped it from the earth. Layers of seaweed and barnacles cling to the massive gem, dimming its ruby glow.

To the left of the mountain, the storied golden galleon *Mercy* lies stranded on her side. At the beginning of the Age of Jeweled Intelligence, Gold gave *Mercy* to the world as a ship to help those in distress on the seas. When loved ones went missing, people gathered, prayed, and blew the breath of the wind into her sails to aid her with their rescue. Now, sea anemones flower among the sheets of her fallen silks—fabric spun from the golden yarn of the earth's heart—fabric as indestructible as the heart itself. Legend says *Mercy* will rise up and cruise the seas again. The Cornish still pray to the galleon when a ship goes down, and often an apparition of the vessel appears on the horizon, shining her light on those in trouble, calming the seas around them. The Coast Guard doesn't doubt these sightings. Many a sailor lives by the grace of the golden galleon.

"I can't find any clues about Mitch or Miriam by looking into the ruins," Tawridge says. "Could you ask the Cycles of Time for help?"

"I'll try, but I can ask only about Miriam at this time." Tamara holds the intention of being the best guide she can be for Miriam, and looks into space. Her vision sweeps through the stars and galaxies and lands on the glittering loops of the Cycles of Time. She bows into the dot in the center, where the past and the future cross over and form the present. "Beloved Time, would you show me a scene from Ruberah that would help me understand Miriam's resistance to her sacred future?"

Moments pass. Tamara holds her gaze steady on the Cycles. A light about the size of a dust mote springs into action in the loop of the past. It darts back and forth through the pink light of Ruberah, then stops. Like a movie released from a freeze-frame, the capitol city of Az'Rayelle springs to life.

Hundreds of tall, bronze-skinned people glide over jeweled pathways that crisscross the city. Others ride the light paths down to the harbor and out to the plains where Mt. Rube glistens ruby red. Men and women wear white gauze robes that billow in the wake of their motion. Many sport necklaces, armbands, and elaborate headdresses made of gold and rubies. To govern their speed and direction, they tap on an astral disk, a thin round of crystal attached to their palms. Athletic and nimble, the Ruberians leap onto and off the light paths, disappearing into white marble buildings and gold-domed houses surrounded with lush gardens and waterfalls flowing with rose-colored water.

Tamara sniffs the scents of the wind, sea, and flowers. No pollution permeates the air. Rube provides energy for homes, industries, and airships that transport a thousand people at a time.

A beautiful woman with honey-colored hair steps off a light path near the Crystal Temple of Science. She wears a pendant shaped like the

Heart of Rube—the first ruby mined on Earth. The gem rests on her forehead, suspended from a golden band. She pauses before entering the temple and looks tentatively at her reflection in the gleaming glass. You are not enough. *Princess Li'ram, first in line to the throne of Ruberah and High Priestess of Sound, chokes back tears and clutches her heart.*

The scene closes, and the Cycles of Time disappear. Tawridge glances at Tamara, a look of surprise in his eyes. "Miriam was Princess Li'ram. Did you know that?"

"Yes, from the moment her sacred future awakened in my river."

"That was obvious," Tavy says, still smarting because Tawridge heard the Deva Chorus and he did not.

"Li'ram didn't feel loved, and that's sad," Tawridge says.

"She didn't feel worthy of her position as a High Priestess of Sound," Tamara says, "and she's suffering from similar feelings today—lack of self-worth—and these feelings will increase until she accepts her sacred future."

Tavy strokes his chin. "Given Dark Master's interest in Mitch and given that he is here with Miriam, I would say that Mitch must have been Da'krah, Prince of the Emerald Kingdom."

CHAPTER TEN

Nighttime in the Tower Suite

Tamara floats into the mists of Ruberah drifting around the west tower of *Penrose Hall*. She asks the mists about Mitch. They affirm that he was Da'krah, Prince of the Emerald Kingdom. Tamara slips inside the tower. Mitch sleeps on in his twin bed, lying on his back. His eyelids flutter and his mouth droops open. Murky vapors from the underworld float above his head. He begins to dream.

He's in a small sailboat, skimming the clear turquoise waters of a calm sea. An island with white sandy beaches comes into view. The beauteous Gwenellen emerges from a gathering of leafy green trees, her curvy body draped in a panel of nude fabric. She saunters to the shore, smiling and waving at him. Her throaty laughter rides on the wind. Sugar-sweet. Mitch loses patience with the slow speed of his boat and leaps overboard, swimming swiftly toward his darling. As he reaches shallow water, he stands and runs toward Gwenellen.

The pink mists speak to Tamara: "Enter Mitch's dream. Appear to him, and try to warn him of Dark Master's hold over him."

Tamara dives into Mitch's dream and comes up by his side as he wades toward Gwenellen on the beach. She taps him on the shoulder, and his spirit vision flashes open.

Mitch shades his eyes against the brilliance of Tamara's light body. "Who are you?' he asks.

"I am Tamara, Spirit of the Tamar, a tributary of the one great river that runs through eternity."

"Why are you here?"

"Your future has been altered by Dark Master, the ruler of the underworld. I advise you to leave Cornwall and return to your home. Leave now, while you can."

"I can't. I have to write an article about the area." Mitch wades into the crystal waters of the River of Life, and gazes into the stars of Earth's galaxy. "Have I died? Am I in heaven?"

"No. You're in your dream world."

"Really?" A wondrous smile fills Mitch's face. "Show me around the celestial skies, will you?"

"Take my hand."

Tamara guides Mitch through the Milky Way and around the moon. Mitch points to a ring of bright-colored spheres circling a clear sphere in the middle. "What's that constellation?"

"Those are the astral orbs of the Jewel Kingdom … rubies, emeralds, sapphires, amethyst, diamonds, pearls, and the sacred metal, gold. Each emits an intelligence which is designed to one day be available to the human family. The clear sphere in the center is Astral Command. It monitors and measures the collective consciousness of the people, checking for the right time to bring forth knowledge from each kingdom."

"Yeah? What are we using now?"

"Gold. Gold is love. Everyone is born with a flame of gold in his heart. Everyone has the capacity to love."

"What about the others?"

"We once could use the power of rubies."

"How?"

"Rubies generate extraordinary creative ideas, but in order to implement them, they must be beneficial to all people everywhere. We used the light of the sun and the sounds of the universe to blend with the intelligence of rubies, and then their force came alive. It was called Rube. Do you remember that?"

"No. What's that green sphere? That light burns so green it's almost blue. That's really beautiful."

"That's the orb of the Emerald Kingdom."

"I'd like to get a closer look at that."

Tamara guides Mitch through the stars and up to the curve of the shimmering emerald orb.

"It looks like a huge piece of blown glass," Mitch says, squinting into the green light. "Look, there a fracture in the side—a hairline fracture. Oh, my God!"

Mitch begins speaking in the language of rubies. He shouts at Tamara, "You didn't help me when I needed you." The force of his fury hits the Emerald Sphere, and the fracture in the jewel splits open. The Soul of Emeralds, a tiny green flame about the size of a minnow, slips through the crevice and vanishes into space.

Tamara reaches into the blue screen of the cosmic mind, grabs a sound wave and tosses an urgent message to Tavy and Tawridge. "The flame of the Emerald Kingdom has slipped from its sphere. Search the universe at once! Find it and return it."

She watches the giants depart Earth immediately, their massive light bodies ascending into the skies. As they speed off in different directions, she returns her attention to Mitch. He's still yelling at her in the language of rubies, blaming her for all his problems. She splashes waves over him, trying to calm him down, but he continues to rant. More painful memories surface, and as he rages at Tamara, he causes a storm in her river. Currents well up and whirl around his neck. "Help me," he shouts. "I'm drowning!"

Tamara reaches inside her own dedicated ray into the earth's heart, hauls up streams of golden light, and filters it into her river. Mitch falls calm. The pink mists of Ruberah advise her to close his spirit vision. She touches his forehead. His illumined sight closes.

He tosses in his bed, punching his fists into his pillow.

CHAPTER ELEVEN

A maid of many talents

Leaving Mitch, Tamara sweeps into the reception hall. She receives a message from the giants saying they've scoured space from the Milky Way to the White Sun Galaxy and found no trace of the Emerald Flame.

"Search the planet," Tamara replies. "You know how imperative it is that we find it."

"We do," Tavy responds, his voice sinking to a low and serious tone. "How did it happen?"

"I'll tell you later." Tamara nears the grandfather clock, and its mechanism cranks and whirs, then strikes eleven gongs. The night deepens. She senses the approach of someone with questionable intentions. Slightly uneven footfalls crunch on the gravel path that hugs the foundation of the house. The person heads in the direction of Lance Penrose's study. Tamara does too.

Kate's father sits in a big, burgundy leather chair inside his study. A bottle of Napoleon brandy stands on a side table. Lance sips the brown liqueur from a balloon glass and gazes at a photo of his family in a silver frame resting on his lap. By Kate's appearance, Tamara suspects it is the last picture taken of them all together. Lara gazes up at Lance, crinkling her nose in the playful air of a happy woman. Kate and her brother look straight into the camera, their sibling green eyes matching their father's. Lance's red hair flows back from his sharp widow's peak. An easy smile covers his strong-boned face.

French doors soften the sound of the sea crashing against the cliffs. Uneven footsteps cross the patio outside. Lance sinks lower in his chair. A haze of fog drifts against the French doors. Lights glow inside the fog—spirits of those lost at sea. Tamara glances to the waters above the ancient kingdom of Ruberah. Tall golden masts rise up and scrape the night sky. Someone prays for someone lost.

Knuckles rap against the glass panes.

Lance jolts his head back. "Who's there?" He looks at the windows. A shadowy silhouette looms in the fog.

Tap-tap. Tap-tap.

Lance grunts and eases himself up from the chair. He places the photograph on his desk, then opens the double doors. Fog creeps into the room but soon dissipates in the warmth of the house. Lance waves his hand back and forth, clearing the mist clinging to the doors. "Who is it?"

"Me." Gwenellen stands on the patio, clutching a cardigan about her. "Can I come in?"

Lance rubs his eyes and ushers her inside. "Is something wrong? What are you doing here at this hour?"

"I ..." Gwenellen crooks a finger through a buttonhole in her cardigan. "I ... Mrs. Penrose ... well, she was good to me." Gwenellen's eyes take on a demure look. She lowers them.

"Yes?" Lance raises a brow.

"I could help out some more, if you like." The singsong of Gwenellen's brogue thickens with every word. "I'm good at figures. I could help with the accounts after my cleaning work. You know, come in here and—"

"Thank you, but that's not necessary. You should go home now."

Gwenellen tilts her head and looks wistfully at Lance. "Being close to you makes me think of Mrs. Penrose. I might even remember something more about her disappearance."

"Are you withholding information?" Lance clasps his

hands together to stop himself from shaking the young woman and forcing her to remember any forgotten details about Lara's last moments.

"I don't know, do I?" Tears glint in Gwenellen's eyes. "All that interrogating by the police. I ..." She heaves a shaky breath. "A girl could forget, couldn't she?" Gwenellen yanks a tissue from her sleeve and dabs her eyes.

"Now, now, don't cry." Lance holds his hand close to her shoulder, debating whether to rest it on her in a gesture of comfort. He abhors tears. He never knows what to do when faced with a weeping woman. He draws his hand back and heads for his desk. "Think carefully, Gwenellen. It's a serious matter to lie to the police."

"I didn't lie to them. I'm always trying to remember to see if I forgot something. I'm just trying to help. I feel awful for you and Kate, but I'd feel better if I could help you more."

"Right. I appreciate that, but we can't afford to pay for—"

"I'd do it for free." Gwenellen tucks the tissue up her sleeve.

"Why? You barely earn enough to rent a room in the village."

"I could move into the loft above the stables. That

would help me, and I'd be here. I could work late."

"The stables? It's a mess up there. No one's lived there for years."

"I'm handy with a paint brush. That's all it needs, a good scrubbing and a coat of paint. Please, Mr. Penrose. I wouldn't feel so lonely if I was close to you and Kate."

Lance looks back at the photo of his family. Lara hired Gwenellen, as she had all the domestic staff. Lance had thought Gwenellen too attractive—well, too buxom—to work at the inn. Men would flirt with her, and that could lead to all sorts of trouble. Lara insisted they give her a chance. The young woman had recently lost her parents in an automobile accident.

She's come to us, Lance. We cannot turn her away.

Lance straightens his shoulders. "Very well, you can live above the stables."

"Oh, thank you." Gwenellen moves closer to Lance. "I'll be ever so helpful, you'll see."

"Yes. Right. That's it then. Off you go."

Gwenellen slips out into the night, but she doesn't head toward the village. She scampers around the house and re-enters through the kitchen door. Tamara lingers in the reception hall, watching to see what's next on her agenda.

Gwenellen dashes across the hall and climbs the main staircase.

Tamara follows her. The young woman's scent smells like sunbaked sand—quite pleasing—until Tamara detects a base note of dried seaweed. Gwenellen takes the second and third flights two steps at a time. On the top floor, she hurries past Kate and Miriam's rooms and stands outside Harry's door. She wriggles her shoulders and giggles like a child about to play a prank. She knocks on the door.

"Harry, it's me."

She doesn't wait for a reply. She uses her master key and lets herself in.

"Oh! I say!" Harry leaps out of bed. A startled, wide-eyed expression freezes on his face. He hauls his robe over red-striped pajamas and knots the sash tightly at his waist. "I ... er ... Why are you here?"

Gwenellen sidles up to him. "Poor Harry, you're so sad. It hurts me to see you like that." She strokes his cheek. "You don't want me to feel sad too, do you?"

"No ... no, of course not." Harry yanks his head to the side, away from Gwenellen's hand.

"That's so sweet." Gwenellen plunks her hands on his shoulders. "Let's dance, Harry." Pushing him backward through the room, she glides after him, swaying her hips like a tango dancer and singing a song about a dark, secluded place called Hernando's Hideaway.

Harry's back hits the wall. He stares into the space above Gwenellen's head, his eyes like those of a sergeant at arms. "I'm not sad anymore," he says.

"No?" Gwenellen cups Harry's face in her hands and forces him to look down at her. "Because if you are, I could be good to you."

"Ah ... well ... er ... um." Harry bites his lip, hating himself for his silly bumbling manner. *I could be good to you!* Oh, why can't he say, yes, please?

"So, you're all right then, are you?" Gwenellen bats her eyes.

"Yes, yes, I'm fine."

"Good ... then will you help me with something?"

"If I can."

"Oooh." Gwenellen squeals a scale of delight and cuddles her arms about her breasts, causing them to jiggle and swell over the top of her bra.

A hypnotic look glazes over Harry's eyes. For the first time since Pammy left, desire floods through him. "What can I do?"

"Mr. Penrose said I could move into the room above the stables. It needs painting. Would you help me with that?"

Harry nods eagerly, wondering if he could ask her to be good to him now. But the opportunity passes before he can find suitable words.

Gwenellen walks to the door. "Thank you, Harry." She kisses the palm of her hand and blows the kiss back to him. "Sleep well."

Harry flings himself on his bed and kicks his legs in the air. The agonizing ache of his divorce shrinks into a manageable event. He's ready to see other women. Of course, Gwenellen is utterly inappropriate, but ...

I could be good to you, Harry.

Tamara follows Gwenellen down the main staircase. As the young woman crosses the reception hall, she veers right and hides in a narrow passage between the kitchen and the stairs leading to the Tower Suite. She cranes her neck and peers up the stairs, seeming to contemplate a visit to Mitch.

"Who's there?" Lance steps into the hall.

Gwenellen draws back into the shadows.

Lance looks around, scratching his head.

Gwenellen bolts to the kitchen. The back door slams shut behind her.

CHAPTER TWELVE

Kate's plan for Miriam

Kate stomps up and down her room, complaining about Tamara, or "T," as she silently refers to her. T harps on and on about what she should and should not do.

Honestly!

The girl grits her teeth. It was all right when she was younger to have T around all the time, whispering in her head. As a small child, she loved playing with T and the giants. It was fun to see them in their light bodies, and her absolute favorite thing in the whole world was to hear them tell stories of Ruberah. Kate's own memory of having lived in the jeweled age came alive as she listened. The symbols of the ruby language drifted into her memory, appearing like chords in music, but made of stars, dots, suns, and waves. As she gazed at them, they burst into pictures. She caught glimpses of her life in Ruberah. She'd been a girl of sixteen and looked much as she looks today. She was super cool; she knew how to filter rays from the sun into Mt. Rube and operate its force. She even saw herself on the day of *The Ending*. She was thrashing around in the water, holding the Scrolls of Knowledge above her head, but they fell and sank into Dark Master's kingdom.

Since then, it's been her one goal to get them back. Now that her mother is a prisoner in the Black Heart, she has double the reason to go there. Kate bites her lip in thought. With Miriam's sacred future coming due, everything is falling into place, but she's got to get Miriam to go to Ruberah with her. She knows Miriam lived as Li'ram in Ruberah—a High Priestess of Sound—and since Kate was a Sun Master, together they could use Rube.

Kate filches a pack of Gauloises from an iron tin beneath her bed. Her brother scored them for her, duty-free in Paris, when he made a quick trip home the day after her mother had gone missing. Dear Christopher, if she nagged him enough he would do anything for her. Then again, poor Christopher— neither he nor her father can see through their spirit vision. They don't know her mother is alive. Kate tried to tell them, but the minute she said she'd seen her through her illumined vision, they both nodded and smiled in the condescending way they always do at any mention of her mystical powers.

Kate rips open the pack of cigarettes and sniffs them. "Mummm ... umm ... umm." The unfiltered tobacco pumps adrenaline into her blood. French resistance fighters had smoked Gauloises, and their slogan had been: *Liberté toujours.* "That's me." Kate thrusts her fist in the air. "*Liberté toujours!*"

Kate leaves her room and raps her knuckles on Miriam's door. "It's me, Kate. Let me in." The hall clock strikes twelve chimes. Kate knocks harder. "Come on, Miriam, you can't be asleep yet."

The door swings opens, and Miriam leans an elbow against the frame. "So, have you found me a room with Mitch?"

Kate barges into the room. "Want a fag?"

"A what?"

"Ciggy." Kate holds up the Gauloises. She notices a flinty, nervous look in Miriam's eyes. She definitely needs a smoke. Advantage: Kate. She pops a cigarette in her own mouth, lights up with a Bic, and puffs smoke in Miriam's face.

Miriam hauls a suitcase from beneath her bed. "So, where's the room?"

"You're not moving, and it's got nothing to do with me. You're not meant to be with Mitch right now. You're meant to be on your sacred future, SF, that's what I call it, and when it's time for SF, things happen, and they happen to help *you.*"

"Yeah? Well … tell SF this. If I'm not moving in with Mitch, I'm going home."

"Don't be daft." Kate kicks Miriam's bag back under the bed. "Do this now, Miriam, or SF will bug the shit out of you until you do."

"What kind of language is that?"

"The kind of language you understand. New York speak, right?"

Miriam glares at Kate. "Give me a goddam cigarette!"

Kate offers the pack to Miriam and flicks her lighter open. She watches Miriam drag in a large draft of smoke.

"Jesus Christ!" Miriam coughs and bangs her hand against her chest. "You'll kill yourself with these!"

"Dying is probably interesting if you're the one doing it, but it stinks if it takes someone you love. My mother's not dead—she's a prisoner in the Black Heart, but she can't live very long in that place. We've got to get her out. I need her. Lots of people need her. I must get her back. You've got to help me!"

Miriam picks a piece of tobacco off her tongue and flicks it on the floor. As crazy as Kate sounds, and as much as Miriam wants to back away from her, she can't. Kate touches a nerve in her—the same kind of hardwired nerve that keeps Miriam connected to Mitch. Even in the face of Mitch's betrayal

117

with Gwenellen, she loves him. Even in the face of Kate's outrageous request for Miriam to rescue her mother, she can't walk away from her. "I'm really sorry about your mother, Kate. I'd like to help, but I honestly don't understand what you're talking about. Sacred futures and river spirits that talk to people make no sense to me."

"Well … I'm here to explain it to you." Kate plunks her butt down on the bed and beckons Miriam to sit beside her. "Come on," she says, softening her tone. "I can help you."

Miriam flops on the bed. Her gut hurts as if being fed into a meat grinder. "I'm not agreeing to anything, but go ahead. Explain away."

Kate produces a little half smile, a slight, pouty upturn of her lips that loans her an air of sweetness and innocence. "You dream at night, don't you?"

"Sometimes, I guess."

"Well … see … you've got an aura of light around you," Kate lowers her voice and speaks with a reverential hush. "Your aura is your spirit force. Sometimes you become aware of its light in your dream world, and when you do, you can do things you can't normally do. Some people, like me, can see through their spirit light when they're not dreaming. My mother can too. That's how I know she's alive." Kate changes her tone to an urgent whisper. "When you crossed the River Tamar, your SF played like a video on the surface of the river. Tamara saw you rescuing my mother from the Black Heart. That's how we know you're destined to meet your SF. All you have to do is be *willing* to embrace it. Then, when you go to sleep, you'll feel the light of your aura, and you'll hear the sound of the ocean. Then just let go and you'll be on your way to the greatest journey of your life." Kate rests a hand on Miriam's. "You'll never be alone on your SF. I'll be with you, and Tamara and Tavy and Tawridge will help us, if we need them." Kate wrinkles her nose in the same endearing manner of her mother. "Will you do that, Miriam? Will you help me save my mother?"

CHAPTER THIRTEEN

A somnambulant journey

It seemed harmless to tell Kate she would help her mother if she saw her in a dream, but now Miriam's not sure, and she dreads going to sleep. She strolls onto her balcony and rests her palms on the battlement. The sea looks black, frigid, and frightening. Miriam shivers. She's a chaise-by-the-pool kind of woman. The idea of even dipping a toe in that ocean scares her, let alone submerging herself beneath it.

Miriam trudges back to her bed, assuring herself that nothing will come of her promise. Kate is just comforting herself with heroic thoughts of saving her mother. She downs a Xanax and massages her face with a regimen of anti-aging products. The routine relaxes her, and the pill begins to kick in. She sinks her head onto her pillow. Self-denigrating thoughts plague her. She's a terrible mother. She left the country while her child is in rehab.

The reality of losing Mitch hits home; she'll have to return to New York and tell her friends he left her for a nineteen-year-old. She'll leave out the blonde bombshell part. No one would believe it. *Oh, the humiliation! Oh, the loss!* How will she fill the vast empty space where hope of a life together had thrived? She tosses from one side to another. Why does she want a man who doesn't want her?

Tamara slips into Miriam's room in her light body, ready to meet Miriam in her dreams and guide her on her sacred future. She sits on her bed and splashes waves of light from the earth's heart into Miriam's. Miriam falls into a deep sleep and finds herself wading into a river of sparkling bright waters.

"Hello, Miriam." Tamara walks towards her with her arms outstretched. "I'm here to help you."

"Who are you?" Miriam looks straight into Tamara's eyes. "I've seen you somewhere before."

"I am Tamara, Spirit of the River Tamar. You saw me as you crossed my river and entered Cornwall. I'm here to guide you on your sacred future. Come with me and no harm shall befall you."

Fragments of Miriam's recent conversation with Kate

return. *Beneath the sea ... Black Heart ... imprisoned mother.* "No!"

"You'll be safe with me, Miriam."

"I don't want to go into the sea. Please don't make me."

"I will never make you do anything. I'm here—"

Tamara stops, as she perceives Kate traveling in her own dream world, striding toward Miriam. Tamara glances into the mists of Ruberah and asks to know what Kate is up to. The mists reveal that Kate has devised a plan to override Tamara's authority and escort Miriam on her sacred future.

Tamara holds a halting hand up to Kate. "Do not try to influence Miriam in her decisions. You will—"

"Blah, blah," Kate says, crashing into Tamara's river and squeezing herself between Miriam and Tamara. "Miriam has promised to help me get my mother back."

"Under considerable coercion from you, no doubt, which as you know—"

"No, Miriam wants to help me." Kate reaches behind Tamara and grabs Miriam's hand. "Come on, Miriam. Let's go."

Kate's defiant attitude disturbs Tamara, but she attributes it to the grief and sense of helplessness Kate feels over the loss of her mother. Tamara would like to whirl energy around Kate and force her to leave Miriam alone, but she must allow

Miriam to make up her own mind. "It will be dangerous to go with Kate," Tamara says to Miriam, but before she can explain why, Kate tugs hard on Miriam's arm and yanks her out of Tamara's river.

Miriam instantly forgets Tamara, but still locked in her dream world, she becomes aware of the glowing energy of her own aura. A sense of empowerment envelops her and she doesn't want to be led anywhere by anyone. "I need to go off on my own for a while," she says to Kate. "I won't be long. I'll see you later on."

"Where are you going?" Kate asks, trailing after Miriam.

Miriam smiles at Kate and gently nudges her back into her own dream world. "I need some space."

Miriam marvels at her own words. She who has never liked being alone suddenly longs to explore by herself. Feeling carefree in her dream body, she affirms to Kate that she will be back soon, then leaves her room. She runs down the narrow stairs of the servants' quarters, relishing the lightness of her body. She pauses at the entrance to the grand staircase, rests a hand on the banister, and descends slowly. She treads happily alone, holding her head high like a woman entering a ball. On the landing, she pauses and looks up at the portrait of Lara Penrose. Lara evokes a sense of déjà vu—a haunting memory that Miriam can't quite grasp. She squints and moves closer to the painting. She detects an accusation behind the smile on Lara's face—an accusation directed at her.

You are not enough.

Miriam gasps, as the painful allegation echoes on and on in her thoughts. She holds her hand up, shielding herself from the portrait. "No. No. No."

Miriam descends the rest of the stairs as fast as she can. Then breathless—she glides across the reception hall, floating in the long somnambulant strides of her dream world. Spacious blanks lapse between her thoughts, and rose-colored memories gather. Miriam pushes open the door to the Atlantic Terrace. She sniffs the scents of rosemary, lavender, and sage drifting in from the kitchen gardens. Her feet sink into the grass, and she feels connected with the ancient roots of oaks and elms. The sky hangs low over the land. She trails her fingers through the stars. Their light glows on her fingertips. Stardust dances in the place where guilt has lain so heavy in her heart. She's invincible!

A phosphorescent, pale pink radiance crests the horizon. It calls her back to another place in time—so far back that it sits on the rim of the future, waiting to loop around again. Waiting for her. Her heart bursts with joy. She's spent her whole life waiting for someone and, all the time something—something bigger than someone—waits for her.

Miriam runs through the rose arches. "Who are you? Speak to me. I'm coming for you."

The heady fragrance of roses drenches Miriam's senses. She fingers their velvety petals in passing, and laughs and scolds them as thorns rip the filmy fabric of her nightgown.

The arches end, and she comes to an abrupt halt at the cliff's edge. A twisting path leads down to the sea. Miriam scales the terrain as sure-footed as a mule on the hills of a Greek island. The corkscrew of time unwinds. She's young, all of life awaits her, and something needs her. *Needs* her! It's written in the pink glow foaming on the waves.

She treads onto the gritty sands of Trellan Bay. The sea frightens her, and the seams of her invincible self split open. The corkscrew of time races forward. She's old, fat, alone, and then dead. Elaine curses her. She can't find a coffin large enough to contain her mother's body. Miriam yells at the top of her lungs, "Give me back the fucking rose-colored glasses!"

Fear creeps into Miriam's dream and dominates her thoughts. The ocean draws up into a massive wave. Its concave gut thrashes down beneath the horizon and floods the continent of Australia. Miriam tries to run, but her feet are glued to the bones of the planet. The wave gathers back up. "No!" Miriam hides her face in her hands. The wave rushes forward, smashes her to the ground, and tosses her around like a garment in a washing machine.

She flails her arms and legs, trying to draw herself up to the surface. A current of blue-black water twines about her and drags her down. Down, down, down. Bubbles explode from her mouth. Her invincible self runs across the ocean and tosses her a handful of pink foam. Miriam grabs it. "T a m a r a!" She yells. "Help me!"

"I'm here."

Tamara appears before Miriam, gathers air, and clasps it to her mouth. Miriam sucks it in like a baby eager for her first breath. Slowly, Tamara eases Miriam to the surface of the sea.

Miriam glances at the cliffs of Trellan Bay. "Take me home."

"You're in your sacred future. You've come to help Kate's mother."

Kate. Miriam feels the girl's ache over the loss of her mother. She looks from side to side, blinking rapidly. "Where is Lara Penrose?"

Tamara shines a ray of light onto a coil of blue-black water. "Down there."

"Ugh!" Miriam hugs her arms around her chest. "I felt that stuff earlier. What the hell is it?"

"It's coming from the Black Heart. It's Lara's despair."

Miriam peers closer into the ocean, fascinated by the coil. "Kate told me the Black Heart holds the collective fear of the whole world. Is that right?"

"Fear, among other unpleasant things, yes."

"And you're asking me to go into that?"

"No. You asked that of yourself a long time ago. I'm here to guide you."

Miriam spurts a callous laugh. "No way."

"I speak the truth."

"Okay. You go first. I'll follow."

"You must take the first step into the Black Heart alone. That's what you envisioned for yourself when you wrote this future."

Miriam slicks her hair off her face. "Why would I do such a stupid thing?"

"You foresaw yourself as a courageous woman, and you are that woman."

"I'm a self-confessed coward."

"I don't think so, Miriam. A long, long time ago you made a mistake. It hurt you and many others. Back then, you asked me if I would grant you a sacred future—a chance to free yourself from the effects of that mistake."

"What mistake?"

"If you need to know that, you will, once you embark on your sacred future."

"I want to know now."

"That's not wise."

"Yeah? Well, I'm not big on wisdom."

"If you insist, I'll see what I can do."

"I insist."

Tamara bows into the Cycles of Time and asks for a scene from Miriam's life in Ruberah, something to help her embrace her sacred future. Currents of pink light flood her waters. "Look into my river, Miriam."

CHAPTER FOURTEEN

Soul Shadow

A young, bronze-skinned woman kneels by a river, her slender body draped in a white gown. Rubies cinch her waist and drip in long threads through her honey-colored hair. Her fine chiseled features reflect on the silver glow of a river, and her blue-green eyes brim with tears. Passion rules her—love for a man she should not love, but a love she cannot give up. The woman determines she will suffer the consequences of this love for many lifetimes to come so that she might enjoy it today. She—"

"Stop it!" Miriam covers her face with her hands, her heart convulsing with pain. "I don't want to see anymore."

"That woman was you, Miriam when you lived as Princess Li'ram. You asked me then to grant you a sacred future, one in which you would redeem yourself for the choice you made. That time has come."

"I can't believe I once looked like that and I was still

miserable."

Tamara laughs, amused by Miriam's sense of humor. "You had more qualities than beauty when you lived as Li'ram. Courage was among them. It took tremendous courage to love as you loved. You have that same courage today, Miriam. It wouldn't be time to meet your sacred future unless you were equipped to do so."

Miriam shakes her head. "I'm not the heroine type."

"You have the opportunity to rescue Kate's mother from the Black Heart. Life will be very difficult for Kate without her."

"Look, I've failed my own daughter. I'm the last person to help Kate."

"You're the only person. This is a debt, Miriam … a shadow on your soul."

Miriam flaps her arms and kicks her legs. "Someone pinch me. Someone tell me this is a nightmare."

"A chance to erase a shadow on your soul is a grand event."

"What shadow?"

"A flaw in your character. Something you've had for a long time."

"I'm not a terrible person. I may bully my clients a bit, but I have to. I have to match apartments to budgets, which in New York often means dashing dreams of tall-ceilinged rooms with fireplaces and terraces. But I'm always aboveboard with my clients, and God knows, I've tried as a mother. Is it my fault Elaine loves cocaine more than her life?" Miriam recalls the affair she had during the last years of her marriage to Elaine's father, but Elaine was just a little girl. *Her rebelliousness couldn't be to punish Miriam for that, could it?* Guilt envelops Miriam. "Are you saying I have to go into this Black Heart to pay for my sins?"

"It's not about good and evil, Miriam. Rescuing Lara is a chance for you to realize a greater love in yourself. That will open the door to your higher consciousness and—"

"U-hum ... well ... they skipped me when they were handing out that stuff. As far as I'm concerned, the best thing God ever did was inspire someone to make butter. That's the extent of my religious belief. So, what's the punishment if I don't go looking for Lara Penrose?"

"The way you will feel about yourself."

Miriam scoffs as if nothing could ever change that.

"You can't avoid yourself, Miriam. Your sacred future is a part of you. You created it, and you decided to meet it at this point in time. Everything is set for that to happen. I will—"

"I want Mitch back, and I want to go home."

"You'll be haunted by—"

"I don't care. I'm already haunted by all kinds of shit. I'm asking you, Tamara, get me out of here."

Ah, spoken like the woman Miriam had been in Ruberah. She has remembered to ask specifically for what she wants, and Tamara cannot refuse her. She touches Miriam's eyes, and Miriam awakens from her dream.

She lies in her small bed, staring up at the ceiling. Phew! She had the mother lode of all nightmares. She releases a breath of relief, but then smells the scent of strong tobacco wafting through the air. She peeps across the room through half-closed eyes.

Kate sits on the floor, her legs stretched out in front of her, puffing on a cigarette.

"Nice dream?"

CHAPTER FIFTEEN

Saturday morning at *Penrose Hall*

A light drizzle dampens the air, and gulls dip into choppy waves, gobbling fish tossed to the surface. Guests on the Atlantic Terrace rock in wicker chairs and stare out to sea, unfazed by a sudden downpour of rain. The walking ladies march along the cliff path, gossiping about Gwenellen—that young hussy who wriggles her bottom as she walks and flirts with anything in trousers.

In the dining room, Miriam discovers the riches of a full English breakfast. She begins with a bowl of porridge liberally coated with brown sugar and cream. She then tackles a fried egg, a couple of thick rashers of bacon, and fried mushrooms. She dabs her mouth with her napkin and eyes a slice of fried bread resting on the edge of her plate. It oozes fat, but Miriam has a rule, she's allowed to taste anything she hasn't eaten before. In fact, she should. Otherwise why bother to leave home? Miriam bites off a small piece of the fried bread. The deity of butter had better watch out—she could be converted. She salivates on the flavors of warm oil laced with bacon drippings and bits of mushrooms. She gulps her coffee and forces herself to leave the table before she can down another bite.

Miriam enters the reception hall just as Kate charges down the main staircase. The girl scowls at Miriam, her eyes full of accusation. Snatches from Miriam's dream of last night come to mind, and she gets the awful feeling Kate knows she met Tamara and walked away from helping her mother. She takes a step toward Kate, feeling wretched and wanting to explain she's just too damn frightened to face that kind of danger. Kate doesn't give her the chance. She darts down a corridor and out of sight.

Miriam rubs her temples, wondering whether to follow Kate, when Harry Treadwell strolls in from the Atlantic Terrace.

"Miriam, how lovely to see you! How about a game of backgammon?"

Harry's eyes, his smile, and his voice dance on a note of conciliation. Miriam wants to throw her arms around him. *Run away with me, Harry.* "I'd like that."

"Good. It's stopped raining, and I've got things set up

on the terrace." Harry ushers Miriam outside.

They sit at a table near the wrought iron trellis. Miriam shakes the dice and moves a chip across the backgammon board. "Have you been to New York, Harry?"

"Many times. In fact, I like it so much I think I'd enjoy having a small flat there. Maybe you could find one for me."

"Just let me know size, area, and price range. If it's available, I'll find it." Miriam feels a tickle of excitement as she imagines herself dating Harry on her home turf.

Harry tips the dice onto the board and contemplates his next move. Miriam recalls the kind touch of his hand on her arm—a touch that had stopped her from lashing out at Mitch. *Wouldn't it be nice to live with such a sensitive man?*

"Coffee?" Gwenellen wheels a trolley onto the porch and parks it beside Miriam. "Harry." The buxom maid bats her eyes. "I meant what I said last night."

Harry blushes, and his hand freezes midair over the backgammon board.

Gwenellen levels a gloating look on Miriam and swans off the terrace.

Miriam pushes her chair out, about to go after the tramp and yank her down to size, but thinks better of it. Tongue-lashing the maid would turn Harry off, for sure. She smiles at

Harry. His cheeks burn red. "What was that about?" she asks, trying to sound casual.

"Um ... er ... Forgive me, Miriam." Harry stands. "I forgot I have another appointment. Can we finish this game later?"

Miriam's jaw drops. Harry's got something going on with Gwenellen. He's no different than any other man. She swipes her hands through the chips, scattering them all over the board. "This game is over!"

CHAPTER SIXTEEN

Saturday afternoon at *Penrose Hall*

Usually, by the time Mitch arrives at a destination, he's firmly entrenched in the role of writer/observer and cannot be budged from that perspective. Not so with this trip, and all because Miriam decided to come along. He travels alone in his work, or not quite, as he often inhabits the persona of his brilliant detective, Jed Flyer. With Jed, flying from one continent to another becomes a riveting experience. Jed always uses the restroom in the rear of the plane, so that he can scan his fellow passengers as he winds his way down the aisle, assessing them for possible suspects in his latest murder mystery. He'll also select a couple of hot-looking women—the lucky ones who will end up between the red satin sheets of Jed's king-size bed.

Traveling with Miriam curtails this sort of research.

Miriam always needs something: a glass of wine, a latte, a little something to munch on, more than a little something to munch on, a better selection of magazines, and worst of all, the need to talk. Fortunately, Miriam seldom wants to withdraw from the fierce competition of selling and listing million-dollar apartments in New York. But when *World Over* assigned him to cover the Tahitian Islands, she harassed, cajoled, and pestered him until he agreed to take her along. "I've always wanted to go there," she said. Then, when his editor postponed that trip and dumped the Cornwall assignment on him, she insisted on coming. "I've made arrangements at the office, and Elaine's father promised to keep an eye on her progress in rehab. I need the break, Mitch."

He sits in the living room of the Tower Suite, balancing his computer on his lap. Now Miriam's raising hell over the accommodations and, of course, his tiny flirtation with Gwenellen. *Cripes*, women never even notice him. Now that a gorgeous young blonde seems to like him, can't he, just for once in his life, have a little fun?

Mitch rubs his hands together, then runs them over his head, a ritual he uses to stimulate the writer within. He lifts his computer onto a table by a window and begins a draft for his article.

The circular-shaped Tower Suite at The Penrose *rates high among the most unique accommodations in the world. Luxurious? No. Clean? Yes. Comfortable? Not if you need the traditional trappings of a first-class hotel. But if you're called to experience the raw and lofty castle-like life of yesteryear, and if solitude be your best mate, this two-story suite reigns supreme.*

Make no mistake about the solitude aspect of occupying this suite. The bedroom provides one single bed, and there are no convertible sofas or fold-up beds to be had. The Penrose family maintains the Tower Suite for those in need of time alone, and its guest book teems with testament to the benefits of having rested here.

A chill creeps over Mitch as he recalls reading some of those writings. Many alluded to a pink mist that drifted up from the sea and whispered stories about a jeweled land called Ruberah, supposedly once a part of Cornwall, now lying somewhere on the bottom of the Atlantic. He dares not quote this sort of thing in his article. Covering this assignment already relegates him a fringe reporter. Prose about a lost kingdom could ruin him. He reverts to the ever-safe subject of scenery.

Unspoiled views of the wild and rocky coastline can be seen through the living room and bedroom windows, slatted deep in the ancient granite walls. A private, turreted roof garden tops the suite. From here you can follow the ever-changing hues of the English Channel as it wends westward into the Atlantic. The inn faces Trellan Bay, a half-moon of sandy beach, bookended with giant headlands. The ruins of Wheal Penrose, a once flourishing tin mine, hug the cliffs close to the shore like a monument to a brotherhood of men who worked and perished in the tunnels below. In addition to the coastal path—which traverses the entire peninsula of

Cornwall—a wide variety of hiking trails meander far and wide from
Penrose Hall. *Some veer through green fields dotted with woolly white sheep
and fatted Guernsey cattle. Others lead into a forest of aged pines, oaks, and
elms that sprawl down to the harbor of Port Issey. Cottages painted in pinks,
blues, and yellows dot the hills around the harbor, loaning the village an air
of the Mediterranean.*

He pauses, remembering Tom Reilly's raspy voice over
the phone lines between Nepal and New York. "Metaphysical
Cornwall is the main angle of the piece, Mitch. Don't sweat it.
It'll come easy. No one is the same after a visit to *Penrose Hall.*"

He thinks of Gwenellen. Could she be the one to change
him? He recalls the way she led him up the narrow stone steps of
the tower, the sway of her hips, and the fleshy curves of her
buttocks. She bent to turn the bed down, and spoke in the
singsong softness of her West Country accent: "Some people
don't sleep well here, but I've a notion you will." He tried to slip
into Jed Flyer's mind and conjure a seductive response, but
thoughts of Miriam plagued him and he became tongue-tied.
Then Gwenellen began talking about the night Lara Penrose
disappeared. A gorgeous girl was telling him about a woman she
had seen standing on the cliff path, a woman who, within
seconds, had seemingly vanished into thin air!

After Gwenellen left, he sat on a loveseat by the south-
facing windows, wondering whether he'd stepped into a pot of
detective-story gold or into a breakup with Miriam. He found

himself angry with Miriam for tolerating him. Women usually dumped him after a few dates, sensing no future with him, but Miriam had kept calling and inviting him to movies, plays, and dinner at her place. She was part tough cookie and part marshmallow, and he's grown to like and need both aspects of her personality.

He senses Miriam wants more from him, but he's always seen himself as a single man. Sometimes when dining in a resort restaurant, he'd notice a family with young children. The ceaseless routine of looking after them horrified him: mopping food from mouths and clothes, efforts to stop screaming fits, threats of punishment for *not* eating and promises of reward *for* eating. He could never do it. Although Miriam has said she's past wanting children, that's not the only issue. He carries an inner darkness, a void where normal human responses like love and the desire to have a family should reside.

He should either confess these things to Miriam or break up with her. Last night, he'd been reflecting on Miriam and Gwenellen when he fell asleep. He rubs the back of his neck, remembering the dream he had. He met a young woman with golden hair and large aqua-colored eyes. She took him to see what she called the spheres of the Jewel Kingdom—a ring of different-colored orbs floating around a clear sphere. He recalled being drawn to the green orb. He can't remember anything after that, but he woke up in a terrible state of anger, punching his pillow.

He sighs and gets back to writing his article. He crooks his fingers over the keyboard and closes his eyes, waiting. Nothing. Why did this assignment have to fall to him? He writes about thread count, bath oils, and cocktails at sunset. It's ironic that he should end up writing about upscale resorts, as he lives in a studio apartment atop a five-floor walkup in a decrepit, old building on the fringe of Harlem. He's lived there all his adult life and will probably die there, which suits him fine. But he's always appreciated good design and well-crafted products, and occasionally he plunks down a hefty sum for a pair of Prada shoes or an exquisite incensed-based fragrance with woody top notes.

He scans the living room of the Tower Suite, readying himself to describe the décor.

Huge tapestries soften the walls of the Tower Suite, curving around them like Cinerama screens. One depicts a banquet in the court of a Tudor king; another shows horses and riders galloping over a moor-like landscape, chasing a fox. A seascape of finely stitched blues, grays, and greens fills the entire rear curve of the room, resembling a reflection of the ocean as seen through the front-facing windows.

He studies the tapestry, and the shimmer of the silk appears to undulate like a living sea. He holds his breath, unable to take his eyes off the waves. Murky, blue-black vapors rise off the tapestry. The darkness inside him stirs, slowly and heavily, like tar churning in a barrel. He tries to get up, but his butt stays riveted to the seat. Blood pounds through the vessels in his forehead. He screws his eyes closed and sinks his face into his hands. His inner terror recedes, the light changes, and as if in a vision, he's transported to the island of his dreams.

He treads over warm sand, heading toward a haven of trees to the home he built of driftwood and bamboo. "Gwenellen, my darling, I'm here." He steps under an arbor of vines. His heart pounds louder than the surf. "Gwenellen, my darling, where are you?"

She appears, and her beauty stuns him as it always does. She licks her plump rosy lips and slinks toward him, swaying her hips. She unbuttons the gauzy fabric of her blouse. Her breasts, luscious and ripe with youth, float free. She lays a hand on his brow. "How was your day, dearest heart?

His insides turn to pulp, and he leads her to the hammock where they sleep at night. A crystal luminosity flashes in the corners of his eyes and everything goes blank. The air turns cold, and he's back in the living room of the Tower Suite. His fingers scale the keyboard of his computer, describing the tingle on his skin at the touch of his darling's fingertips, but nothing appears on his computer screen except his description of the *Tower Suite*. Did he slip out of his skin and become someone else? He recalls a moment of confusion when he drove over the Tamar Bridge. He'd felt something huge and foreboding shadowing him. It vanished so quickly he dismissed it as not being real, but now he's not so sure.

He looks outside. A light rain splashes against the window, and clouds scurry low to the sea. His heart wallops as he spots Gwenellen strolling arm-in-arm across the fields with Harry, her face tilted brazenly to the wind and the rain.

He leaps to his feet, grabs a rain slicker from a hook by the door, and scrambles down the stone stairs. He misses the bottom step and stumbles forward, bumping into someone. In his rush, he shoves the person aside and tears down the corridor to the kitchen.

CHAPTER SEVENTEEN

To the stables

To the amusement of two village girls shelling peas, Mitch storms through the kitchen and into the vegetable gardens. He sprints along brick-paved pathways and leaps over beds of cabbages, lettuce, and rhubarb, all the while calling Gwenellen's name. Miriam trails after Mitch, yelling at him for crashing into her and running away.

Panting, Mitch catches up to Gwenellen and Harry as they near the stables. He swings a possessive arm around Gwenellen's waist and scours her face. "What are you doing?"

Gwenellen lolls her head on Harry's shoulder in the manner of a woman luxuriating in the presence of the man who loves her. "I'm moving into the loft above the stables. Harry is going to help me paint it. Aren't you Harry?"

Mitch gasps. *What the hell is going on?* Yesterday, Harry was looking all dewy-eyed at Miriam. "Gwen—"

"Shush!" Gwenellen puts a finger on Mitch's lips, smiling her most generous smile.

Mitch feels shamed. How could he doubt her? She's just being friendly to Harry—as is her nature. "I can help too."

Gwenellen squeals with delight. "Lucky me! Two big strong helpers."

"So, what do you do, Harry?" Mitch asks, making an effort to befriend the man.

He couldn't have picked a worse subject. Uncomfortable with his current lack of employment, Harry mumbles his way through the story of selling his business. "I'm considering several different investments."

Shit, he's rich. Mitch raises a brow. "Married?"

"Harry's divorced," Gwenellen says, like a mother answering a painful question for a child. "And he was sad about it, but he's not sad anymore."

Mitch gulps a breath. Gwenellen belongs to him. He's got to get Harry out of the picture. He leans in close to Gwenellen. He wants to tell her that with her by his side, he'll write great novels. He'll be rich and shower her with jewels and clothes. He's about to pull her away from Harry when he feels a hand slam down on his shoulder.

Miriam glares at him, her eyes bulging with rage. "How dare you treat me like that!"

"Like what? What are you talking about?" Mitch rubs his temples, trying to fathom what wrongdoing he's committed now.

Miriam drags him by the arm away from Harry and Gwenellen. "I need to speak to you, alone."

"We're leaving," Gwenellen says as she tucks her hand into Harry's hand. "We'll be in the stables."

Mitch takes a step to follow Gwenellen, but Miriam hauls him back. "Listen to me." She wrinkles her brow the way she does when she prepares to handle a client dithering over a deal. Mitch can hear the words forming: *Listen, Mr. Buyer, if you hesitate now, this apartment will be gone in an hour—off the market, and there's nothing else out there. Nothing.*

"We should go home, Mitch ... now. If we don't—"

"I can't leave. I haven't finished my article."

"Since when can't you write it at home?"

"This place is different. It's off my beat. I've got more research to do."

"For God's sake, Mitch, Gwenellen is playing you for a fool ... you *and* Harry. She's flirting with both of you, and she's

147

probably laughing at you with her girlfriends at the pub at night."

"No, she's not like that. Gwenellen knows about the local myths and legends. She's helping me with my article, and she's just being kind to Harry."

"You're an idiot!" Miriam spins around and starts walking toward the inn.

Vaporous drifts of blue-black energy surge up from the Black Heart—tiny tentacles—millions of them, invisible to the human eye—and flurry around Mitch. He looks at Miriam marching across the fields. By her gait, he knows he's done something to upset her, but he can't remember what. His equilibrium falters. He needs Miriam. She's always there—solid as a steamroller—mowing down life's disappointments. He should gather some wildflowers for her. He needs to see the happiness that floats in her eyes when he brings her flowers.

He starts to run after Miriam, but the energy from the Black Heart seeps into his brain. He halts on the spot and shakes his head like a man who can't remember what he set out to do. Gwenellen's laughter peals in his ears, and his love for her fills in the blanks. He runs to the stables, leans against the outside of the barn, and closes his eyes.

The thought of Gwenellen lying in Harry's arms makes Mitch want to place his hands around Harry's neck and squeeze the life out of him. His conscience prickles, and with the ease of habit, Mitch takes on the persona of his cool-headed detective.

He rests his hand on his hip, Jed style, and swaggers inside the stables. Jed packs a high-speed, 9mm gun—a Sig Sauer X-Five. Mitch shifts his hand to the place where the detective sticks the X in his belt. The power to kill shivers over him like frost on a bitter morning. Jed kills at least once in every novel. Mitch balls his hands into fists, flexing his muscles, searching for the detachment he feels when writing those scenes. Aah, there it is—the feel of a cool, wide-open space, cutting across the planet like a highway with no stop signs. No beginning. No end. No depth. Just like him.

Mitch treads over the straw-covered floor of the stables, sniffing the smells of animal sweat and urine. He listens to the soft stomp of horses shuffling in their stalls. Gwenellen and Harry stand at the far end of the old brick building next to a flight of wooden stairs, their heads bent over a can of paint. A tapestry bag with wooden handles lies on the floor close to Gwenellen's feet. An envelope sticks up in the outside pocket—cream, like the stationery in his room. Mitch thinks of when he first talked with Gwenellen about Lara's disappearance. He asked her if Lara left a note. She inferred Lara had. He salivates. Could it be in that envelope?

Mitch hides behind a tall tier of shelves laden with saddles and bridles. The mystery of Lara's disappearance excites him, and his mind runs riot with plots and red herrings. A piercing whinny yanks him out of his reverie. A few stalls away, a black horse thrusts his head over the half door—the same beast that Kate rode, galloping across the fields as Mitch arrived at the inn. The stallion's nostrils flare. He looks in the direction of Gwenellen and Harry and releases another bone-chilling whinny.

Harry glances up. "Easy there." He walks up to the stallion with Gwenellen in tow. "There, there." He approaches the horse, his hand outstretched, ready to caress the beast. "This nice lady is going to live upstairs."

The stallion rears onto his hind legs. His underbelly glistens, and he kicks his front legs, showing his power to mangle, to kill.

Harry grips Gwenellen's arm and guides her away from the stall.

Stepping out of the shadows, Mitch rests his hands on his hips, ready to rescue the maiden in distress. "That's a feisty beast, Gwenellen. He looks dangerous. I don't think you should move in here."

The stallion's ears shoot straight up, and a palpable line of tension forms between the beast and Gwenellen. Both Mitch and Harry feel it and back away from the horse. Gwenellen moves closer to his stall. A smirk twists over her lips. Her eyes look dark and mysterious, like medieval glass.

"I'm not afraid."

Her mocking tone strips Mitch of his bravado. He falls back into his old self—a man longing to be on a highway leading from nowhere to nowhere. He catches Harry's glance and senses an unspoken question passing between them. *Who is Gwenellen? What makes her tick?* As if answering them, the stallion bucks and tosses his head. His whinny becomes an adamant warning.

"Shush, Firebrand!" Kate trudges into the stables, her hair dripping with rain and straggling over her shoulders. The horse grunts and lowers his head. The girl nuzzles his forehead.

Gwenellen nudges Kate. "Why does horsey look so sad?" she asks, a goading tone to her voice.

"You'd better stay clear of Firebrand."

Gwenellen chuckles. "Or else?"

"Or else, he might trample you to death."

"I say, girls." Harry moves between the women, gently pushing them apart from each other. "Let's calm down. Maybe we should go back to the inn and have some tea."

"Not now, Harry!" Gwenellen yanks on his arm. "I need you to help me paint the loft."

"Oh … all right."

Kate leads Firebrand from his stall, and Mitch backs further away from the beast as they pass him. Kate slips a bit in the horse's mouth, climbs onto his back, and rides him bareback into the rain.

Mitch wrings his hands, hating the frightened man inside. Jed Flyer would have swiped the horse from Kate, swept Gwenellen up by the waist, and galloped off with her into the rain-sodden yonder. Why can't he be like that?

At the foot of the stairs, Gwenellen squeezes a ribbon of ultramarine coloring into the white paint. "Sea blue." She chants and paces around the can, stirring the paint with a long stick. "Sea blue. I want sea blue walls."

"I'd better check on the condition of the loft." Harry turns and climbs the stairs.

Mitch lowers his glance to the envelope in Gwenellen's purse.

Gwenellen stops chanting. "What are you thinking, Mitch?"

"Is that ...?" Mitch points to her bag. "Did you ...?"

"I told you there was a note, didn't I? It was by her scarf in that thicket of gorse."

Mitch's mouth goes dry. "What does it say?"

"What'll you do to find out?"

"Anything. I love you, Gwenellen." Mitch recoils at

having blurted that out, but he has no time to recover his dignity.

Harry bounds down the stairs, reporting on the state of the loft, totally unaware of his inopportune arrival. He picks up a pad and draws a map of the room. "There are lots of little cracks in the walls but nothing too serious." He shows the drawing to Gwenellen.

Mitch caves into his inner darkness. Being happy in the place between places has created an exalted idea of being alone. If Gwenellen runs off with Harry, he'll be stranded on that highway leading nowhere. But he won't be alone—he'll have the memory of her, of losing her. Then all the feelings he's stuffed away for all the years since his mother died will clobber him, and the misery that came before that—the wretchedness he must have brought with him into this life. He coughs under the stress of trying to avoid his pain.

"You'll fix the cracks in the walls, won't you, Mitch?" Gwenellen brushes her lips against his cheek.

The feel of her skin against his revives Mitch's hope for a life with her. "Yes, of course, my darling."

"And you can drive me into the village to get my things, Harry."

"I could drive you," Mitch says.

"Um, but Harry's got a big car ... a Mercedes ... biggest

they make. Isn't it, Harry?"

Harry blushes, embarrassed by her reference to his wealth. "It's not very practical for moving furniture."

"Mine is," Mitch says. "It's a hatchback."

"But it's red." Gwenellen pouts. "I don't like red."

Gwenellen's petulant outburst offends Harry. "I say, Gwenellen, that's a bit much."

"No, it's not. I don't like red. It can hurt me."

"It's okay." Mitch picks up a can of Spackle and heads for the stairs.

Harry gapes at Gwenellen, expecting her to follow Mitch and apologize. Gwenellen misreads his expression, and thinking he's impatient to leave, picks up her bag. "Let's go."

Her lack of sensitivity appalls Harry. His attraction to her dies on the spot. "I'm sorry, Gwenellen, I've got some business to attend to." He stalks off, pulling up the hood of his jacket against the rain.

Gwenellen falls to the floor, pretending to faint. Mitch dumps the can of Spackle and runs down the stairs. He kneels by Gwenellen's side and strokes her hair off her face. "My darling, are you hurt? Should I call a doctor? Please, tell me what I can do to help you!"

Gwenellen flutters her eyelids with the delicacy of a dying gazelle. "You can punish Harry. The color red could harm me, and he walked away without any care for my suffering."

"Yes, of course, my darling, I'll talk to him about it."

Slowly, Gwenellen hauls herself into a sitting position. The porcelain tint of her skin grows muddy, and harsh lines settle around her lips. "I want you to kill Harry."

"What?" Mitch steps back in horror, staring at Gwenellen, searching for some trace of the adorable her. The cold gleam in her eyes causes chills on his scalp. His earlier thought of murdering Harry fades into a sea of fear—a sea walled in by prison bars. He swallows hard. "You're not serious?"

"Oh!" Gwenellen clasps her hand to her mouth and closes her eyes as if searching for some vital information. Slowly, her features begin to soften again, and the glow of her beauty returns.

Mitch sucks in air between his teeth. "You really scared me there for a moment," he says, laughing with relief.

Gwenellen grips Mitch's hand and climbs onto her feet, pulling him up with her. "You said you loved me and you'd do anything for me. Is that true?"

Her breath falls warm on Mitch's lips, and she parts

hers, flicking her tongue over them.

"It is, my darling. Anything, you name it and I'll do it. "
Mitch leans forward ready to sink his mouth on hers, but she
chuckles her little cotton-candy laugh and pushes him back.

"Kill Harry."

Before Mitch can express any objection, Gwenellen
locks him into her gaze—a bright blue gaze sparkling with the
clarity of fine sapphires.

Mitch senses some part of him crumbling, free-falling
away from him. His world wobbles. He can't lose Gwenellen, but
surely he can't kill Harry. *Can he?*

"You don't love me." Gwenellen stalks away.

Mitch runs after her and catches her at the stable door.
"I do love you, but—"

"But?" Flecks of steel gleam in Gwenellen eyes. She
raises her chin in a challenging manner. Mitch tries to think of
how Jed Flyer might handle Gwenellen, but the detective doesn't
fall in love—doesn't let anything come between him and the
person he hunts.

"Harry's mean. He could come after me with something
red. Then I could die, and you wouldn't care!" Gwenellen shoves
Mitch aside and storms outside.

He gazes after her. *She could die from something red? How?* Rain pelts down and plasters her cotton dress to her body. Her golden tresses drip into the small of her back. His heart drums in his chest, telling him he must defend his lover against this threat. He sprints into the rain. Mud sloshes over his shoes. He slips, falls, hauls himself up, and runs flat out, following Gwenellen onto the cliff path. "Wait!" he shouts.

Gwenellen turns and walks back to Mitch, a beatific smile lighting up her face "Yes?"

One thought pounds on his mind: He can't live without her. A newfound power surges through him, assuring him he can do anything for her. "How will I kill Harry?"

"Ooh." Gwenellen strokes Mitch's cheek. "How sweet." She leads him down the cliff path and stops at Devil's Neck by the narrow passage that leads out to the giant headland. The sea rushes through the rugged archway beneath, and rain lashes down on the angry waves. "This is a good place. It's easy to fall off the cliffs here."

Mitch studies the ledge where Gwenellen said she had found Lara Penrose's scarf in a thicket of gorse. Wind blows a tiny yellow flower off the thicket. It lands on the lapel of Mitch's jacket. A frightening thought threatens his happiness. Could Gwenellen have had anything to do with Lara's fall?

"Mrs. Penrose was good to me." Gwenellen wipes rain

from Mitch's cheek and looks at him out of wistful eyes.

Mitch chides himself for doubting her, and in a hurried move, presses his lips to her mouth.

"No!" Gwenellen turns away. "I can't. Not until you prove that you love me. Men are always saying they do. But they don't."

"I love you, Gwenellen. I really do. Marry me."

"You know my terms."

Mitch feels dizzy. Gwenellen will marry him if he kills Harry. His life is larger than fiction.

"Bring Harry here tonight," Gwenellen says. "Nine o'clock. Just the two of you."

CHAPTER EIGHTEEN

Lunch in Port Issey

The weather changes abruptly as Harry approaches the steps to the Atlantic Terrace. The rain stops, and sun streams onto the porch. Harry takes it as a good omen. He needs to make amends with Miriam. He tosses his windbreaker on a chair and looks around the porch. The walking ladies sit at a round table playing poker. They wave at Harry and invite him to join them.

"Sorry, I'm looking for Miriam. Have you seen her?"

The women shake their heads. "No, but do come and play a hand or two."

"Another time." Harry swings into the reception hall and spots Miriam at the foot of the grand staircase. "Miriam." He strides up to her. "I'm so sorry." He shifts his weight from one foot to the other. "I was foolishly attracted to Gwenellen, but I now realize she's just a silly girl. I'm desperately sorry for having been so insensitive to you earlier when we were playing backgammon. I would consider myself lucky if you would forgive me and have lunch with me."

Harry's eyes shine with sincerity, and his honesty impresses Miriam. She dawdles before accepting his apology, enjoying the moment. Mitch never apologizes. Mitch doesn't appear to be aware that such niceties exist.

"Well ... I *am* a bit hungry."

"Ah ... lovely."

Harry whisks Miriam outside and into his car. They drive to the village in silence—the contemplative silence of a man and a woman out together for the first time. They enter *The Ship*, a restaurant on the pier of Port Issey. Harry ducks his head, avoiding fishnets draped over the entrance. A waitress leads them to a table by a window with a view of the harbor. Harry declines the menu and suggests they have crab salad and light ale.

Harry's take-charge attitude pleases Miriam. She's exhausted from two years of Mitch's inability to decide when and where they should eat. Even after she chooses a restaurant, he squints at the menu and shakes his head as if food might be alien to him. She unfolds her napkin on her lap and listens attentively as Harry talks about the history of mining in Cornwall. His cell phone rings. He glances at the ID screen. At once, Miriam suspects his ex is calling him.

Harry's face breaks into a wide smile. "Excuse me for a moment, Miriam. I've got a call from my daughters."

He leaves the table, and a pouty-faced waitress saunters by and deposits a basket of bread in front of Miriam. The heavenly aroma of garlic wafts up her nose. She rests her hand on a baguette. It's warm, and butter oozes onto her fingers. The gaping hole of hunger opens inside her, made even bigger by Mitch's betrayal. Tears well up. He had never been very demonstrative, but he also had never been unkind to her before. His infatuation with Gwenellen has rendered him completely insensitive to her feelings. Well, two can play at his game. She lifts the baguette from the basket, but then wonders what if the afternoon leads to romance and she reeks of garlic? She's still ten pounds overweight—maybe more, since her eating binge yesterday. Getting naked for a new man is hard enough, let alone worrying about her breath. She glances at Harry standing by the door with his back to her. If his ex gets on the phone, she'll probably drag him down, and sex won't be a likely option. But if he's having a happy conversation with his daughters—oh, what the hell, she shouldn't go to bed with him on a first date anyway. Miriam rips off a chunk of bread and stuffs it in her mouth. Butter drips onto her chin. She dabs it off with her napkin.

Harry returns to the table, chatting happily about his

daughters. "Susie just turned fifteen," he says, describing the lavish birthday party he and Pammy threw for her in his London home. "And Joanne is thirteen. Both talk about boys all the time. Susie wants to start dating. I'm against it, but I'm not sure I can withstand the pressure."

Miriam laughs. "I know what you mean. At fifteen, Elaine nagged me constantly. 'All my friends are allowed to date,' she whined." Miriam omits any reference to Elaine's loss of her virginity at thirteen. Miriam found out because the boy, two years older than Elaine, bragged, and the word got back to Miriam. Elaine met her mother's outrage with a bored shrug. "So what?"

"When did you let Elaine start dating?" Harry asks.

"Oh, I don't remember." Miriam avoids Harry's eyes. Controlling her daughter's social life had never been an option. Miriam had ended up stuffing Elaine's backpack with condoms and sent her off to school, threatening to ground her forever if she got pregnant. Miraculously, Elaine took this as a sign of having attained her mother's approval and promptly gave up sex. Instead, she verbally abused every man Miriam dated—until Mitch came along. *Mitch and Elaine.* A lump swells in Miriam's throat. Losing Mitch is losing a lifeline to Elaine.

Harry sips his lager. "And where is Elaine now?"

"Spending the summer with her father." The lie rolls off Miriam's tongue smooth as sheen on satin. After all, Elaine's rehab is but a few miles from her father's home. Miriam quickly fills in some facts about her ex-husband, Mark Lewis. She'd like to avoid any deep probe into the failure of her marriage. That usually puts her in defense mode, as she had an affair with his best friend. No good has ever come of confessing to that indiscretion.

"Mark is a dermatologist." She talks in a lively, chit-chatty way. "He lives in Westport, Connecticut and is re-married and has three more kids. I guess his biggest fault is that he gives Elaine more money than is good for her." Miriam makes this sound light and airy, as if Elaine waltzed through the mall spending it on little gingham dresses the color of sunshine instead of using it to grease the palm of her drug dealer.

Their salad arrives accompanied by slices of spongy white bread lavishly buttered and cut into triangles. Sucking in her stomach, Miriam forks a healthy chunk of crabmeat into her mouth. Harry squeezes lemon over his and dusts it with a grinding of black pepper. Miriam sets her fork down, resolving not to devour her food. Only yesterday, Harry had observed her wolfing down an entire bowl of clotted cream. She picks up a slice of bread and nibbles off a corner. "How long are you staying at *Penrose Hall?*"

"I'm driving back to London on Monday."

"I'm thinking of leaving then. It doesn't look like Mitch will." She musters a casual attitude. "Maybe I can hitch a ride with you. You could show me the town before I go home."

Harry's mouth wavers in and out of an uncertain smile. "Susie and Joanne will be staying with me then, and I'm not sure what I would tell them."

"You're divorced, Harry. Your kids know their mother is dating that young Norwegian guy."

"No, they don't. Pammy thinks they're too young to understand."

"You don't think they know their mother fell in love with another man?" Miriam's voice rises with shock. "Kids are smart, Harry."

"Look, I just don't want them to think badly of their mother. She's a wonderful person, really. If you met her, you would like her."

Miriam stuffs bread in her mouth to stop herself from telling Harry she would hate Pammy. She perceives her as a manipulative and selfish woman. It takes two mouthfuls to avoid voicing her opinion. She swallows the last piece of crust. "I just offered to be with you, Harry."

He lowers his eyes. "I ... well—"

Miriam draws on her former brazen dating self, "You need to move on, Harry. If you're not attracted to me, say so."

"Oh, I am attracted to you, Miriam. It's just ..."

"Let's get out of here."

"All right." Harry leaves some money on the table and leads Miriam to the door.

Outside, Harry's cell phone rings again. "Yes, of course, sweetie. Yes, if it's all right with Mummy."

Miriam clenches her teeth. She guessed correctly. Pammy is behind the phone calls. She fumes and looks around the harbor. Fishing boats bob on a low tide. Tourists stroll along the quay, licking ice cream and eating fish and chips wrapped in newspaper. Gulls wail. The smell of fish permeates everything. Miriam's heart skips a beat. Across the harbor, Gwenellen saunters down a narrow cobbled road and onto the quay.

"That was Susie." Harry says, tucking the phone back in his pocket. "She saw a pink dress in the window of Harrods—a must-have dress."

"Girls." Miriam smiles. She suspects Pammy put her daughter up to this. She probably keeps a hold on Harry through the girls. Otherwise, why wouldn't she just buy Susie the dress? Her attention returns to Gwenellen. The little tart bounces onto the quay. The humid air frizzes her golden curls around her face, giving her the look of a cherub in a renaissance painting. She wears a denim skirt and a short, tight-fitting lavender sweater. Her breasts wobble as if crammed into a bra a couple of sizes too small. Heads turn. Men gawk at her in the same stupefied way Mitch did upon first seeing her.

Miriam steers Harry down an alleyway heading in the opposite direction. They walk out onto the main road of the small village of Port Issey. Shops front onto the narrow street, their windows laden with figurines, fishermen's sweaters, and all manner of fudge made with the inevitable clotted cream.

"Hello, Harry." Gwenellen appears from out of nowhere, thrusting her breasts at Harry. "Have you finished your business calls?"

Harry blushes and stammers. Gwenellen chuckles her deep, throaty laugh. "I forgive you, Harry, dear sweet Harry." She kisses his cheek and smiles at Miriam. "Shall we all do something together?"

An undercurrent of sexual intent waves off her like heat from a blistering furnace. Miriam douses it with an icy reply. "Harry and I have plans."

Gwenellen walks her fingers up Harry's chest. "You could come to my place and help me pack my things."

Miriam smacks Gwenellen's hand. "Did you hear me? I said we have plans."

Harry looks from one woman to the other in dazed confusion. He wonders if he should help Gwenellen. She is, after all, young and seemingly without friends and family. No doubt her flirtatious manner is a shield against some insecurity, but he knows there will be no going forward with Miriam if he does help the girl. He sighs, longing for the sanctity of marriage—for life lived in clearly defined boundaries.

Glaring at Harry, Miriam waits for him to back her up and blow off Gwenellen. Harry hesitates, and Miriam storms into the crowded street, burying her hopes of a future with Harry in the same grave as her future with Mitch. At Village Square, she hails a taxi. "Take me to *Penrose Hall.*"

Sensing Miriam's distress, Tamara sweeps into the village and slides into the front seat of the taxi. The driver—an ancient soul she's known since Ruberah—tips his cap to her, then speaks to Miriam.

"How do 'e like the inn?" he asks, his voice lilting in a heavy brogue.

"It's fine." Miriam stares out the window. She'll leave today and get back to New York—back to work.

"'E can't leave. 'E's not slain the past."

"What?" Miriam meets the driver's wizened old eyes in the rearview mirror.

"The river's in you. Tamara 'olds your future. 'Tis magical—wrapped in the pale pink light of Ruberah. But 'e's got to slay the past before 'e can 'ave it."

"I don't understand. Who has to slay the past?"

The driver pulls off the road and onto a grassy ledge. He stops the taxi, swings his arm over his seat, and taps his finger on Miriam's shoulder. "You, my 'andsome."

The old man's bony finger feels heavy on Miriam's skin. Her thoughts scatter and she falls into a contemplative mood. She slumps back against the seat. Her eyes begin to blink uncontrollably. Pink light sparkles before her, and a round-shaped hand mirror appears. Cabochon rubies frame the glass and form a handle shaped like a serpent. Miriam looks into the mirror. The old man's face stares back at her. His eyes become her eyes, and his wrinkled skin turns smooth and stretches over her cheekbones. Sweat pearls on Miriam's forehead. A blaze of pink light bounces off the mirror. Time reels back—way back. Miriam shields her eyes. "River Spirit!"

Tamara leans over the back seat of the taxi. "I am here, beloved princess. How may I help you?"

"I'm not a princess. I'm me, Miriam, and I don't want to see anything in this mirror."

"But you remember the old man," Tamara whispers. "He lived in the Time of Ruberah. He served you and your family. He carries the truth mirror, and he's trying to help you."

"I don't want to be helped." Miriam covers her face with her hands.

Tamara nods to the old man. He removes his mirror and the pink light wanes. Miriam's ancient memories fall quiet. The loss of Mitch, her disappointment with Harry, and her heartache over Elaine come crashing back.

She yells at the driver, "Why have you stopped here? And get your hand off my arm."

"Don't 'e be afraid of me, miss. I'm your friend."

"Take me back to the inn at once, or do I have to walk?"

"Aye, my 'andsome, fear will be the end of 'e."

The old man starts the engine and drives up the hill. He speaks telepathically to Tamara, dropping his heavy brogue. He uses that pattern of speech to distract those about to embark on a scared future—distract them enough to slip his truth mirror before them.

"Almost had her there for a moment," he says. "She almost slipped into her jeweled intelligence."

"Thank you for trying."

"What's going on with young Kate? I see her looking through her spirit vision without you beside her. She feeling her oats, is she?"

"I should say so. Have you, by chance, caught sight of Mitch in your mirror?"

The old man shakes his head. "Not a chance. Can't get past the vapors of the Black Heart. They swirl around him day and night. Poor devil, eh? "

Mirror man steers the car to the right at the top of the hill. The wheels crunch onto the dirt road, and they ride down to *Penrose Hall.* He parks and looks back at Miriam, wrinkling his sea-stained face into a smile.

"Don't leave before 'e's meant to go. 'E's too young to die."

Miriam shakes her head, trying to prevent his words from registering in her thoughts. "Here." She slaps some money in his hand, jumps from the cab and runs into the hotel.

The entry hall looms large and quiet as a funeral parlor. Miriam stops in her tracks at the foot of the stairs. Lara Penrose looks down at her from her portrait on the landing. Miriam waves a finger at the painting. "Don't give me that look of disapproval. My own daughter needs me. I've got to get home to her."

Miriam keeps talking to herself, justifying her need to leave. How could anything bad befall her if she does what any mother would do? Looking after her child must come before everything else. She catches sight of the sign on the reception desk: RING FOR SERVICE. She marches across the hall and bangs her fist on the brass bell. "I want to check out. *Now!*"

In the city of Truro, some twenty miles from *Penrose Hall*, Kate halts her shopping basket in the food halls of Marks & Spencer. She giggles, thinking of her plan to make sure Miriam stays at *Penrose Hall*.

She sidles her shopping cart up to the cheese counter, where her father bends over a display of Stilton. He seems permanently bent over and frail these days. She lays a gentle hand on his shoulder. "Stand up straight, Daddy."

Lance prods a wheel of Brie. "Not ripe enough for tonight."

Kate reads the sorrow behind his eyes—grief he so valiantly tries to hide. She wishes her brother would come home to help ease his pain. But Daddy insisted Christopher finish his summer studies at the Sorbonne in Paris. As neither her father nor her brother can see through their spirit vision, they've never looked into the lost kingdom—never heard the soft, spatial music of Mt. Rube, or felt the power of Rube Force sleeping inside it. The power she needs to rescue her mother.

She drums her fingers on the display case. "Daddy, I saw a cardigan in a store down the street. It would be good for when I go back to school. Do you mind if I go and try it on?"

"Of course not, darling." Lance Penrose glances at his watch. "I'll be here for another fifteen minutes or so. If I'm gone when you return, I'll be in the car waiting for you."

Kate kisses his cheek and bounds off. She dashes through the crowded streets, heading toward the soaring gothic towers of the cathedral set smack-dab in the center of the town. She climbs the stone steps of the church, and files inside with a group of tourists. Kate sits on a bench near the back, listening to the shuffle of feet and the murmurings of foreign languages floating on the cool, musty air. Light rays shine through the stained glass windows, bathing the nave in hues of crimson and royal blue.

Kate closes her eyes and looks through the beam of her spirit vision. She follows a ray of light as it shines through a crimson pane and passes through the elegant granite arches. The beam splashes onto the aisle, seeps through the cracks in the worn-down floors, and bleeds into the tributaries of the subterranean.

"Tavy, Taw." Kate directs her breath into the ray. "I need your help."

CHAPTER NINETEEN

Love spell

Miriam smacks the bell on the reception desk for the second time, shouting. "Someone, get out here! I want to check out!"

Tamara swoops in close to Miriam and strokes a finger over her forehead, hoping to ease her fears. But an ear-blasting roll of thunder rumbles across the bay, causing Miriam to rush out to the Atlantic Terrace. Tamara glances to the sky. A ring of silver-bright storm clouds gathers over Trellan Bay. Tamara shifts her gaze to the pink mists circling the west tower, "What's causing this disturbance?" The mists show her Kate in Truro cathedral, calling upon Tavy and Tawridge to help her keep Miriam in Cornwall.

Oh, Kate, how could you?

Following Miriam onto the terrace, Tamara sends a message on the wind to Tavy and Tawridge. "Do not act upon Kate's wish." But she's too late; the giants have already embarked on their mission, and Miriam has fallen under the allure of the energy rolling toward her.

Rows of empty rockers sway back and forth from the force of the wind. Thick clusters of lead-gray clouds hang over the cliffs. Two wide streams of silver water burrow across the ocean, cutting through waves like a couple of combines. They splash onto the shore, then rise up as rivers and cascade beneath the clouds. Tavy and Tawridge float inside the silver light—their faces rough and forthright like carvings in a prehistoric cave. They open their arms and spread their reach over the land for as far as the eye can see.

Miriam's teeth chatter with fright, as light radiates from the giant men, nearly knocking her to the ground. She grips the rail surrounding the terrace.

Tamara looks on helplessly. She has told Tavy and Tawridge of Kate's new rebelliousness, but they've not seen it firsthand. They still think of her as the darling little girl of yesteryear, and they would do anything she asked of them.

She watches Tavy and Tawridge round their lips and blow the golden light of their giant love into Miriam's heart. Miriam feels a dreamy sensation of being loved—a love bigger and grander than anything she has ever imagined. Love, free of want or longing—love for her—forever—just for the taking. She flings herself into a chair and rocks back and forth, drinking it in. *I am perfect just as I am.*

Harry bustles onto the terrace in search of Miriam. He can't believe he's hurt her again, and all over that heartless Gwenellen. He spots Miriam in the rocking chair and heads toward her, but he's suddenly overwhelmed by a floating mass of energy circling above him. He shades his eyes from what looks like two giant men hovering over him. Harry trembles as Tavy and Tawridge breathe the golden breath of their love into his heart. Then he melts into the wondrous feeling of everything being right in his world—and most of all, Miriam. He opens his arms to her, noticing a new glow of happiness on her face. She gets up from her chair and falls into his arms. They kiss—a long and passionate kiss—feeling as if they've always belonged to one another and always will.

Tamara speeds through the sky to Truro, her light body gliding on the wind. She catches Kate as she bounds down the steps of the cathedral, a wide grin on her face.

"How could you, Kate? How could you use Tavy and Taw in such a deceitful way? Sooner or later, Harry and Miriam will wake up from their love spell, and then—"

"So what?" the girl scowls. "You told me Miriam has two possible futures, and in one she finds true love. It's only fair that she should know what that feels like."

"But she doesn't know. The love she feels is borrowed, and when she loses it, she will suffer greatly."

"Um … well … maybe things will work out with Harry anyway," Kate says, dashing into the busy streets.

The girl's sudden callous attitude stuns Tamara. Though often willful, Kate would not knowingly cause harm to another person. Tamara checks with the mists of Ruberah to find out what could be affecting her.

The mists reveal a blue-black vapor rising within Kate— the very same vapor Dark Master cast upon Sol'aria on the day of *The Ending*. Tamara's light body dims with anxiety as she realizes Dark Master is behind the change in Kate.

CHAPTER TWENTY

Saturday night at Penrose Hall

The grandfather clock chimes three times, announcing fifteen minutes before the hour of nine o'clock.

Mitch leaves the Tower Suite and descends the stairs. He wears jeans, a black sweater, and his favorite Prada athletic shoes. He steals through the reception hall with the agility of a panther prowling for prey. His eyes look dull, dead—no longer the eyes of the man who once strutted among others with the swagger of a world traveler. They are the eyes of a man ruled by Dark Master.

Mitch stops by the door to the Atlantic Terrace and peers outside. A light mist dims the stars. The young honeymooners sit on a loveseat, resting their heads together. Mitch leans against the doorway, crossing his legs in casual repose. "I'm looking for a game of backgammon. Have you seen Harry around?"

The newlyweds turn and glance at Mitch, then look back at each other. They snicker. The little intimacy denotes a deep union—the kind Mitch has never known and never thought he could have, until Gwenellen.

"We saw Harry a few minutes ago," the young woman says. "He went to the bar for a nightcap. He was with Miriam."

So, Miriam's hooked up with Harry—pity for her. Mitch bids the honeymooners goodnight and heads for the bar. He reviews the plan he made with Gwenellen. He'll lead Harry to Devil's Neck, and Gwenellen will cause a distraction, enough to enable Mitch to shove Harry over the cliff's edge. Mitch smacks his fist against the palm of his hand. This will bind Gwenellen to him forever.

He lingers at the entrance to the bar. The bitter smell of beer hangs on the air. Ruddy-faced men raise their tankards and tell stories, stopping from time to time to indulge in loud bouts of laughter. The inevitable legion of elderly ladies occupies the tables, their big veined hands clutching at drinks, their smiles receding into multiple chins.

Miriam and Harry perch on stools at the far end of the bar. Gone is the socially inept Harry whose brow had seemed permanently dimpled in confusion. He whispers to Miriam and leans his body against hers in the manner of a lover at ease. And gone is the restless Miriam always butting in before anyone can finish a sentence. She gazes at Harry with the devotion of a disciple to a saint.

Mitch folds his arms. Only a few hours ago, Miriam had been begging him to return to New York with her. Now she looks as if she's fucked the afternoon away with Harry. His chest tightens. He'd like to have Miriam waiting in the wings. What if something goes wrong with Gwenellen? His childhood haunts him.

He's eleven years old and being marched up to his father's house, which is big and cold like the man himself. He's handed over to Miss Maine, the stone-faced housekeeper. She looks him over, sniffing. Her nose twitches as if meeting with a foul smell. "A bath." She points up the stairs. He's naked in the tub. He stops wanting God to give him his mother back. He no longer believes in God. No benevolent deity could be so scathingly cruel as to burn his mother to death before his eyes. All he wants is for Miss Maine not to come in.

She swings the door open, looks at him, and laughs.

Panic thumps in Mitch's breast. The heat of the flames that ravaged his mother's house smolders beneath his skin. Miriam has been a safe place—a retreat from that horrific memory. In her own crazy way, Miriam can be a very stable person. Every day she pounds the streets, phones, and the Internet, scoring listings for apartments, making sales—and being there for him when he wants her. He mops his brow with the back of his hand. Somewhere, beyond his vast inner void, he senses he might love Miriam, but he just can't connect with those feelings. He sighs, and Gwenellen returns to his thoughts. He beats his childhood fears into remission and saunters into the bar.

The walking ladies clink their glasses, congratulating each other on the day's hike. Mitch skirts around them. One grabs his arm.

"Oh, do join us, Mitch. Tell us what you've discovered about the area."

"Later." Mitch shakes her off and strides up to Harry and Miriam.

"Sorry to intrude." He looks from one to the other. Miriam greets him with an irritating air of nonchalance.

"Harry." Mitch taps the man's shoulder. "I need a favor of you. It's Gwenellen. She feels awful about the way she acted when we were at the stables, so awful she asked me to ask you if you'd come outside for a minute so she could apologize."

"Oh, that's not necessary," Harry says.

"It is to Gwenellen. She's young, you know. She's trying to do the right thing. It's important to her. It won't take long. I'll have you back with Miriam in five minutes."

Harry squeezes Miriam's hand. "I think that's admirable of Gwenellen, don't you?"

Mistrust glimmers in Miriam's eyes. "I don't know—"

"Hey, come on, Mir," Mitch cajoles, "Gwenellen wants to set things straight. Cut her some slack."

"I'm willing to do that," Harry says, glancing at Miriam for confirmation.

Miriam concedes grudgingly. Mitch turns away from the sight of her and Harry smooching goodbye, thinking there must be some kind of magic in the beer they pump up from the cellar.

Tamara swoops into the bar, having just learned of Mitch's plan to kill Harry. "There is magic, Mitch," she whispers. "Black magic, and it's coming from the sea, from the Black Heart, and it has a hold on you." Tamara brushes as close to Mitch's aura as possible without infecting herself with the rays of Dark Master's tyranny. She speaks of the night she met him in his dream world and of how he'd seen the spheres of the Jewel Kingdom, but Mitch's mind remains closed to her and open only to Dark Master's bidding.

Harry eases off his stool, and Mitch hangs an arm over his shoulder, steering him through the bar. Mitch stops by the walking ladies. "Order me a Grand Marnier." He flashes a smile. "I'll be back shortly. Then you can tell me all about your day."

Harry and Mitch stride through the rose gardens toward the sea. The dewy blossoms release their perfume into the night air, further intoxicating the men with their desires for love.

Tamara sends a message to her giants on the wind, telling them of the peril about to befall Harry. Tavy responds, his voice trembling with regret for having granted Kate's wish for Harry and Miriam to fall in love.

"Kate just wanted to help Miriam," Tawridge says, ever defensive of the girl.

"But I said we should ask Tamara first," Tavy insists. "I warned—"

"Forget what is past," Tamara says. "Mitch intends to kill Harry. You must remove your spell of love from Harry so he can think clearly, or his death will be upon our legend."

Tawridge's great bell tone rings up through the ocean. "Consider it done."

Tamara notices a haze of gray mist creeping along the horizon line—a scenic prompt from Dark Master. Whenever a sacred future comes due for an old Ruberian, Dark Master does everything in his power to force that person into that future. He monitors their every move, plotting to capture them. He has a complex computer system designed to extract ancient knowledge from their brains, which he hopes to use to restart Rube. With the force of Rube under his control, he'd have a lethal hold on the world.

Mitch and Harry clip along the footpath, chatting like old friends. Mitch waves at Gwenellen, who stands barefoot, wriggling her toes at the rocky edge of Devil's Neck.

Harry slows his pace, falling behind Mitch. He senses a change in the air pressure—a swirling sensation that feels as if some huge, unseen presence stalks the ocean and could, at any time, rise up. The hairs on his scalp prickle. Clouds cease to move. The banging of the wind in his ears falls mute. All is quiet, deathly quiet, like in the seconds before an earthquake.

"What's the matter? Why have you stopped?" Mitch steps back beside Harry.

Clouds flurry and part, and the sea swells up, splashing high over the cliffs. Tavy and Tawridge stream across the ocean bed, the combined force of their rivers momentarily disrupting the natural rhythm of the sea. At Devil's Neck, they thrust their rivers up over the cliffs and into the air above Harry. They inhale deep breaths and withdraw the golden light of their love spell from Harry's body, and then dive back into the ocean.

The wind rises. Clouds drift high in the sky, and the sea drops to its normal level. Harry feels empty, like a sheet of blotting paper suddenly erased of a lifetime of treasured etchings. He wipes sea spray from his brow and looks at Mitch. "What just happened? I feel … I don't know … strange."

"Just another freak storm, I guess." Mitch glances out to sea. "They sure have a lot of them around here. Come on, Gwenellen's waiting."

"Waiting? For what?" Harry asks.

Mitch cocks his head to the side, puzzled by the confused look in Harry's eyes. "You said you'd give Gwenellen the chance to make things right with you. You can't go back on that, Harry. You want to do the right thing, don't you?"

The right thing—ah yes, the phrase brings Harry back to reality. The ache of his broken marriage comes first. He wonders, as he often does, where he went wrong with Pammy. This self-scrutiny comes to a halt as he recalls his afternoon of lovemaking with Miriam. He writhes with discomfort. Miriam is on the rebound from Mitch and much too vulnerable to become involved with another man. He should not have made love to her. Whatever possessed him?

Mitch slings his arm over Harry's shoulder again. "Come on. Let's get this over with."

Harry walks on, thinking of the consequences he will surely face as a result of his indiscretion with Miriam. Oh, good heavens! He'd even told her he loved her and they'd talked of marriage!

Fog thickens on the horizon and billows into the sky like black smoke rising from a furnace. The dark vapors gather momentum as they roll to shore and swamp the cliffs and land, all but blinding Harry and Mitch. Harry stands close to the cliff's edge, staring into the eerie substance, comfortable in his discomfort—deserving no less.

Standing a couple of steps behind Harry, Gwenellen slips her hand in Mitch's and drags him to her side. "Do it now, Mitch."

"Tell me you love me. Tell me you'll marry me."

Gwenellen opens her mouth to speak but hesitates, searching for the exact words to inspire Mitch to kill for her. Mitch stares at her like a robot needing the turn of a key to spring into action.

Tamara catches sight of Miriam walking along the cliff path, her face twisting in angst as she calls out to Harry. The fog thickens. She staggers, swaying her arms in circles, parting it as she moves slowly forward. Still under the spell of Tavy and Tawridge's love, her heart has warned her of the danger surrounding her lover. Tamara would ask her giants to rise up again and remove the spell from Miriam, but with Dark Master lurking close to the shores of Cornwall, she needs the giants to remain in the sea. Without their light, the ruler could upset the balance of the oceans surrounding the peninsula.

Miriam yells Harry's name as she traipses along, but her voice is drowned out by the moan of a foghorn hooting across the bay.

Gwenellen rubs her breasts against Mitch's arm. "Kill Harry," she whispers, "and I'll be with you forever."

Forever. Mitch caresses the word, losing himself in the wonder of his good fortune.

Beyond the headland, a current of roiling blue-black waters cuts through the waves. The ceaseless back-and-forth motion of the sea falters for a second as Dark Master surfaces from his kingdom. The black immensity of his great cape shadows the bay, and fog blankets the whole peninsula, muffling the breeze, and muting the sea. The ruler swivels his hooded head in a complete circle, his camera vision clicking and taking note of every detail. Dark Master skims back beneath the ocean, but leaves his shadow lingering over the land—an aid for the deadly deed about to happen.

Tamara foresees disaster lurking close to Miriam. She shouts into the wind, "Tavy, Taw! Remove your love spell from Miriam at once!" But the giants don't receive her message. Dark Master's shadow bounces it back to her.

Miriam gropes her way along the cliff path and arrives at Harry's side. "Oh, Harry, my darling, I had the most terrible feeling that something awful was going to happen to you." She burrows her head against his shoulder. "I wouldn't want to live without you."

Harry's nerves run ragged. He quivers in his skin and takes a quick step away from Miriam. He hoped he'd have time to think things through before seeing her again. He wanted to let her down as kindly as possible.

"You know I love you, Harry," Miriam says, nudging in close to him again. "I love you with all my heart and soul. Nothing can part us."

Harry searches his conscience for the right thing to say, while Miriam gazes at him, fearless in the arms of boundless love.

Behind them, Gwenellen gives Mitch a little push and he moves closer to the cliffs. The ever-thickening fog disturbs him, but he got a good glimpse of Harry a moment ago. Mitch rams his fist straight ahead aiming for Harry's back. Horror strikes as Mitch hears the high-pitched screams of a woman's voice.

CHAPTER TWENTY-ONE

Into a golden parachute

As it turns out, Dark Master did Tamara a favor when he interrupted her message to the giants. Still under their love spell, Miriam plummets over the cliffs and lands in an upside-down parachute of golden energy created by Tavy and Tawridge. She bounces up and down, happy as a child on a trampoline. The giants lower her slowly down the cliff face, speaking soft-spoken words, assuring her she is safe in their care. The parachute flops onto the sea, and Miriam floats on her back and stretches her arms out wide, flowing the golden light of the love spell to everyone, everywhere.

Tamara swims to Miriam's side, and rests a sparkling hand on her shoulder. "Miriam ... it's me ... Tamara. I've come to take you back to shore."

"Not yet, please. I hear something exquisite." Miriam lays her cheek on the surface of the sea. "It's a boy singing. It's the purest voice I've ever heard."

Tamara beckons to Tavy and Tawridge, and they surge toward her joining their rivers together. "Miriam is listening to the chorister," Tamara whispers. "Let's sweep her up and rush her back to Trellan Bay."

"Leave me alone," Miriam shouts, shoving Tamara away. "I love this song." She hums as the boy sings Mendelssohn's *Oh, for the wings of a dove*. Her pleasure is short lived. The Mermaid of Zennor cuts a swift crawl beneath Miriam and rips the shark-like fin at the tip of her tail through the fleshy underside of Miriam's arm. Miriam lets out a shrill, ear-splitting scream.

The sea turns red.

CHAPTER TWENTY-TWO

Sunday morning in Trellan Hospital

"Get out!"

The sight of Mitch touches a wound so deeply etched in Miriam's soul that she slips a little from the soaring heights of her love for Harry.

Mitch grips the metal frame at the foot of Miriam's hospital bed, trembling with relief that Miriam survived the dreadful fall. "For God's sake, Mir, what happened?"

"You son of a bitch! You tried to kill me! That's what happened. Get out!"

"No way, Mir. You know me. I'd never do that." Mitch tugs on the ends of his hair, unable to recall the details of what happened. "All I remember about last night was hearing you scream. Then Harry appeared out of the fog and said he'd called for help. He said you must have fallen over the cliffs, that at one moment you were there, and then you weren't."

Miriam screws her face in anger. "It was you. I would know you anywhere. Even on the foggiest night. I could smell that fragrance you splash all over yourself. Get out!" She stabs the call button by her bed.

"Miriam, please—"

"Get out, you idiot!"

"Look, Mir, the police questioned me for hours last night. I told them we'd broken up, but that you'd gotten involved with Harry and that I'd never seen you looking so happy. I also told them that Gwenellen and I were together. So why the hell would I want to kill you?"

The door swings open. A squat, forty-something, broad-beamed nurse bustles into the room. She folds her fingers around Miriam's wrist, checking her pulse. "You need something, my 'andsome?"

Miriam directs her finger at Mitch. "Him out of here."

The nurse swings a sideways glance at Mitch. "Are 'e deaf or just stupid?"

"Mir, if I'm in any way to blame for this, and honestly, I

don't know—"

"Out!" Miriam yells.

The door closes behind Mitch, and the nurse beams at Miriam. "Good news. Doctor has signed your release. Your arm's swollen and you've got some stitches. Nasty cut, that ... many a dangerous thing in the ocean. You'll wear the sling for a while. Keep the arm rested. Kate Penrose is here with her father to take you home."

Miriam flinches. Where's Harry? She lowers her eyes, thinking of yesterday, when everything between them changed. She recalls a sudden swing in the weather, and then Harry rushed onto the Atlantic Terrace. Their eyes met, and they fell in love. She laughs to herself. It sounds as corny as a B movie, but she's never felt any emotion as strongly as she felt their love. They kissed, and her whole being fused with his. The past died. Harry no longer mourned the loss of Pammy. They dashed up to Harry's room and made love on the narrow single bed. Afterward they lay in each other arms and talked for hours. Harry confessed that he feared he might lose his daughters if he loved anyone other than their mother. Now he realized that to be unfounded. Of course, his girls would want him to find happiness again. And Mitch vanished from her memory altogether. Then Harry said, "We belong together. Marry me." She said, "Yes," without question or doubt. Everything seemed perfect.

Miriam looks up at the nurse. "Is there someone else with Kate and her father? Another man?"

"Kate will look after you. She's got the gift, just like her mum." The nurse shakes her head, causing her short curls to wiggle. "Aye, 'tis a terrible thing about Lara Penrose. You be careful. You nearly came to the same end. Someone's after you, but don't run away. You signed your initials beside a departure date when you arrived at Penrose Hall. Stay until then."

Miriam shivers, noticing a distinct change in the nurse's expression—a tightening of her lips—a haunted cast to her eyes. First the taxi driver warned her not to leave early, now this no-nonsense woman had implied her life was in danger. There were either a lot of crazy people here or ... "What do you mean? Who's after me?"

The nurse sits on the edge of the bed. "Some say Lara ran off with another man, but she never would. Lara's like an angel, kind to everybody. She loved Lance. They've been sweethearts since they were kids. Mark my words: Lara's not dead. That mermaid's got her, and it was her who took a bite out of you. I've seen her teeth marks before." Tina touches the bandage wrapped around Miriam's upper arm. "The river's in you. That's why you're alive. Tamara looks after you until the scheduled day of your departure. Some would say you're lucky for that, others that you're cursed."

Miriam rubs her temples. A nervous trill of laughter

escapes her. "Cursed? How could I be cursed by a river?"

"You're on your sacred future. Correct?"

"Oh … that," Miriam sighs. "I don't—"

"Understand," the nurse says, nodding her head. "They never do."

"What do you mean?"

"One minute you know it's real and the next you can't remember a thing about it. You see Tamara, and then you don't see 'er, but if you signed the guest book with the pink ink, you'll go. Everyone does."

Miriam shakes her head. "No. I'm in love. I'm not going anywhere except to London with Harry."

Tina pats Miriam's hand. "There … there. Don't fret."

"But I didn't agree to any of this."

"You did. You've just forgotten."

The door opens. Kate rushes in. "Hi." She dumps a large brown carrier bag on the floor and studies Miriam's arm, fingering the bandage. "Fab, you'll have a scar. That's sooo sexy."

"Where's Harry?" The memory of their time together lifts Miriam right back into the love spell.

Kate digs in the brown bag, rummaging through clothes she brought for Miriam. Tamara forbade her to say anything to Miriam about Harry. She's on slippery turf with T over the love spell, and T will be here any minute to look after Miriam, so she'd better not cross her again. Kate pulls a clingy spandex shirt out of the bag, turquoise and dotted with orange spangles. "Here, this is mine, but it's made of stretchy fabric. It should fit you." She hands it to Miriam. "Your things were too boring."

"Where's Harry?"

Miriam sits up front in the Land Rover beside Lance. Her wounded arm rests in a sling. Kate's shirt clings to her body—stretched to the max. Miriam yanks the garment down to cover a roll of fat bulging over the waistband of her pants, while trying to convince Lance that Lara could return to him.

"Look at me. Yesterday, I spent a few hours with Harry and fell in love. Last night, I fell over the cliffs, and death seemed imminent. Then I found myself bouncing in streams of golden light, feeling happier than I've ever felt before."

Miriam raves about how Tamara and her giants rescued her. Lance frowns, wondering if the fall affected Miriam's sense of reality. Men, generally—with the exception of seafaring men, who naturally revere the forces of nature—find it difficult to give credence to Tamara's legend. Lance relaxes his grip on the wheel. Miriam's unexplainable survival does raise his hopes for Lara.

Tamara and Kate sit side by side in the rear of the car. Tamara tries to commune telepathically with Kate, suggesting ways she might be of help to Miriam. The girl ignores her.

Outside a china-blue sky domes the land, and the sea splashes to shore, dusting the sand with foam—some of it pale pink, glittering from cove to cove in long wavy lines. Tamara whispers to her giants, still flowing in the sea, "Remove the love spell from Miriam as soon as possible."

Tavy and Tawridge surge up from the ocean and float their rivers across the sky. As Lance steers onto the circular driveway of *Penrose Hall*, Tamara feels the giants suck in a great breath, and then watches the light of their love leave Miriam's body through the top of her head. Miriam scratches her scalp and yawns.

Entering the inn, Miriam glances in a mirror by the door. The dread of aging alone looks back at her. The ticking of the grandfather clock in the reception hall further reminds her of time passing. She shudders. Why isn't Harry here? Harry said he loved her. He asked her to marry him. Miriam lays a hand on her heart. It feels suddenly empty of the passion she felt for Harry. She gulps, and reasons it will come back as soon as she sees him.

"Come on, Miriam." Kate drags her toward the stairs,

but Miriam frees herself from the girl.

"I must see Harry, now."

"It's tea time. He's probably on the terrace."

"What! I nearly died, and Harry's having tea! Go and get him. I don't want to see all those people."

"Let me take you to your room," Lance says. "There's a service lift in the rear. We'll ride up in that."

"Go on," Kate urges. "I'll send Harry up."

"What the hell is going on?"

The front door opens. Harry's laughter precedes him— laughter Miriam recognizes, but coming with such gaiety that it stuns her. A woman hangs on Harry's arm. Wire-rimmed glasses magnify her small dark eyes. Her face is jowly and devoid of makeup. Her brown hair falls to her shoulders in a style she's probably worn since high school. She's a good twenty pounds overweight, and she doesn't give a damn or she wouldn't be wearing cargo shorts, their baggy pockets stuffed to the gills with god knows what.

"Miriam!" Harry coughs in his nervous manner. His brow puckers. "I ... well, this is Pammy. We ... er... well ...we're getting back together."

CHAPTER TWENTY-THREE

Sunday afternoon at *Penrose Hall*

That's Pammy?

Miriam stares at the woman in disbelief. The difference between the winsome female she'd imagined and the dumpy woman hanging on Harry's arm dumbfounds her. Rage and desperation crowd in on her. She storms up the stairs.

"Kate," Tamara nudges the girl. "You're responsible for Miriam's distress, and her state of mind could affect your mother's chance of a safe return. Go after Miriam and console her."

"Can't. I promised to go riding with a friend."

Tamara gasps. Kate's sudden lack of concern about the

rescue of her mother reveals the extent of Dark Master's influence on her. Tamara scours Kate's aura hoping to catch sight of the vapor the ruler inflicted on Sol'aria back in Ruberah. No luck. The darkness lies deep in Kate's subconscious, beyond the boundaries of Tamara's reach.

Kate runs off and Tamara follows her onto the Atlantic Terrace, but the girl vanishes behind a row of trees obscuring the fields that lead to the stables. Tamara lets her go, and she also decides to leave Miriam alone for a while. She searches the terrace for Mitch, wondering how he's faring after last night.

He sits in a wicker chair rocking back and forth, away from the crowd gathering around the tea trolley, a haze of blue-black vapors drifting around him. Tamara gathers a handful of pink mists hanging close to the west tower and looks through them into Mitch's thoughts. He's thinking of the awful moments after Miriam sailed over the cliffs instead of Harry. He'd stood frozen and horrified, the sound of Miriam's screams piercing his eardrums. Gwenellen shook him and spoke to him like a dictator to a subordinate. "It was an accident," she said. "That's what you will tell people. You don't know what happened. The fog was dark and very thick. You heard someone stumble, then scream. That's all you know. Harry has called the police. Go back to the inn. The detectives will be there when you arrive. When they question you, tell them what I just said. Say no more." Then, as if in afterthought, she added, "And don't forget to act bereaved and confused."

Mitch had never been more confused in his life. The flames that killed his mother blazed back to life, and the pain of losing her nearly choked him to death. He barely had control of himself when the police began asking him questions. Then his mind went blank to everything except the words Gwenellen had told him to say. He repeated them over and over. Eventually, Constable Trewarren, a scrawny young man with an olive complexion, walked him back to Devil's Neck. Mitch's knees trembled when he found Gwenellen hugging Harry. She stroked Harry's brow, bestowing on him the very tenderness Mitch had imagined she would give to him when they lived in their island life. A couple of patrol cars roared over the fields. Sirens blared. High beams and emergency lights lit up the foggy night.

Gwenellen pulled herself away from Harry and threw herself on the ground, banging her fists against the rocky path. As Mitch wondered why, the ever-astute Jed Flyer spoke to him. *She's pretending to be hysterical so she won't be questioned until later.* Jed was right. Constable Trewarren helped Gwenellen into one of the police cars and ordered the driver to take her to the hospital. Sitting in the back seat, Gwenellen smiled and waved at Mitch like a princess to an adoring crowd.

Tamara leaves Mitch to his thoughts, and flies across the fields, gliding low to the ground in her light body, pursuing Kate. She draws alongside the girl as she approaches the stables. Tamara tosses strands of her sparkling hair around Kate like she used to when they played together, pretending to be goddesses of the jeweled kingdom—women who hurled power through their hair, capturing those who caused harm on behalf of Dark Master.

Kate looks down, avoiding Tamara's eyes. "I said I'm sorry about Miriam and Harry," she says, sounding a little more like her old self.

"I know you're suffering over Miriam's resistance to rescue your mother, but she can't help it. She's too devastated over the loss of Mitch ... and now Harry ... to cope with anything else. You need to help her recover."

"Why doesn't she just go on her sacred future, which is what she's meant to do?"

"Miriam doesn't have to do anything, Kate."

"You mean she could just go home and be miserable?"

"Misery is relative. To some it's better than change."

"If Miriam's too scared to go into the Black Heart, I'll go."

"To rescue your mother is Miriam's sacred future. You must not rob her of the chance to meet it."

Kate kicks her heels into the ground, huffing and complaining, then sighing and coming to terms with herself. "Okay. What can I do to help Miriam?"

"Be kind to her. Listen to her. Do thoughtful things for

her, small things like the way you used to clean your mother's reading glasses before she sat down with a book."

"But that was for Mummy. That was different."

"It can't be different, Kate. Your mother's life depends on it."

"That's not fair."

"Ah, well—"

"Don't lecture me. I'll do it, but I've got to do it my way."

Tamara eyes the girl closely. The light of her volition reflects deep violet in her aura, telling Tamara there will be no way but her way.

Looking out from the terrace, Mitch observes Kate tramping through the rose arches, heading for the inn. He thinks of what Tom Reilly said about her before Mitch left New York on this assignment. "As you approach *Penrose Hall*, you'll see a girl with long, red hair, riding a black horse." Mitch hits his fist against the palm of his hand, wishing he'd asked Tom more about that. Kate disturbs him. She sits on the edge of the darkness inside him like a vagrant spirit ready to drag him down.

He'd better try to make friends with her. He leaps from his chair and sprints toward her.

"Hey, kiddo." He slaps a hand on Kate's shoulder and smiles his widest smile. "Great about Miriam, isn't it?"

Kate raises a brow.

"How do you think it happened? I mean that she's okay."

"Just not her time to die, I suppose."

"You're cool, honey, a really cool kid."

"What do you want?" Kate asks flatly.

He runs his hands through his hair, tugging the ends over his collar. "You're something of a legend, you know." He laughs and tells her what Tom O'Reilly said about her, then rests his hands on his hips.

"So, what about it?"

"Aw, come on, honey, I'll write about you. Make you famous."

"What do I need with that if I'm already a legend?"

Mitch shakes his head. "You're tough."

"And you're …" Kate bites her lip, stopping herself from call him a wimp.

"About Gwenellen." Mitch moves closer to Kate. "She doesn't seem to have any family. Do you know anything about that?"

"No. My mother hired her. All she told me was that Gwenellen needed the job." Kate pauses as if to say something else, but decides not to. "Why don't you ask her yourself?"

"That might bring up hurtful memories for her. What else were you going to say about what your mother told you?"

"I wasn't." Kate strides past him.

Annoyed, Mitch watches the girl. She obviously knows something about Gwenellen, and she's hiding it. He glances at the terrace and finds himself in the beam of Gwenellen's smile. She giggles and raises her shoulders in an adorable little sugarcoated shrug. How sweet. How innocent. How could he doubt her?

Kate deliberately bumps into Gwenellen as she passes the tea trolley on the terrace, and she smirks at the young woman as if implying Mitch had told her a secret about her. Tamara flees after the girl. "Be smart, Kate. You know Gwenellen has connections with Dark Master. Don't pick a fight with her."

"I'm on my way to help Miriam. Isn't that what you want?"

Kate crosses the reception hall and begins to climb the stairs. Tamara keeps close to her. "You're among the fortunate people in the world, Kate. You know that to act out of anger or revenge opens your energy field to the Black Heart."

The girl puts her hands over her ears and walks on. Tamara watches the first pellets of psychic energy spin forth from Gwenellen's mind, whiz through the reception hall and hit Kate in the spine. The girl flinches and draws to a halt. "That was a direct ploy from Dark Master—an attempt to draw you into a battle that only he will benefit from," Tamara says.

"I don't care. Gwenellen had something to do with Mummy's disappearance, and I'm going to hurt her."

Tamara starts to advise Kate against that, but stops herself. Dark Master goads the girl's rebellious behavior. Tamara decides to give her enough space to make her own mistakes and learn by the consequences. It's a hard choice, for as gifted as Kate is in her spirit sight, it remains undeveloped to a large extent. Kate can see how Gwenellen uses her mind to direct her weapons of attack, but she cannot see into Mastermind Control in the Black Heart—the place where Gwenellen receives her power from Dark Master.

The girl narrows a cold, calculated gaze on Gwenellen and creates a vision of her receiving a blast of Kate's fury. She pulls a handful of violet light from her aura, wraps the vision inside it and hurls it across reception. It flies through the doors leading onto the Atlantic Terrace and lands in the pit of Gwenellen's stomach. Gwenellen drops a teacup, and doubles over in pain.

Unable to resist, Tamara leans in close to Kate. "You could soften your will, Kate, and withdraw some of that energy. I could help you—"

"Never. I'm going to kill Gwenellen."

"No, you will not," Tamara says. "The job at hand is to get your mother out of the Black Heart. You must focus on helping Miriam as we talked about earlier."

The girl fumes, slipping from feeling all-powerful and back into her fourteen-year-old self. Her fiery thoughts mingle with Tamara's light, and clouds of mist froth up between them. Tamara reaches into her river, all the way back to Ruberah, and hauls long streams of pink mist into the present. She layers it over the stairs and through the reception hall, forming a barrier between Kate and Gwenellen, preventing the possibility of an all-out psychic battle between them.

CHAPTER TWENTY-FOUR

Sunday night at *Penrose Hall*

Kate kicks aside shoes scattered around her bed, kneels, and yanks out a black metal box from beneath the mattress. She flips the lid open. Three packets of cigarettes lie side by side: filter-tipped Players, Gauloises—her favorites—and Virginia Slims, the packet Mitch tossed in the litter bin by reception while Miriam was signing the guest book. Kate selects those and steps onto the tiny balcony outside her room.

"Hey Miriam," she shouts across the short distance to Miriam's balcony. "Come out. It's time for us to talk."

Miriam adjusts the sling on her shoulder and storms outside with the aplomb of a wronged queen in a Greek drama. "I'm not making any deals with you."

Kate sticks a Virginia Slims cigarette between her lips.

"Those are mine." Miriam stares at the packet. "Give them back."

"Finders keepers." Kate lights up and puffs smoke in Miriam's direction. "I brought you vodka at teatime, and you agreed we'd talk later. Shall I come to your room?"

"You're a brat. You know that, don't you?"

"I know. Here." Kate hands Miriam the cigarette, then heaves herself onto the battlement and swings her legs over to Miriam's balcony.

"For Christ's sake!" Miriam drops the cigarette and uses her good arm to grab Kate and help her over. "You could fall and kill yourself."

Kate wipes grit off her hands. "What's more exciting than a little near-death-experience?"

"You're depraved."

"I know."

Miriam retrieves the cigarette from the floor. "I'm mad at you." She inhales smoke. "You knew Harry had hooked up with his ex again. You should have told me when you came to the hospital." Miriam scoots into her room, trailing smoke.

"Sorry."

"I'm leaving in the morning." Miriam slumps on the bed. "I've got to get to the office. I'm in the middle of selling a big apartment, and I can't afford for anything to go wrong. I need that commission."

"You won't get across the Tamar, Miriam. You signed the guest book and agreed to stay until Tuesday morning."

"I know you've got a lot of weird rules around here, but let me tell you something, signing a hotel register does not legally bind anyone, anywhere in the whole goddamned world, to stay in any hotel for any length of time."

Kate plunks herself on the bed beside Miriam. "Do you know who bit you in the arm?"

"What do you mean who? It was a shark or something."

"That was a nice ride down over the cliffs, wasn't it? When I was a little girl, Tavy and Taw used to create a great, golden parachute for me, bundle me inside it, and fly me over to the north coast. Then they'd lower me onto a surfboard. Everyone thought I was born to be a champion surfer, as I never fell, even when I rode the biggest waves." She swipes the cigarette from Miriam and takes a puff, "Inside the parachute I could hear the sounds of nature that Tavy and Taw hear. I listened to the voice of the winds, and minerals deep inside the earth, to birds and fish, and all the creatures that live in the ocean. Did you hear a boy singing when you landed on the sea in that parachute?"

Miriam's gasps, remembering the sweet sound of the boy's voice, "Yes."

"Then the Mermaid of Zennor had a jealous fit and bit you."

"Excuse me?" Miriam's voice rises with disbelief.

"Ages ago, the mermaid heard the boy singing one Sunday in church and fell in love with his voice. She's a shape-shifter, so she came up from the sea and stole him. The boy sings for her and for her alone. If you hear him, she'll try to kill you because you stole that time from her."

Miriam drags on the cigarette, trying to cope. Obviously, she wouldn't be alive but for some kind of magical help, and she had felt something fleshy, almost human wrap around her in the sea, but a mermaid? "I'm still leaving in the morning."

"Um ... well ... about signing our guest book. Remember the red pen with the pink ink that you used?"

"What about it?"

"That's special ink. Only those about to go on a sacred future use that pen. When you signed your name with the pink ink, the Cycles of Time opened your record from the Time of Ruberah, and your life changed. Everything that's happened to you has been to help you enter your sacred future."

"Listen, Kate." Miriam faces the girl square on. "Can't you just let me go home?"

Kate slides an arm around Miriam's shoulders, "If you were anyone but you, yes. But you're special to me, and not just because I need you to help me get my mother out of the Black Heart, but …" She pauses, locking Miriam into her gaze, "because back in the Time of Ruberah, we were sisters."

A soft, rose light shimmers in Miriam's vision, and ancient memories return. Her love for her darling sister, Sol'aria, washes over her like the root cause of her being. "Sisters?" Miriam whispers, her voice quavering.

"Yes, the royal sisters of Ruberah. We could ignite Rube, the energy of rubies—the most powerful force ever to exist on planet Earth. I filtered light from the sun into Mt. Rube, and you streamed in sounds from the cosmos. We can still do that."

Miriam wavers between understanding the things Kate describes and falling unconscious to them. But as Kate speaks, her senses tune up, and she becomes distracted by the sound of slightly uneven footfalls. At first, they seem far away, as if submerged beneath water, but then they become louder and stiff like the sound of someone walking on stilts. Finally, they stomp along the corridor outside her room.

Miriam nudges Kate. "Someone's coming!"

"Who cares? I'm talking about Rube ... about you and

me waking up a force that's been asleep for millions of years."

"I'm sorry, but someone frightening is coming to my room." Miriam reaches for the Xanax on her bedside table.

Kate knocks her hand off the bottle. "Don't muddle your mind with that stuff."

Miriam looks at Kate, aghast. "Don't tell me what to do." She lowers the shoulder of her injured arm, trying to free herself of the sling so she can reach the pills with her other hand.

Three raps hit the door, three knocks with a spine-chilling space between them.

CHAPTER TWENTY-FIVE

A fateful lie

Miriam clings to Kate. "Who is it?"

"It doesn't matter. Just tell me you'll come back to Ruberah with me."

"What are you talking about?"

"Gosh, Miriam, have you forgotten already? You really are impossible."

Another three raps hit the door. It opens slowly, and Gwenellen glides in. She licks her lips over a little gleeful smile. "I've been working with your father on the books, Kate. He wants to see you in his study."

"That had better be true, or you'll be sorry."

Gwenellen grips Kate's arm. "Try hurting me again and you won't be a pretty little girl anymore."

"Oh, I'm so scared." Kate bares her teeth like a snarling beast and stalks from the room.

"That girl has a wild imagination." Gwenellen moves close to Miriam. "It's best to take what she says with a grain of salt."

The need to protect Kate surges back to Miriam. "I think she's a terrific kid."

Gwenellen strolls toward the balcony. "Mr. Penrose said I was to help you pack."

The mention of Kate's father, the one seemingly normal person at the inn, relaxes Miriam. "No need. I'm already packed."

"It's stuffy in here." Gwenellen throws the French doors all the way open and stands with her back to the sky. Sunlight blazes behind her.

Shading her eyes with her hand, Miriam detects a dark blue haze waving around Gwenellen like a reflection off the sea. She slides to the foot of her bed to get a closer look, but Gwenellen steps inside and into the shadows.

"About Mitch." Gwenellen buffs her fingernails on the sleeve of her cardigan. "He couldn't help falling in love with me.

Men just do."

"Mitch, in love? Give me a break. The only thing he's in love with is an image of himself as a best-selling author."

"He'll become that with me."

"Please! He's a hack and always will be." Miriam gets off the bed and paces over to Gwenellen. "Mitch tried to kill me. What do you know about that?"

Gwenellen's eyes turn ice blue. "He didn't. It was the river. Tamara wants you dead."

The breath goes out of Miriam as the image of the glittering young woman with the aqua eyes pops into her mind. Strange as it is, she'd like to believe in Tamara as a benevolent guide—one who will always protect her. Gwenellen's lie shakes the foundation of that hope. "Why would Tamara want to kill me?"

Gwenellen moves into the long shadow of the armoire. "Harry used to come here when he was a boy. Tamara once told him he would fall in love, marry, and share happiness with that woman forever. Harry's divorce casts a cloud on her prophecy and nothing is dearer to Tamara than her legend. So, when Harry got smitten with you ... well ... there went Tamara's love-for-one-woman prediction." She buffs her nails some more on her sweater sleeve. "She had to get rid of you, didn't she?"

"That sounds ridiculous."

"It's all about power, Miriam, and Tamara gets hers from fools like you."

"How do you know what Tamara told Harry as a boy?"

"You think you're the only woman he's told his pathetic little love story to?"

"How do you know what Tamara thinks and does?"

"Lots of people here know about her—her and her stupid giants. But you being from New York and all ... well ... I thought you'd be smarter than them." Gwenellen ambles to the door, swaying her hips. "If you've got some sleeping pills, take a couple tonight and knock yourself out. Get a good night's rest and leave tomorrow." She slips from the room.

Miriam chews on her thumbnail, wondering what to believe. Feeling exhausted, she lies down for a nap before dinner. Soft, rose light colors her vision, and she falls into a deep sleep, dreaming of Ruberah.

Princess Li'ram catches her reflection in the glass façade of the Crystal Temple of Science, and marvels at how she gives off the air of a carefree young woman. Rubies sparkle in her hair, at her waist, and in the straps of her sandals. Gems that love her, love she doesn't deserve, but love that's always there because she is Li'ram, High Priestess of Sound. Her throat tightens as she enters the Temple of Science. She looks away from the adoring glances and bows she receives from those passing her in the lobby. She does not deserve them.

She hurries into her private lift. The doors of the crystal cube close, and the glow of rubies spreads beneath her feet. She speaks her destination into the astral disk on the palm of her hand, and the cube glides upward. She gets off at her private sanctuary, a room where she prepares herself to work as a High Priestess of Rube. She slides off her sandals, folds their ruby laces carefully beside them, and treads on floors of solid gold. Normally, she would kneel, surrender to the Goddess of the Ruby Sphere, and close her mind to all but the heavenly sounds of the Deva Chorus. She delays that duty, as she can't free herself from thoughts of Da'krah and their plan to ignite the power of emeralds. She walks to the windows facing north.

Mt. Rube rises from a high plain outside the city. Streams of rose light fan out from its base, feeding power to the homes and industries of Az'Rayelle. She follows a ray over the hills to a white marble palace. Sol'aria stands on the wide, gold base beneath the sundial in the gardens. Her flame-colored hair falls free to her waist, blowing in the breeze. Li'ram's heart bursts with love for the girl, who is only sixteen and so at ease with being a Sun Master of Rube. Sol'aria looks up as if knowing Li'ram thinks of her, which no doubt she does. Her jeweled intelligence shines clearly in her thoughts, in a mind where no cause reigns higher than working with Rube— not even E'am, the young man she loves and will soon wed in the rings ruby fire.

A sense of dread strikes Li'ram. What if she's doing the wrong

thing in helping Da'krah bring the Emerald Force to life? E'am and
Sol'aria fought bitterly last night. E'am asked Sol'aria to withdraw from the
Emerald project. Sol'aria refused. Agony presses on Li'ram's heart. She
must never let anything bad happen to Sol'aria. Her father charged her with
her sister's safety in the moments before he died. "All beings are blessings
from the universe," he said. "As a High Priestess of Sound, you are
exceptionally valuable to mankind. As a Sun Master, Sol'aria is rare
among us. Few will accept the responsibility to draw energy from the star that
gives us life. They fear they will disrupt its natural flow. Sol'aria knows she
is one with the Sun."

Miriam wakes up with a start, her dream so vivid only a moment ago, gone as if it never happened. Her heart aches as if bludgeoned with a blunt instrument. The sight of her luggage lifts her spirits. She will get out of here tomorrow.

Miriam hurries downstairs to the dining room. She'll have shepherd's pie with mashed potatoes and gravy, and treacle tart with a dollop of vanilla ice cream for dessert. At least the Brits have great comfort food. As she steps onto the landing, Harry and Pammy cross the reception hall, hands clasped, arms swinging, like a couple of kids on their way to the playground. Miriam rubs her wounded arm. She removed her sling in order to eat more easily, but considers going back to her room to get it. Harry ought to see her physical suffering, at least.

"Miriam." Lance calls from the foot of the stairs.

"Would you do me the honor of dining with me?"

Miriam hesitates but accepts as she catches the shocked glances of the walking ladies scurrying past Lance. The thought of giving them something to gossip about pleases her, and she all but runs down the stairs. She slips her good arm through Lance's in the manner of a possessive woman. As they pass the old biddies, Miriam flashes them a brazen smile. A collective gasp of disapproval rises behind her.

Lance leads her to a table in a small bay with heavy leaded windows. Their thick panes distort the view of the cliffs near Devil's Neck, making them seem larger—nearer. Two tables behind Lance, Mitch sits alone. He faces Miriam, but he's got his head buried in the menu. The hurt of being dumped for Gwenellen burns Miriam to the bone.

A bent-over elderly waiter looms beside their table, snaps up the white linen napkin from Miriam's place setting, and spreads it on her lap.

"A cocktail?" Lance asks.

"Sure. I'll have a gin martini. Make it a double, straight up, olives."

Lance orders a gin and tonic. He recommends the grilled Dover Sole and a chocolate soufflé for dessert.

Hmmm. Fish is a far cry from comfort food. Miriam

manages a smile. "Sounds good." She sucks in her stomach. Shit, she probably weighs more now than she did before she went to the spa a couple of weeks ago.

"Everything is arranged for your departure in the morning." Lance straightens the cutlery beside his plate. "Pete, our handyman, will drive you to the Newquay Airport. I'm afraid you'll have to leave here by five-thirty to catch your flight."

"Not a problem." Miriam peeks at her watch. Nine hours, and she's out of here. She adjusts her wristwatch to sit straight on her arm for easy checking. This time tomorrow she'll be in the air on her way back to New York.

"Bread?" Gwenellen swings a basket in front of Miriam. The smell of warm yeast swamps her nostrils. Miriam swipes a brown, loaf-shaped roll—the largest one in the basket.

Gwenellen leans over Lance. "And an olive roll for you ... your favorite." She dumps one on his plate, brushing her breast against his shoulder. "I'll come to your study again later on. There's still work to do on the accounts." She smirks at Miriam and sails off to Mitch's table.

"Is there anything she can't do?" Miriam asks.

"She is a bit much, isn't she?" Lance sighs. "My wife thought she needed a helping hand. Lara ..." His voice breaks. "Lara liked to help people."

"She sounds like a lovely person." Miriam cringes at the patronizing tone of her voice, but hopes it's enough to dissuade Lance from talking about his wife. She's not willing to endure yet another wonderful-woman-lost story.

Their drinks arrive, and Miriam clinks her glass to Lance's. She takes a long slosh of her martini. *Jesus!* It's barely cold and way too heavy on the Vermouth. Still, it's booze. She swigs another gulp. Lance bears the quizzical look of a man wondering if he might share his heartache with her. *Shit!*

"Have you always lived in New York?" Lance asks, seeming to pick up on her discomfort.

"Yeah, sort of. I grew up in New Jersey, just over the George Washington Bridge." Miriam slathers butter on her roll, bites into it, and munches and talks at the same time. "My dad was an accountant. He was dark, squat, and hairy, but oh, god, he was funny." She swallows a mouthful and continues, "Mom was a beauty. She had auburn hair and a Baywatch babe body. She reminded me of a wildflower reaching for the sun. Men adored her, but she loved Dad. He could make her laugh even when she was really pissed at him." Miriam dollops more butter on the roll. "My older sister Beatrix looks like Mom. Me, well, I got my father's looks."

Lance laughs. "You can be very amusing, Miriam, but you're certainly not short, squat, and hairy."

"I was in high school." Miriam gulps the ghastly martini, blotting out the memory of her really fat years.

"Everyone's awkward in high school." Lance beckons for the waiter. "Another martini?"

"I'll just have gin on the rocks, on ice," Miriam emphasizes the word ice.

Lance orders a bottle of wine, a Montrachet, to go with their fish. He probes some more into Miriam's life. Eager to keep clear of his missing wife, Miriam plows through the story of her early marriage. "My husband Mark Lewis could have doubled for Robert Redford when Redford was young. Anyway, I met Mark in college. He was a med student. I was nineteen. By then Mom had waxed away the hairy beast of my adolescence, died my hair hooker red, and convinced me I was knock-dead exotic. Mom was bowled over when she met Mark. Redford was my mother's heartthrob. 'We want him for your husband,' she said. 'Imagine waking up to that every day.'" Miriam laughs. "Be careful of what you wish for, eh?"

Her drink arrives. Miriam sips on it, shaking her head. "Poor Mark."

"Oh, I don't agree with that." Lance smiles, tilting his head in a kindly manner. "It sounds like you were a delightful, spirited young woman."

"Tell me something. Is this polite stuff inbred, or do you

learn it?"

Lance chuckles and his eyes sparkle. Without his hangdog expression, he's quite handsome.

Miriam glances across the room at the walking ladies sitting at a big, round table. She catches a couple of them with their heads bent together, obviously watching her. Smiling into their disapproving looks, she flips her hand through her hair in a flirty gesture and bats her eyes at Lance.

Miriam loses interest in the old biddies as the waiter scoots up to the table, carrying a large, round tray. He sets the tray on a side table, slits the bellies of two golden grilled fish and lifts out their backbones. He serves them each a fillet and adds a bowl of vegetables and a platter of French fries to the table— thin, golden-crisp fries—just the way Miriam likes them. He opens the wine. Miriam locks her hands together in her lap, stopping herself from gorging on the food while Lance tastes the wine. As soon as he nods his approval to the waiter, she helps herself to liberal amounts of everything. The succulent sweet flesh of the fish melts in her mouth, and the fries ooze with the delectable flavors of hot fat and salt. She wolfs it all down between utterances of delight, even forgetting the slight throb of the gash in her arm.

Finishing, she looks up and catches Mitch's glance. Dark circles smudge his eyes. He smiles a pathetic smile. Miriam looks away. The police no longer suspect him of pushing her over the cliffs. Miriam thinks back to that night when she had stood next to Harry. She had been dreaming of a future with him, when someone rammed his fist into her back. Terror seized her and time slowed down. She began falling forward. Fog swirled. She reached for Harry, but he wasn't there. Her body ached from the violent force of her would-be murderer, and she could still feel him nearby. Back then, she didn't think it could be Mitch. Mitch wouldn't kill a spider. He coaxed them into a jar, then took them outside and released them. The man who punched her in the back did it with the kind of resolve she could not associate with Mitch. She'd wondered if it had been Harry. *Or had Gwenellen been right? Had Tamara pushed her over the cliffs?*

She catches sight of Harry and Pammy chatting and canoodling. Pammy's cheeks glow, and her hair is mussed. She snuggles up to Harry, cooing in his ear. Miriam wonders what the hell happened to the young sailor guy Pammy was so madly in love with. From their big, round table, the walking ladies nod and bestow smiles of approval upon Harry and Pammy's reunion.

Miriam empties her wine glass. Gwenellen swishes up to her. "Don't forget what I told you about Tamara."

"What was that?" Lance says, looking at Miriam.

Gwenellen floats off, grinning over her shoulder at Miriam. Miriam huffs with annoyance. "Oh … nothing important, I'm sure."

Lance continues eating, cutting his food, nudging small amounts onto his fork, munching methodically. *Jesus!* Miriam has already gobbled down everything in sight.

Lance eyes her empty plate. "It's so nice to see someone enjoy their food the way you do."

That's a polite way to say pig out, Miriam thinks. "Has Tamara ever harmed anyone?"

"Oh, why do you ask? Yesterday, you were so full of how she saved your life as you fell over the cliffs."

"I'm just curious."

"I don't understand these mystical matters, Miriam, but Lara believed absolutely in Tamara as a guide for those who find her, but then ..." He looks out the window. "Lara always said there are many shades to good and evil, and you cannot have one without a tint of the other."

"So you're saying Tamara is capable of evil?"

"Aren't we all?"

Miriam slides her sleeve up and peeks at her watch. Eight hours to go.

The soufflé arrives—a wonderful puff of chocolate confection rising from a white dish.

"Hot chocolate sauce." The waiter places a small jug in

front of Miriam and another next to Lance.

Lance heaps a generous portion of soufflé onto a plate and hands it to Miriam.

Dear God, please don't let me eat it all.

CHAPTER TWENTY-SIX

Dangerous decisions

Mitch circles the living room of the Tower Suite, taking the same short, measured steps that Jed Flyer takes as he concentrates on a murder suspect. He recounts the facts that led up to Lara's disappearance. His gaze burns bright with excitement as he paces close to the curvature of the walls, trailing his fingers over the surface. A burning sensation shoots through him as he touches the tapestry of the ocean, and his longing for Gwenellen rears up, but it's clouded by suspicion. He pauses near the coat hooks by the door. Had Lara really dropped a note on the night of her disappearance? If so, why did Gwenellen keep it from the police? Did she really have it? Gwenellen works late tonight. They made a plan to meet in her loft above the stables at nine o'clock. Mitch checks his watch: eight-fifteen.

He spins on his heels and descends the ancient stairs, taking them slowly so as not to trip and fall. He steals through the kitchen, mercifully empty of staff, and out the back door. He jogs over the brick pathways through the kitchen gardens and then runs flat out to the stables. He leans against the old building feeling exhilarated. He loved to run as a boy—it was the one sport he did well. He dreamed of scaling hurdles and winning prizes. His father called that sissy stuff. "Football, my boy, that's a man's sport."

Mitch fights off a moment of panic as he remembers the cowering boy of his youth. He proceeds into the stable and eases past Firebrand's stall, resting his hand on his hip near the place where Jed Flyer packs his gun. Firebrand stomps and whinnies. Mitch dashes up the stairs to the loft.

Dark blue velvet curtains cover the entryway to Gwenellen's room. Mitch leans his ear against the thick fabric, listening in case his beloved has returned early from work. He parts the draperies, scans the loft, and tiptoes in.

"Gwenellen, are you here, my darling?"

The aquamarine walls and Prussian blue floors smell of fresh paint, happily applied by his hand. Azure netting floats beneath the wood-beamed ceiling like a summer sky. Pale blue light shines through the waxy shade of a table lamp.

He knocks on the door to the tiny shower stall.

"Gwenellen, are you in there?" No answer. He moves to the kitchen area and grips the sink. The idea of searching Gwenellen's possessions suddenly repels him. He turns to leave, but his fictional detective nags his conscience: *leave no clue unexamined.* Mitch steals back across the room, looking for places where Gwenellen might hide the note. He peers inside a vase on a shelf and under some books and magazines. He searches under the area rugs and beneath the sofa cushions. He approaches a nightstand with two drawers. He kneels and yanks the top one open. He glances over earrings, lip gloss, combs, and hair clips. He opens the bottom drawer and rummages through sweaters. He feels beneath the lining paper. His fingers land on an envelope. He slides it out. The notepaper inside is of cream vellum embossed with *Penrose Hall* in light brown letters. He unfolds the note.

> *Dearest One,*
> *You're so mysterious. I love that about you.*
> *Of course I'll meet you tonight at Devil's Neck.*
> L

Mitch whistles in surprise. That's got to be Lara. Did she have a lover? Mitch returns the envelope to its hiding place and rearranges the sweaters to look as they did before he disrupted them.

He stands and stretches his arms above his head, thinking. Maybe his first suspicion had been right. Maybe Lara's husband Lance found out about Lara's lover and killed her in a jealous rage. But where did he put the body? The Coast Guard and the police scoured the area for weeks searching for Lara.

Mitch scratches his head and reasons the killer may not have been Lance. If Lara had a lover, he could have been the killer, having grown tired of waiting for her to leave her husband. Whoever murdered Lara did not do it on the cliff path. He snatched her there, and as she struggled for her life, she dropped the note and her scarf flew off and caught in the thicket of gorse on the side of the cliffs. Gwenellen said Lara had disappeared in an instant.

Of course, he had completely discounted Gwenellen's story about a mermaid coming up onto the land and kidnapping Lara. Mitch laughs, but she's so adorable when she says things like that—so childlike and innocent. Getting back to Lara, he wonders if the guy who killed her might have hidden her body in a mineshaft beneath the sea. Had anyone thought of looking there?

He picks up a pad and pen from the bedside table and scrawls a message to Gwenellen.

> *My darling,*
> *I can't bear it that some suspect you of*
> *harming Lara Penrose. I'm going to find her*
> *body and her killer. I'll clear your name, my*
> *angel.*
> *All my love,*
> *Mitch*

Mitch leaves the loft, folding the velvet curtains carefully behind him. He descends the stairs two at a time and runs through the stables and outside. The lingering light of the summer day affords him a clear view of Trellan Bay. He sprints all the way down to the cliff path near Devil's Neck. Catching his breath, he crouches down and looks through the arch of craggy rocks. On the other side, a ruin stands on a ledge near the base of the cliffs—a small tower, looking like the bombed remains of a Norman church. From the old photographs of Wheal Penrose that line the hallways of the inn, Mitch recognizes the ruin as what was once the water tower. He also recalls a photo of a ladder inside—the ladder that leads down to mining tunnels beneath the sea.

He walks toward the mine, taking extra care as he crosses the narrow passage over Devil's Neck. Hoping to impress Gwenellen, he dressed Jed Flyer style tonight, donning the tight-fitting jeans he bought eighteen years ago—the day he created the detective. He's gained a few pounds since then and had to suck his gut in to zip them up. He strides to the other side of Devil's Neck and stoops to tie a loose shoelace on his black leather sneakers—Prada, Jed always wears Prada. Jed goes commando too, as does Mitch tonight. He regrets that now as the jeans cut into his butt. He stands and yanks down on the crotch.

The sea rolls calmly to shore, and the wind barely blows. Mitch suspects a stronger wind lurks between the headlands that sprawl into the ocean, waiting to gust up at any moment. He rounds a curve in the path and spots a trail that leads down the cliffs to the ruin. A wire fence and a gate block the entrance. A sign warns:

DANGER! CRUMBLING CLIFFS. DO NOT ENTER.

Mitch whistles a cautious note. In contrast to the sheer drop of the cliffs on the other side of Devil's Neck, the terrain slopes outward, softening in descent. A person could drag a body down to the bottom. He fingers the padlock on the gate. It falls open. Mitch eases through. Gorse and bracken overgrow the path, but someone has cut it back in places. Fresh rock fall has been raked off to the side. He slaps his hand against the flashlight in his pocket. He'll need that once he gets inside the mine.

Mitch steps onto the trail, lodging one foot firmly on the ground before swinging the other forward. He scales back and forth crossing the cliff face. His foot slips, and he scrapes the arm of his jacket against a jutting boulder before regaining his balance. The crashing of waves against the shore thunders in his ears, causing him to feel slightly unstable.

The terrain continues to grow steeper with each step. Water sloshes against the rocks below. Mitch withdraws his flashlight and directs the beam down the cliffs. He stares at a huge rock jutting out from the others, forming a sheer drop to the sea. He inches forward. The grounds beneath his feet shifts, and he fights to gain control. The earth all around him begins to slide. *"Shit!"*

Mitch wobbles but manages to stay on his feet, plummeting downhill like a skier out of control. He reaches out for something—anything—to stop him. He must not fall. He shoots across a curve in the trail and skids onto the huge rock protruding over the sea. He lunges for the stunted trunk of a tree, breaks his speed, and plunks flat on his butt. The jagged surface of the rock rips his jeans, and the seam in the back splits open. He scrapes to a halt on the cold hard granite. His ass burns as if raked over a bed of nails.

Mitch buries his face in his hands and tries to collect his thoughts. He looks up to assess the situation. His right foot dangles over the edge of the cliff. Sea spray soaks his leg. He slides his foot back onto the rock, rolls onto his stomach, and crawls back to the trail. He grips the tattered fabric at the seat of his jeans and pulls the pieces together. Something sticky covers his hand. Blood! He swishes his hands in a pool of seawater, then wipes them dry on his T-shirt. He's tempted to call it quits, but he can't. Jed Flyer would never crawl home defeated with his ass hanging out.

He glances up the cliffs. New formations of rocks and boulders nestle on the path behind him. Goddamned place. He's beginning to feel it's punishing him for setting foot on it. But he must help Gwenellen. He plows on. The trail ends. He's about two feet above sea level. Waves roar in and out of Devil's Neck as if controlled by a different hand than the rest of the ocean. The wind gusts out of hiding. Clouds scurry across the sky, darkening the land. He aims his flashlight on a plaque by the entrance to the ruin.

IN MEMORIAM OF THOSE WHO DIED IN
WHEAL PENROSE

He reads a list of names engraved below, men with romantic sounding names: Trelawny Carew. Breock Penryn. Tristan Delabole. He feels the burn of shame. These guys had put their lives on the line to make a living, when all he does is travel, write, and complain about it. He scrunches his shoulders and passes through the narrow doorway.

Inside, an enormous grate covers the hole of the mineshaft. He kneels, grips the metal bars, and heaves. The iron shield doesn't budge. He gets a firmer grip and tugs again. His arm muscles ache, and blood throbs in the vessels of his neck. The grate moves a little. He kicks his foot under it, holding it in place. He rests for a couple of seconds, then pulls again and again, inching the frame off the huge opening. It clangs onto the stone floor and produces a cacophony of pitch-perfect sounds like notes bouncing off a tuning fork.

Mitch stares into the black hole of the open shaft. The muted roar of the ocean and the acrid smell of damp rock assault his senses. He shakes the ladder clamped to the side of the shaft. Though rusty, it feels solid enough. He swings a foot onto the top rung and lowers himself into the shaft. Step after step, he descends, finding his way into the rhythm of the journey—into the place he likes best in the world—the place between places. He recalls strolling the decks of Queen Mary 2, sipping a Bloody Bull before lunch. Flying over the Pacific, sometimes sleeping in a luxurious recliner seat, and sometimes wedged in the middle seat near the rear of the plane. Sitting in crowded old trains as they rumble across India, the comforting clickety-clack of their wheels telling him he's safe—no one will find him.

CHAPTER TWENTY-SEVEN

Working in the dream world

Gold's whisper-soft voice travels to Tamara through her dedicated ray into the earth's heart.

"If Miriam does not meet her sacred future now, she will never cross your river again, and the gift of being a High Priestess of Sound will desert her. Do everything you can to take her on this journey tonight."

Tamara rises from her river in her light body and skims through the skies to *Penrose Hall*. She finds Miriam asleep in her bed, a velvet mask covering her eyes. A bottle of sleeping pills stands on the night table. By the peaceful expression on her face, Tamara assumes she's taken at least one.

Gold's message adds pressure to an already difficult

situation with Miriam, mostly caused by Kate's interference. Miriam accepted the order of High Priestess of Sound before her birth as Princess Li'ram, and she vowed to treasure that ability above all else. That oath lives in her soul. It's what tells her a cause greater than herself needs her. It's her covenant with the human family. Tamara will do everything in her power not to let it die.

She steps into Miriam's dream world. "Miriam … it's me … Tamara." She extends a hand of light to Miriam. "You have important work to do. Speak my name so that I might guide you on your sacred future and then bring you safely home."

Miriam sees and hears Tamara clearly, but steps away from her. "I'm not going anywhere with you. Gwenellen told me it was you who tried to kill me."

"Gwenellen lied to you." Tamara glances into the pink mists and reviews Miriam's recent meeting with Gwenellen. "She also made up the story about Harry meeting me when he was a boy. I did not predict a future of perfect happiness for him with Pammy. I would not predict that future for anyone. Perfect happiness can only exist with one's awakened awareness. For you, Miriam, that's your jeweled intelligence—more specifically, your gift as a High Priestess of Sound. You—"

"I think you did something to mess Harry up. That's why he's so confused … that's why he left me and returned to Pammy. I lost Harry because of you."

"Let go of wanting love, Miriam. It blocks you from receiving the love that is already yours. Enter your sacred future with me as your guide, and you will know this for yourself. Come." Tamara holds both hands out to Miriam. "I will carry you to the entrance of the Black Heart, and I will—

"Wait!" Kate comes bounding toward Miriam, traveling in her own dream, appearing as Sol'aria, Miriam's younger sister in Ruberah. "Come back to Ruberah with me, and all will be well between us."

"Sol'aria!" Miriam flings her arms around the girl, her love for her swelling in her heart. "I have not known a moment's peace since I last saw you."

Tamara speaks to Kate mentally, scolding her for manipulating Miriam. "You're deceiving her and playing on her emotions by appearing as Sol'aria. That's not right, Kate."

"I don't care."

The wild gaze burning in Kate's eyes reminds Tamara of Sol'aria's eyes on the day of *The Ending,* right after she wrote her sacred future.

I will retrieve the Scrolls of Knowledge from the Black Heart. It shall be my one purpose in my every life until it is done.

Amidst the turmoil of volcanic fire, raging seas, and the screams of the dying, Sol'aria called upon Tamara to guide her on that sacred future. Tamara told her that the River of Life could not accept her promise, but before she could explain why, Dark Master directed that blue-black vapor into Sol'aria's intended vow, which caused its promise to rise up like a jealous god and blind Sol'aria to Tamara's guidance. Sol'aria tossed her sacred future into the River of Life and then drowned, clutching the scrolls to her breast.

Now Dark Master's vapor convinces Kate she can accomplish the sacred future she wrote as Sol'aria. Tamara seeks Gold's advice. The whisper-soft voice of the earth's heart tells her she can do nothing to change Kate. "Let her go, Tamara."

"What about Miriam?" Tamara asks. "Kate has all but persuaded Miriam to travel to Ruberah with her."

"Try to reason otherwise with Miriam, but if you can't, let happen what will."

Gold's advice calms Tamara, and she dips her hand in the golden light from the earth's heart and trails her fingers over Miriam's cheek. "You chose me as your guide when you lived as Princess Li'ram. You knew I would look after you on your sacred future. You trusted me, and that trust forms a field of energy that will protect us. Travelling back to Ruberah with Kate could be dangerous."

"Dangerous? How?" Miriam asks, reverting to her fearful self.

"Kate has some awareness in her jeweled intelligence, but she —"

"We're talking about saving my mother, Miriam." Kate pushes Tamara aside and flings her arms around Miriam. "I'm connected to her like you are to Elaine. I hear her in my heart, and she wants you and me to go back to Ruberah to awaken Rube Force and use that to come and get her. She wants this because it will help us heal the wounds we carry from that time. And who would you trust more than me, your sister from Ruberah?"

CHAPTER TWENTY-EIGHT

Monday night

Kate sits astride Firebrand and backs him up to the stairs leading to the loft in the stables. "Stand on the third step, Miriam, and then climb on."

A gust of wind blows into the stables and swishes the velvet curtains at the top of the stairs. Miriam wonders if Gwenellen is in the loft—and if Mitch is with her.

"Gwenellen's not up there," Kate says, interpreting Miriam's pained expression. "Firebrand doesn't like her. He'd be kicking up a fuss if she were anywhere near him." She reaches her hand out to Miriam. "Don't be afraid. I'll be with you the whole time. We'll go into the Black Heart together."

"You'll come in with me?"

"Yes. Why wouldn't I?"

Miriam frowns as she recalls meeting Tamara in a previous dream. "Tamara said I had to go into the Black Heart alone, because that's what I wrote in my sacred future."

Kate thinks hard and fast. "We're the royal sisters of Ruberah, Miriam. We can always help each other."

The girl's confidence buffers Miriam's doubt, but then the things Gwenellen said make her fearful again. Tamara is very powerful, and she might have forced Mitch to deliver the punch that sent her flying off the cliffs. "Do you think Tamara is dangerous? Gwenellen told me she tried to kill me because my affair with Harry ruined a prediction she made that Harry and Pammy would be together forever. Could that be true?"

Kate casts her glance away from Miriam, wondering how to answer her. She cannot tell a lie about T. Although T promised to be Kate's constant guide until she turns eighteen, there are conditions to that. Kate hears her mother's voice saying, "Tamara's legend helps people find her. It speaks to something they've forgotten about themselves. To cast a shadow on its truth is to cast a shadow on the people of Earth. If anything becomes more important to you than them, you should ask Gold to be released from Tamara's guardianship."

Firebrand snorts and tosses his head, warning Kate to be wise. She feels torn. She must get the Scrolls of Knowledge away from Dark Master, but she knows, deep in her soul, that she must not lose T. She decides to avoid a direct response. "I'm a Sun Master, and you, Miriam Lewis, are a High Priestess of Sound. Together, we can do anything."

Kate holds herself very still, feeling the fright in her breath as she wonders if T heard her. No response from T. Goosebumps crawl over Kate's scalp, her heartbeat quickens, and she can feel the color draining from her cheeks. "I didn't lie," Kate says speaking mentally to T. A long, frightening silence hangs in the place where T's voice ought to be. She sends T a message: "I'll tell Miriam the truth about you before the time runs out for her to complete her sacred future. Okay?" She waits. No response. The girl harrumphs, and then reverts to her purpose of the moment.

She reaches her hand back for Miriam again. "Get on Firebrand. Aren't you tired of being afraid?"

Miriam envisions herself hiding in the corners of her life, afraid of this and that—afraid of every damn little thing. Sickened by the insight, she slaps her hand in Kate's and mounts the horse.

"Ready?" Kate asks.

"Hell, no. This is insane!

Kate laughs and guides Firebrand into the field outside. "Hold onto me and don't let go. Okay?"

Miriam folds her arms around the girl's waist. "Consider me glued to your skin."

Kate digs her heels in the stallion's belly, and they charge forward, galloping into the night wind, heading straight for the cliffs. The ocean glistens, looking dark and threatening under the light of the moon. Kate's hair billows in Miriam's face, tinting the world red. A rush of excitement works its way up from Miriam's gut. Slowly, she releases her body into the rhythm of the horse's stride. The earth speeds by. The dauntless girl of Miriam's early childhood rushes to meet her—daddy's little darling—a fearless, dazzling girl, laughing out loud: fab, utterly fab!

The brink of the perilous cliffs stretches before Miriam. If Kate doesn't change directions or stop Firebrand in the next few seconds, they'll ride over the edge. But the child in Miriam doesn't care. Her laughter peals over land and sea. If they sail off the cliffs, they'll plunge headlong into the Black Heart, duel with the magicians of the underworld, and drag Lara Penrose out by her long, willowy arms. Or the stallion will spread his wings and fly through the heavens like a black satin Pegasus, calling all gods to their aid.

"Go, Firebrand!" Miriam hollers.

Firebrand thunders up to the cliff's edge, draws to a halt and rears onto his hind legs. The fearless child of Miriam's youth slinks back into hiding. "Kate! Get this damn horse under control. He's scaring the shit out of me!"

Kate pays Miriam no heed. The fiery girl yells into the night like a chief leading a tribe into battle. Miriam stares down at the stallion's hooves just inches from delivering them both to certain death. *Dear God, whatever you want. I'll join a nunnery. Just knock some sense into Kate.*

Kate pats the stallion's neck, and he swings his great body sideways, landing his front hooves safely on the ground. "To Wheal Penrose!"

CHAPTER TWENTY-NINE

Into the mine

With Kate in charge of Miriam, and Mitch wandering into the mine by himself, Gold asked Tamara to follow and observe them all for the duration of Miriam's sacred future. Gold avoided any direct reference to the do-not-interfere rule, but the word "observe" brings it front and forward in Tamara's mind.

Tamara speeds over the cliffs in her light body, heading for Wheal Penrose, passing Firebrand as he gallops toward Devil's Neck carrying Kate and Miriam. Tamara dives down the mineshaft and finds Mitch about two hundred feet below sea level, near the bottom of the ladder.

His nostrils burn from the bitter smell of ore, and the damp cold eats into his bones. He finds it hard to distract himself with dreams of Gwenellen as the churn and drum of the sea pound against the shaft. One of the books Mitch read on Wheal Penrose told of ghosts and strange lights that haunt the mine. Several miners claimed to have seen a ball of crystal, bright-red light floating through the tunnels. They had nicknamed it "The Head," as it sometimes spoke and warned of disasters about to happen. According to local lore, The Head comes from the lost Kingdom of Ruberah and carries the consciousness of the wise ones who once lived there.

Mitch pauses and wipes sweat from his brow. "Facts, Mitch, facts. Jed always sticks to the facts." He recites a few that he's learned about mining.

"There's more tin left in the Cornish ground than has ever been excavated. Tin and copper have been mined here from as far back as 2000 BC. The deep lodes beneath the sea lay dormant until the development of the steam engine in the eighteenth century."

Red light edges into the tunnel below as if coming in from the sea—a strange, neon-bright light. Mitch closes his eyes, and his heart hammers somewhere up by his throat. Even with his lids firmly closed, he can see the brilliant glow. Perhaps it's one of the mystery lights common to the area. His teeth chatter. He knows the tectonic flexing of the earth's crust sometimes causes electrical and geomagnetic changes. He's been in places where this happens and produces light phenomena. It's usually around megalithic sites. *Yeah, that's got to be the explanation. Cornwall is one big megalithic site!* He rests his forehead against a rung of the ladder, still shivering with fright.

The red light recedes, and Mitch whistles with relief. He drops his foot to the last rung on the ladder, lowering his weight slowly to test it for safety. He glances up the shaft. The pale disk of the moon hangs directly over the pump station, appearing like a blank face from another galaxy. He looks back down. Sea water sloshes over a rocky passage. Lara Penrose's murderer could have thrown her body down the shaft, then left—he'd have had no reason to risk his life by dragging it further into the mine. Her body must be right there beneath that water. He eggs himself on, thinking this time next week he could be honeymooning with Gwenellen, perhaps in Tahiti.

He digs in his pocket for his flashlight and swivels the beam around, searching the water. It appears murky and shallow, but he can see the rail tracks once used by a pulley-system to haul the ore from the mine. He scours the water for Lara's remains, reminding himself that she's been dead for almost a month. Her body would be badly decomposed—and probably eaten by fish and other scavengers of the sea. Still, there should be a skeleton.

He aims the light down the tunnel, and his gut curdles at the thought of entering the long, narrow space. He'll have to duck to avoid huge overhangs of rock. The rough walls of the mine look like the result of gunpowder explosions of long ago. The stench of stale seawater permeates the atmosphere, but every now and then a vein of quartz crystal sparkles in the beam of his flashlight. He cranes his neck, noting that a few feet away the passage curves to the right. The red glow wavers in the distance.

He clicks off his flashlight and swallows the fear lumping up in his throat. The sea drums in his ears. Maybe he could tell Gwenellen he tried to find Lara but couldn't. No, he can't lie to her. Their happiness depends on his clearing her name.

He thinks of Miriam and misses the predictability of her—the way she's always a little mad at him, and not without reason. He misses her daughter too. Moody and troubled, Elaine feels lost, much like him. Somehow, they have an unspoken understanding about this, so he doesn't react to her antics. He just lets her remarks bounce off him. She usually smiles in response. Then he knows she will be all right. Then he knows his life is worthwhile. *Strange.*

Gwenellen's smile floats before him, and thoughts of Miriam and Elaine disappear. Gwenellen wipes away his loneliness. He'll trudge through the mine until he finds Lara's body. He'll face the strange, red light if he has to, but he's not dragging his best Prada shoes through that mess.

He eases them off and wedges them behind a rung in the ladder.

CHAPTER THIRTY

Journey to Ruberah

On the other side of Devil's Neck, Kate and Miriam ride beneath a cluster of palm trees. Kate dismounts and helps Miriam off the horse. "We'll walk from here," she says.

Glad to have her feet on the ground, Miriam looks out to sea. Her mind drifts back to her life in New York. *Would she have stayed home if she'd had any clue as to what was going to happen in Cornwall? She'd like to have missed the pain of losing Mitch to Gwenellen, but would she forego meeting Kate?* No. The irascible girl has wormed her way into her heart. She pats the outsides of her pockets, hoping to feel the bulge of a protein bar. Nothing. Why is she always famished?

Kate presses her nose against Firebrand's nostrils, sharing breath—passing secrets and promises in the pink mist.

"Stay right here." She strokes the stallion between his ears. "I'll call if I need you."

She walks over to Miriam and taps her on the shoulder. "Time to go."

They clip along the cliff path in the light of the moon. Kate chats about the boarding school she attends and her various girlfriends—even sharing the comical horrors of her first kiss. They laugh and entertain one another like an aunt with a favorite niece.

Miriam tells Kate she was a shrinking violet at Kate's age, but her mother had convinced her a little fat around the middle was sexy. "She told me to walk tall and shake my tummy like a belly dancer."

"Your mother sounds really nice."

Miriam swings her good arm around the girl, "So does yours, and we'll get her back home safe and sound."

"You're pretty super, too. I bet your daughter thinks that, you know, deep down where you can't see it."

"I hope."

They arrive at the wire fence, and Miriam reads the sign:

DANGER! CRUMBLING CLIFFS. DO NOT ENTER.

Miriam looks askance at Kate. "Looks like we can't go—
"

"Oh, pay no attention to that sign. It's just to keep the tourists out. I come down here all the time. It's safe. Honestly."

"Jesus Christ, Kate!"

"What? Is he down here walking on the water again?" Kate giggles and fingers the padlock. *Unlocked?* She scratches her head. This morning she had brought supplies for their journey. Had she forgotten to snap the lock after she left? She swings the gate open.

Miriam dithers, looking back through the night in the direction of the inn.

"Don't freak out now, Miriam."

"I'm really out of my element here," Miriam says passing through the gate. "Give me a break. Okay?"

"Okay." Kate leads her onto the trail. "We're lucky, we'll have a full moon tonight. Stay close to me."

The wind howls. Miriam stops. "This seems pretty darn dangerous ... I don't know."

"Shake your fat roll, Miriam."

"I knew I'd be sorry I told you about that."

"Shut *up!*" Kate giggles. "I love the way Americans say shut up to one another. It's considered rude over here. Daddy has a fit when I say it. I tell him I mean it like an exclamation … you know, instead of … 'you don't say' … but he's so old school, he doesn't get it."

"Yeah, and I bet he'd be more than upset if he knew what you're doing out here."

Kate shrugs, and then talks about the miners who walked this path every day for years. "Their wives cooked them pasties for lunch, and the men would always leave some small pieces for the Piskies before they descended into the mineshaft. You know about our Piskies, don't you? They're our faerie folk, mischievous little sprites who delight in playing tricks on the unwary. So by leaving them some food, the miners kept the little imps from playing pranks on them while they worked." Kate pats her pocket. "I brought Mars Bars. We'll leave one for them, so we'll be safe."

"Great, I feel so much better." Miriam wonders if she might convince Kate to feed her a candy bar for the same reason.

"I hope you don't see one," Kate says. "They're ugly little brats. They have broad faces with round, owl-like eyes shaded by shaggy eyebrows and wide mouths that reach from one horrid-looking pointed ear to the other. They like to charge at you and—"

"Enough already. I'm plenty scared as it is."

Kate tosses her hair and laughs. "You worry too much. Go with the flow. Isn't that the American way?"

"Yeah, but being with you feels like wading against a riptide."

"Come on, Miriam. We're the powerful sisters from Ruberah. Think about that."

"Uh-hum."

They pick their way down the same path that Mitch traveled a short while ago. At the sharp bend in the trail, Kate notices a fresh fall of rocks and boulders. She's been on the cliffs during several landslides and hopes she doesn't have to deal with one now. Miriam would have a conniption. She glances at a ledge overhanging the cliff and narrows her eyes. A piece of fabric flutters on a sharp rise in the rock. Someone's been down here since she came this morning. Her mind skips to Gwenellen, her mother's betrayer—of that she's certain. She trembles. Her resolve to kill Gwenellen knots in her stomach.

Miriam stays close behind Kate, treading warily over clusters of rock, bracken, and the thin roots crawling beneath them. She stops when Kate veers off the track and climbs onto a giant rock that protrudes over the ocean. "What's out there?" Miriam shouts. The wind howls and blows her hair across her eyes. She brushes it back and holds her breath as the girl bends to examine something on the surface. "What is it?"

"Nothing." Kate tosses the shred of blue denim into the sea—best to keep her suspicions to herself. She steps back onto the path and points to the ruin below. "That's the old water tower. It's the entrance to the mine. Come on."

The moon sheds light on the broken tower, and the angry waters beneath Devil's Neck thrash against the land. Old Dracula movies reel through Miriam's mind. She imagines monsters lurking in the caves. A cold breeze whips off the ocean. Miriam hugs her arms about herself. Under the glow of the moon, she studies a memorial plaque by the entrance to the ruin. "All these men died here?"

"Yes."

The girl's head-on acceptance of a painful truth reminds her that Kate is brave, just like she was as Sol'aria. Brave like their mother, Queen of the Ruby Kingdom. An awful memory from *The Ending* rises in Miriam's thoughts, clear as if it happened a few moments ago. She, Li'ram, was supposed to go with Sol'aria to save Mt. Rube, but her mother, old and fragile, went in her place. Still a powerful High Priestess of Sound, her mother insisted, giving Li'ram time to stand in the ruby circles with Da'krah and be mated for life.

"What's the matter?" Kate asks. "You look weird."

"Nothing." Miriam shoves regret aside and follows Kate

through the entrance of the ruin.

Moonlight floods the interior of the old water tower. Kate stops short at the sight of the open shaft and the iron grate resting off to the side. Thinking Gwenellen must be down in the mine, she kneels and peers into the darkness, searching for signs of the demon woman.

The hole in the ground terrifies Miriam. She glances through the arched doorway. *Could she make a run for it?* But run where and to whom?

"I brought some warm things to wear." Kate says, walking to a dugout in the wall. She pulls out a duffle bag. "Put these on." She hands Miriam a fleece jacket, a pair of knee-high rubber boots, and a headband with a flashlight on the front. "I've got extra batteries." She slaps the pocket of her jacket.

"I'm scared, Kate."

"Scared is good. It'll pass as soon as we get started. Just put on the clothes and follow me." She fishes a Mars Bar from the bag. "Here, unwrap it and place it by the shaft for the Piskies."

For once, Miriam's desire to eat fades beneath anxiety. "Nah, I don't believe in ugly fairies." She kicks off her shoes and hauls on the jacket and rubber boots.

Kate lays a Mars Bar at the top of the shaft and sets a

foot on the ladder. Miriam thinks of the men who died in the mine. The terrible fear of being trapped beneath the sea crawls over her skin. She snatches the candy, rips off the paper, and gobbles it down, swooning over the sumptuous blend of chocolate and caramel.

"Honestly, Miriam." Kate dumps another Mars bar on the rim of the mineshaft. "It's important to leave that one there. We've got enough to occupy us without—"

"Okay." Miriam takes a couple of steps away from the shaft, half hoping the damned Piskies will jump out of the walls. Then she would have an excuse to run away—anything rather than follow Kate into that awful dark hole.

Propping an arm on the edge of the mineshaft, Kate notices Miriam darting anxious glances at the doorway. "Many more people died in *The Ending*," she says, "many more than all who ever died in all the accidents in the whole county of Cornwall in all its long history of mining."

Guilt hits Miriam full throttle. "What exactly did we do with Rube Force to cause such a disaster? I don't seem to have any recall of that."

"Doesn't matter. We can't undo it, but we can free my mother from the Black Heart. Come on."

Remorse cuts into Miriam's soul, and she kneels on the hard stone floor and lowers a leg onto the ladder. Already a few feet down, Kate guides Miriam's foot onto a rung. "Hold on tightly. The ladder is still strong."

Miriam grips the iron railing. "This is crazy. I can't—"

"When Rube comes for you, and it will as soon as we enter the tunnel, you'll feel invincible. You can do this, Miriam."

Miriam stares down into the darkness. The lunar glow catches Kate's face and slows the hammering in Miriam's heart. "Remind me of what we did wrong with Rube. I need to know."

Kate descends at a slow pace, tilting her head back so her voice carries up to Miriam.

"There was to be an Age of Jeweled Intelligence on Earth. It began with rubies because they carry a great force for nurturing life and creating things. We used Rube like we use electricity and oil today. There are seven jewel kingdoms, and each one brings different abilities to the human family. Each kingdom has a jeweled mountain, but they remain submerged beneath the sea until we've progressed enough to use their intelligence. The Ruby Mountain surfaced at the beginning of the Time of Ruberah, and halfway through that era, the Emerald Mountain began to rise up from the sea. A large peninsula of land developed beside it, and people started to be born in the Emerald Kingdom. We Ruberians had fully developed our ruby intelligence, and many thought it was time to help bring the Emerald Force to life. Our father, King of Ruberah—a terrible sweetie who adored us, especially me 'cause ... well, never mind. Anyway, he said the human race was not yet ready to harmonize its consciousness with the elements of emeralds. He said the Goddess of the Emerald Sphere would tell us when the time was right. But, Da'krah, Prince of the Emerald Kingdom, disagreed with him. He wanted Daddy to use Rube to help him ... well ... force the mountain to surface completely and jump-start the power of emeralds."

A thunderous sound drowns out Kate's voice. Miriam freezes mid-stride on the ladder. "Oh, my God! What's that noise? Is the mine caving in?"

"No, it's just rocks bouncing on the tide. Did you hear what I said about Da'krah?"

Calmed by the girl's casual attitude, Miriam says, "Do you remember Da'krah? What was he like?"

"Interesting, in a dark, brooding way. Sort of like Heathcliff." Kate giggles. "He was also very ambitious. Our father absolutely refused to help him start the Emerald Force. He said it would be too strong for us to handle. Emeralds bear the life force of the earth—their consciousness flows in from all the stars and planets in our universe. Man did not understand enough about their cosmic energies to use them wisely. Unfortunately, our father died just as Da'krah set his sights on marrying you."

Miriam's heart gongs in her chest. The long echo of her love as Li'ram reverberates through the tunnels of time, telling her that she gave in to Da'krah and helped him. Worse, she talked Sol'aria into helping her. Miriam bows her head. "So, we ... I ... helped Da'krah and we developed a force beyond our control that destroyed everything?"

"Yes, but remember, a lot of people thought it was the right thing to do." Kate holds onto Miriam's ankle and yanks her foot down to the next rung. "Just because you were older than me back then doesn't make it more your fault. I was loads smarter than you. You knew that. I could have talked you out of it."

"Nice try, kiddo, but I was obviously bent on pleasing Da'krah. Seems like nothing would have stopped me." Miriam moves more easily down the shaft. "What else can you tell me about him?"

"Da'krah sent you two love birds in an emerald cage— exquisite white birds with pale blue bills. They rocked on their little perches, chirping the sweetest song. You fell in love with them upon first sight, as you did with Da'krah."

"A couple of birds and he won me over?"

"Um ... well ... you said he was fantastic in bed."

"I wouldn't have told my kid sister that."

"I wasn't a kid. Sol'aria was sixteen and in love with a boy called E'am."

"How do you remember all this?"

"You never forget someone you loved."

"Okay. If you say so."

Kate laughs, and then falls silent as they approach the bottom of the ladder. She notices a pair of shoes wedged between the wall and the railing. She jerks them out and traces her finger over the red strip of leather running down the back of a shoe.

"What is it?" Miriam asks.

"Men's shoes." Kate peers inside and reads the label. "Prada."

"Prada! Give me one."

Miriam reaches her hand down to Kate. "Oh, my God! This belongs to Mitch. What the hell is he doing down here?"

The shoes evoke a familiar feeling of dislike in Kate, the same feeling she got when she first met Mitch. She's wondered off and on if Mitch might have been Da'krah in the Time of Ruberah, but always dismissed the thought. Surely, the once powerful prince of the Emerald Kingdom could not become such a wimp as Mitch. But Miriam loves Mitch in the same insane way that Li'ram loved Da'krah, and Mitch is here with Miriam. Old lovers often come to Cornwall together.

She glances at Miriam a few rungs above her on the ladder, clutching Mitch's shoes to her heart. Kate doubts Miriam has ever questioned whether Mitch had been Da'krah, but that's not unusual. T says people learn facts about their sacred futures when the time is right. "I'm going to have a look around the mine, Miriam. You wait here. I'll be back in a couple minutes."

Miriam barely hears Kate. A whiff of the fragrance Mitch wears drifts up from his shoes and sinks into her olfactory nerve. Memories unfold. Weekends spent in her apartment. Waking up late on Sunday mornings, making love, reading *The Times*. Eating brunch in a neighborhood bistro. *How great was that?* She strokes the leather of the shoes. Mitch wouldn't wear his Pradas down here, unless ... unless he had dressed to impress Gwenellen. What idiotic thing was he up to now?

"Kate." Miriam peers down the dim passage. "What's going on? Where are you? Can you see Mitch?"

"Not yet. Be quiet. I have to concentrate."

Kate steals down to the bend in the tunnel and leans her back against the rocky wall. The base of her spine burns, and her temples throb. She can feel the faint vibration of the Ruby Kingdom pulsing in the ocean. Her whole life flashes before her. She looks into the blaze of pink light that illuminated the delivery room at the moment of her birth—the light that colored her sight and her longing to return to Ruberah. She sees herself as Sol'aria, waving her arm above a stormy sea—her fist filled with scrolls tied with ruby ribbons.

I will retrieve the Scrolls of Knowledge from the Black Heart. It shall be my one purpose in my every life until it is done.

"Yes!" Kate waves her freedom fist high above her shoulder, the thrill of her promise shivering over her skin. Right after they rescue her mother, she'll search the Black Heart and find the scrolls. She closes her eyes and chants a mantra from ages past.

"Beloved jewel of my soul, crown of my being, I give you my life."

She repeats the chant, looking through her jeweled vision. Her words stream through the ocean and into the pink seas of Ruberah. Ruby light shoots out from the base of Mt. Rube, answering her call. The rays skim across the ocean bed and flood into the mine. Multicolored lights sparkle and bounce off the minerals in the walls. Ghosts of long-dead miners drift into the tunnel and reach for them like children chasing balloons.

Kate mingles with the ghosts, asking if they would like to move on. Some nod in agreement, and she tosses ruby light at their foreheads and watches as they vanish. Others choose to stay, saying they are not ready to leave the memory of those they worked and died with.

Unaware of all this, Miriam steps down to the last rung of the ladder. Pale blue eyes shine back at her from the stream of shallow waters.

CHAPTER THIRTY-ONE

Globes from Ruberah

Lara's eyes make a flash appearance to Miriam, just as they once did to Mitch, but they remain clear and constant in Tamara's view. Lara's concern for Kate surges through the barriers of the Black Heart and into the light of Ruberah. She hears her daughter chanting to her jeweled consciousness, and asks Tamara how she knows to do this.

Tamara unfolds scenes in the ruby light, showing parts of Kate's life since her mother's disappearance. Lara blinks with fright as she watches her daughter using her spirit power, using it to rebel against Tamara. She also glimpses scenes from Miriam's visit to Cornwall. "I recognize Miriam," she says. "She was Li'ram, my daughter in Ruberah."

"Yes," Tamara says. "As Ruberah sank, Li'ram wrote a

sacred future. To redeem herself for having chosen Da'krah over her duties as High Priestess, she insisted she one day rescue someone from the Black Heart."

"And her sacred future is happening now," Lara says. "And that person is me?"

"Yes."

"I am heartsick, Tamara, to see that Miriam bears guilt from her actions in Ruberah. I did what any mother would do when I took Li'ram's place and went with Sol'aria to save Mt. Rube on the day of *The Ending*. My life neared its end, and I had already lost my beloved husband. Li'ram stood at the beginning of her journey in love." Lara sighs but wastes no time on regret. "Please don't let Kate use Rube Force without your guidance. Please, Tamara. Please."

"Now that Kate has use of her spirit light, I cannot stop her from using it as she chooses … lest I break my vow to Gold … lest I die to my life as a guide for the human family."

"Forgive me." Lara's eyes fade from the ruby light.

"Beloved jewel of my soul, crown of my being, I give you my life."

Kate resumes her chant, remembering the many times her mother told her that it's the intent behind a song that carries

266

its message to the desired source. Kate sings, all the while envisioning herself rescuing her mother from the Black Heart. Once again, her song wends through the Atlantic and touches Mt. Rube. Two globes of crystal-bright, red light—slightly bigger than a human head—emerge from the mountain and zip back to Wheal Penrose, travelling on a thin line of ruby light.

The globes sail into the mine, filling the tunnels with the celestial sounds and the brilliance of Rube. Kate dashes to the ladder where Miriam stands on the bottom rung. "Our globes are coming. They'll be here in a jiffy. Get down here beside me."

"I saw blue eyes in the water down there." Miriam points to the shallow water. "What's that about?"

"Maybe you imagined them. Forget about that. You're about to meet your globe from Ruberah."

"My what?" Miriam tucks Mitch's shoes behind the ladder and steps down beside Kate.

"Your globe. You'll wear it on your head, and it will help you stay connected to your ruby intelligence."

"Did you see Mitch in the mine?"

Kate shakes her head and tugs on Miriam's arm. "Look!" She points down the tunnel.

Ruby light swerves around the bend in the passage, piercing the darkness like a probe from another planet. Two brilliant spheres emitting a fiery red radiance float into view. Miriam hears music flowing from one of them—a sublime sequence of notes rising and falling—sounding at once familiar and yet brand new. That sense of being needed returns, but this time it's accompanied by a feeling that she has a unique talent, a way to serve the need. She feels secure—even joyful. Then she glimpses Mitch standing near the bend.

"Mitch!"

Her longing for a loving relationship with him overtakes her, and she wades into the tunnel, straining her eyes past the globes for a clearer image of Mitch. Her foot slips. She stumbles and sinks into deeper water. It trickles in over the tops of her boots. "Help!"

A slippery form slithers around her ankles, and she screams, knowing it's the mermaid who attacked her in the ocean. She hops from one foot to the other, yelling to Kate for help. If the mermaid cuts Miriam with her sharp fin here in the mine, she'll probably bleed to death.

She glances over her shoulder at Kate, but the girl looks straight past her, her eyes locked as if she's in a trance. Miriam dodges the swish and swirl of the slippery woman as best she can, shouting for Mitch. "Mitch … wait … it's me!" Her voice falls mute beneath the music emanating from the ruby globe. She dares not step backward, for fear of losing her balance and being gobbled alive by the mermaid. Then the brilliance of the globes shines on the mermaid, and she paddles her tail and scoots off like a torpedo out of a cannon.

Shivering with relief, Miriam leans a hand against the wall for balance and sloshes back to Kate. She shakes the girl by the shoulders. "You little shit, why didn't you help me?"

Kate looks wide-eyed and innocent. "Help you with what?"

"That mermaid was here. She swam around my ankles. She could have killed me."

It suddenly occurs to Kate that if Miriam got hurt down here, they wouldn't be able to travel back to Ruberah and she'd lose her chance to retrieve the scrolls from the Black Heart. "Gosh, Miriam, I didn't hear you. I'm sorry you were so frightened. Are you all right?"

Miriam detects the false note in Kate's voice and brings her to task. "Look, kid, my daughter has pulled every trick in the book on me, so cut the act. Why didn't you answer my call for help?

"I'm sorry. I didn't purposely ignore you. I had to concentrate on my chant to our jeweled minds. I have to bring the globes right to us, and look, they're almost here.

"So you did see me?"

"Well … yes and no. You see—"

"Okay, never mind. Now you listen to me. You're young and you probably can't understand this, but I want Mitch back. I saw him in the tunnel, and I ... I need him."

"We're on our way back to Ruberah, Miriam. Our jeweled minds are getting closer to us by the second. How can you think about stuff like that?"

"You'll understand when you're older, but—"

"Look! They're here!" Kate removes the elastic band and flashlight from her head and opens her arms wide. The ruby globes stop in front of her, and she taps one with her forefinger and eases it a little to her left until it rests in front of Miriam. "That one's yours. Hold it, Miriam. Tell it how much you love it. Welcome it back to you."

"I don't think so." Miriam stares at the thing, cowering away.

"Go on, Miriam," Kate insists. "Your ruby mind will respond to being loved. Put it on. Just pull it down over your head. It looks like crystal, but it's not. It's made of a substance from the Ruby Sphere—a material that can collapse and fold around your neck in ruby rings. Totally fab."

"I'm not putting it on until you tell me what I can expect."

"I can't tell you much, because yours is the globe of a

High Priestess of Sound. Mine is that of a Sun Master. See, mine is a bit brighter than yours, but yours vibrates more than mine because it's full of sound. As a High Priestess, you filter that sound into Mt. Rube. I expect you'll hear the Music of the Spheres, because those notes emit a very fine and very high vibration. My globe will transmit the brilliance of our sun, and if necessary, the light of a sun beyond our sun, from a galaxy on the edge of another universe. Mummy says that sun is billions of times more powerful than ours, and those who live in that galaxy have attained diamond awareness. They were once people like us, and they lived on a planet similar to Earth. Of course, that was ages ago in a round of time long before Earth was born." She laughs. "That's why they say there's nothing new under the sun. Get it?"

"Yeah. That really clarifies things."

"Good," Kate says, apparently missing Miriam's sarcastic tone. "I think I know how to get to that galaxy at the edge of our universe. We could go there after we get back from the Black Heart. Maybe even have a peek into the next universe."

"No, that's okay. I'm good with this one."

The girl shrugs and turns her attention to her globe. She runs her hands over its curves, caressing it like a connoisseur examining a rare treasure. Her mirrored image smiles back at her from inside the ruby radiance. The girl and her reflection gaze at one another like old friends filling in the years of their long separation.

It suddenly dawns on Miriam that nothing could stop Kate from going back to the lost kingdom. If her mother appeared in this moment—unharmed and ready to resume their lives together—Kate would still return to Ruberah. A palpable intensity vibrates off the girl, telling Miriam all else is secondary.

Miriam feels a bit duped, until her ancient memory reminds her that she once loved Da'krah with the same ferocious determination. That dynamic flares up again, only this time over Mitch. He must return to her. They belong together. She'll do whatever it takes to get him back.

She watches Kate lift her globe high above her and then lower it back down over her head. The girl smiles at Miriam from inside the rosy radiance. In her knee-high boots, jeans, and oversized jacket, she looks like a model posing for a line of clothing from outer space.

"Put yours on, Miriam. It's weightless. You won't know it's there except for the way you see things, which is super cool."

Miriam grips Kate's shoulder for balance, yanks off her boots and empties them of water. "About Mitch ... I meant what I said, so let's make a deal. I'll help you get your mother out of the Black Heart if you'll help me get Mitch back."

"That's daft. Mitch has got nothing to do with your sacred future."

"Take it or leave it, Kate."

Kate briefly considers telling Miriam that Mitch had been Da'krah, but decides against it. Miriam might be impossible to manage if she knew that. "Um ... well ... I have to get the Scrolls of Knowledge out of the Black Heart too. So if you agree to that, then okay, deal." She holds out her hand, ready to shake on the arrangement.

"Deal." Miriam shakes her hand, and sneaks a last glance up the mineshaft. Clouds float across the moon. *Dear God, please allow Mitch and me to return to our lives in New York.*

"Come on, Miriam." Kate rips off Miriam's headband and light and plunks her ruby globe onto her head. The girl and the woman look at each other, their faces awash with the rosy glow of Ruberah. Their hearts swell with the remembrance of sisterhood.

As Tamara waits by the curve in the tunnel, she receives a message from Tavy and Tawridge. "We need to be with you. We're on our way." Within moments, they gush into the mine, flooding the narrow passages with the light of their astral bodies.

Tamara warns them that they can only observe. "We must not jump in and help or advise Kate as we have done in the past. If you don't think you can—"

"We can do anything for Kate," the giants say in unison. "And for Miriam too," Tawridge adds. "She was such a lovely princess."

CHAPTER THIRTY-TWO

Encounters in the mine

Miriam grows comfortable inside her globe, fascinated by rings of light unfolding in all the colors of the Jewel Kingdom. She hears the Deva Chorus of Mt. Rube. Ten thousand voices chant a love incantation to the Ruby Goddess. Miriam chants with them, just as she did when she lived as Li'ram. A plane of silver-blue light appears. Patterns, sounds, and symbols run across it like electronic equations. She has only to decide to assemble them into something for use in the world, something for the well-being of all, and Rube will show her how to manifest it in the physical world.

Her old fear of being essential to the lives of others creeps in, and her heart falls heavy. Her ruby globe begins to grow dim.

"Stay positive, Miriam." Kate leans her face next to Miriam's, pressing her globe against her cheek until Miriam's globe blazes back to full brilliance. "No matter what you see, don't panic. Trust your jeweled mind. It will bring you everything you need to return to Ruberah."

"Yes, but will that be the best for all people?"

"The world needs my mother, Miriam. She's kind to everyone. She's an angel helper for mankind."

Miriam nods. "All right. I'll try to think about that."

Kate trudges into the tunnel, wading through the murky waters. She weaves to the right to avoid the dip in the ground that Miriam fell into earlier. Miriam measures her steps to match Kate's and once again begins to enjoy looking through the pink skin of her globe. Music plays softly in the background of her mind—beautiful as if plucked on a harp. Long pauses rest between the notes, and other more distant sounds play in the pauses. Or perhaps the sounds are very close, so close that they come from her heart. Or perhaps they're a collision of both something out there and something inside her. Whatever, she feels wonderful—complete—connected to all things.

A ghostly figure of a man looms up from nowhere, and the feeling of happiness dies. He towers between Miriam and Kate, but he's little more than a skeleton with a miner's lamp clamped to his skull. He gives the impression of being able to see from the black hollows where his eyes had once been.

"Kate!" Miriam yells. "Look behind you!"

Kate glances over her shoulder. "Oh, hi, Timmy. How be 'e?" She speaks in a thick Cornish accent and listens attentively to the ghost as he describes the condition of the mine—of repairs that need to be done.

"I'll see to it, Timmy. Don't 'e be worrying about things."

The ghost points a bony finger at Miriam. Miriam's insides cramp up. The glow fades from her globe and it falls down to her neck, leaving her face to face with the ghoulish being.

Kate bends her ear to the ghost and giggles. "Timmy fancies you, Miriam."

"Tell him to go away, *please*."

"He can't hurt you. He's dead."

Great, she's finally hit the jackpot—a dead guy digs her! The ghost traces his finger across Miriam's cheek. She muffles a scream.

"Oh, go on." Kate nudges her. "Give Timmy a smile—make his day, as you Yanks say."

"You're such a little bitch! Help me get my ruby mind

back."

"Not until you're nice to Timmy."

Kate strides off, and Miriam rushes after her but catches her foot on a rock. She stumbles. Her world spins. She pictures herself splashing into the filthy waters, open prey for that deadly mermaid.

Cold hands grip her arm. Miriam regains her balance. The ghostly presence lingers beside her.

"You take care, my 'ansome."

His voice is smoky and low—almost not there at all, but somehow more there than any voice she's ever heard. He turns and starts walking away.

"Timmy."

He stops. Miriam looks directly into the hollows of his eyes and smiles. The features of his face fill in. Dust smuts his forehead. Dark stubble covers his cheeks. His nose is big and humped. His hair is black, without a trace of gray. He died young. He smiles a generous smile and walks on.

Miriam's globe surrounds her head again, and her jeweled consciousness floods back. She treks after Kate, wondering if Timmy left a wife and children behind, and if his name is on the plaque outside the mine.

Kate waits for her at the bend in the tunnel. "Timmy's sweet, isn't he?"

"Why is he still here?"

"He loves the mine. Many of the miners did, you know. In my family, we bear a great sorrow for those who died in Wheal Penrose. It passes from one generation to the next. We'll never forget them. We love them, but that's not necessarily the best thing for them. It's partly what keeps them around. "

"So, stop loving them." The words no sooner pass Miriam's lips than her affection for Timmy overtakes her. How could she feel so strongly about someone from such a brief encounter? "I'm sorry, Kate. That was insensitive."

The burdened look of a much older person settles in Kate's eyes—an expression Miriam has often detected in her own daughter's eyes. Miriam wonders if she herself suffered such untenable emotions as a teenager. Not really. She had been preoccupied with being fat, a painful condition alien to both Kate and Elaine.

They round the corner, and another dark passage stretches before them. Miriam searches the darkness for Mitch. No sign of him. Rock presses in from all sides. The thrashing of the sea grows louder. Miriam detects the same clomping sound she once heard in the corridor outside her room—a sound like someone staggering along on wooden stilts. Miriam asks her ruby mind to show her where Mitch is, and her vision soars down the tunnel on a ray of pink light. She glimpses Mitch, his jeans shredded in the rear, his butt exposed and bloodied.

Idiot! Why isn't he wearing undershorts?

"Kate." She taps the girl's shoulder. "I saw Mitch. He's hurt. We've got to help him."

The clomping sound starts again. They both stare down the tunnel. The wooden footfalls get closer and closer. "Stand back." Kate swings her arm in front of Miriam.

"Why? What is it? Tell me!" Miriam's globe flickers as she fights to stay calm.

"You stay here and stay calm. We're a team. Listen to the Devas and think of me. That's very important, as it will help me stay connected to my ruby mind. Okay?"

Miriam nods. "Just bring Mitch back to me."

Kate strides down the tunnel, her aura spiraling around her in shades of flame. The clomping ceases, and the outline of a woman emerges in the shadows of the passage. Close-fitting, shiny black fabric covers her body from head to toe. A black heart shimmers on her chest like a breastplate. Dark waves whirl around her. Her rigid stance gives the appearance of a cardboard cutout of a movie superwoman. Kate recognizes her as the Mermaid of Zennor in her demon body, courtesy of Dark

Master.

Kate's globe swirls around her, sifting through her ancient knowledge. She asks for permission to attack the woman in return for her deadly actions against her mother. Listening to her jeweled mind, she pulls a handful of ruby light from her globe and raises the weapon above her shoulder.

"Mermaid of Zennor! Prepare to fight for your life."

CHAPTER THIRTY-THREE

A change of heart

The mermaid leaps and dodges Kate's ruby fireballs with the precision of a professional gymnast. Kate asks her jeweled mind for permission to create a sword of light. She receives it, and imagines a long, gleaming blade. It takes form, and she charges down the tunnel swiping it through the woman's aura, trying to loosen her connection to the Black Heart. "Give me my mother back or I'll cut off your head."

The mermaid sneers, "Give up, little girl. You can't win this battle."

"Just you wait and see." Kate touches the tip of her sword to the mermaid's neck, but the woman does a back flip and dodges the blade.

"Come on then … come and get me." The mermaid moves backwards, taking swift, small steps down the tunnel, drawing Kate closer to her turf—the sea.

The girl lunges after her, striking at her legs. Flames sear through the fabric of the woman's body suit, and she wobbles and loses her balance. Dashing in for the kill, Kate pokes the tip of her sword against the mermaid's breastplate, about to thrust fire through her heart. The woman sucks up blue-black vapors from the Black Heart, and then with a soaring leap, jumps over Kate and begins climbing the wall, dragging her injured leg behind her.

Kate races after her, scaling the rocky surface and whacking her sword at the woman's foot. Energy steams up from the underworld, and the mermaid fans it onto Kate. The vapors cling to the girl's skin, covering her from head to toe in a net of slime. Laughing, the woman drags the imprisoned girl up to an iron door.

Kate slashes at the netting with her sword, but it grows back as fast as she destroys it. She kicks and rages at her captor, shouting, "I'll kill you!" Her globe flashes like lights on an emergency vehicle, and her ruby intelligence warns her she must not use its power to take the life of another unless her own is at stake. Kate fails to hear the gentle voice and continues to threaten the mermaid. The light in her globe dims, then goes out, cutting her off from her jeweled intelligence.

"Look at that … ruby thing has gone dead. Who's got the upper hand now?" The mermaid shoves the door open and hauls Kate through it.

The roar of the ocean fills Kate's ears. She peers through the slime of the underworld, trying to discern the geography. Moonlight glows on a deep pool of seawater cradled in the cliffs. She's out at the far end of the headland behind Devil's Neck, and Mitch is there too, leaning against a ledge overhanging the sea. Oily, black chains bind his wrists and ankles. His eyes beseech her help.

Kate meets his glance as the mermaid drags her over the reef to the edge of the pool, and memories from Ruberah flash through her mind.

In the dark of the night, she stands beside Li'ram on the marble steps of the palace. They wait for Da'krah. Tonight he will ask their father for permission to stand in the ruby rings and be mated for life with Li'ram. Sol'aria has come to support her sister in this cause, although she does not feel Da'krah is worthy of Li'ram.

Li'ram's love for Da'krah shines in her eyes and heightens the glow on her skin. Happiness radiates from her as if coming straight from the heart of the Jewel Kingdom. Mistrust of Da'krah mounts in Sol'aria's breast. He will hurt Li'ram—she can read it in his aura. She tries to warn Li'ram, but her sister will hear no words against her lover.

"I need you to believe in my love for Da'krah. Promise me that,

Sol'aria."

The memory closes, but Sol'aria's promise lives on. It is now Kate's to keep. The hard shell of her anger at Mitch softens, and with her change of heart, her ruby globe lights up again. The net of slime covering her body evaporates into thin air.

Kate directs light from her globe into her feet and kicks the mermaid in the shins, knocking her into the pool of deep waters.

"If you kill me, Dark Master will torture your mother. She will die a slow and painful death."

"You kidnapped my mother."

"That's her fault. She dropped her guard."

Revenge beats in Kate's breast, but when her globe begins to flash again she heeds its warning. She walks slowly away from the mermaid and treks to the end of the headland. Still bound to a rock by the slimy chains of the Black Heart, Mitch cries out for her help.

Kate consults with her ruby mind, and it tells her she can try to assist Mitch but must not be upset if she fails. Dark Master has an iron grip on him. Kate stands up straight to her full height, pulls a flare of ruby light from her globe, and tosses it to Mitch. "Grab it, Mitch, and I'll tug you to safety."

With his hands bound together, this proves impossible for

Mitch. The netting of the Black Heart coils around his neck, and an agonizing ache rips through him. His body crumbles, and he falls into an endless black void. The sound of his suffering reverberates on the wind, gusting and blowing over the headland.

CHAPTER THIRTY-FOUR

Riding the ley line to Ruberah

During her moments alone in the mine, Tamara thought Miriam might become frightened enough to remember her in a kindly light. Not so. Miriam obeyed Kate's request to listen to the Devas, and she stood as she stands now, happy inside her globe. The celestial voices calmed her and evoked that feeling of being needed, but as Kate strides toward her that changes.

"What happened?" Miriam asks, running up to Kate. "Where's Mitch? Where's that strange woman you were fighting with? Who was she?"

"The Mermaid of Zennor. She's a shape-shifter, which means she can grow legs when she wants to and come up on the land. We saw her in her demon body—the part of her that belongs to the Black Heart. I tried to help Mitch, but—"

"Oh, no! Has the mermaid taken him? Is he in the Black Heart?"

"Uh-huh … but that's not as bad as you think. Mummy says we all belong to the Black Heart in one way or another. Every time we go against our better judgment, we draw energy off it, and so it owns that part of us. So, see, Mitch won't feel so strange there."

Miriam gasps. "Is that supposed to make me feel better?"

"Sorry. It came out the wrong way. What I meant—"

"I don't want to know. What happens now?"

"We go to Ruberah and ask for permission to use Rube."

"Ask who?"

"The Goddess of the Ruby Sphere. We can reach her from inside Mt. Rube."

"Where is it … the mountain?"

"I don't know, but our ruby minds do. We have to work as a team, like we did in Ruberah. I'll ask for directions while you listen to the Deva Chorus." She presses the skin of her globe against Miriam's. "This is vital to getting Mitch out of the Black Heart, Miriam. You do realize that, don't you?"

Miriam vows that if she ever gets back to her ordinary life, she'll never complain about her job again. She doesn't work hard just because she needs the money—she loves what she does, and it's the one thing she's good at. She can sense which apartment fits which client, and she drives a deal through all the petty grievances that could destroy it. She makes people happy and likes her life, but she's got to have Mitch in it. "Go for it, kid. I'm already listening."

Kate asks her ruby intelligence how they should travel back to Ruberah.

"Use the power of the sun flame in your heart."

Kate remembers the practice she used every day in her life as Sol'aria, and dips her head low toward her heart. She directs a ray of her sun flame into the rocks beneath her feet. The land splinters, and the ley line rises up from its ancient grid. Particles of minerals and sediment from the ocean swirl inside the ray of red crystalline brilliance, and the voices of all who have ever traveled on it rise in a chant that fills the mine. Ghost travelers from ages past huddle into the tunnel to stand in the light of the one link that connects the earth to Ruberah.

"Foretune to travel well," the ghosts whisper to Kate and Miriam.

"What does that mean?" Miriam asks Kate.

"It's how Ruberians said goodbye to each other. It

means prepare for things to work out well."

"I'm all for that."

The light of the ley line locks onto their feet and forms straps similar in style to the sandals they wore in Ruberah. Kate grins. "Cool, right?"

"Cool."

"Ready?"

"No. Just kidding. Yes."

A thundering sound like the drumming of kettledrums blasts through the mine, and the ley line shoots forward. Kate and Miriam hold hands and whiz down the tunnel on the beam of red light. Huge rocks at the end of the mine slide apart, and the girl and the woman skid into the ocean. The ley line expands and encases them in a bullet of light that looks like a futuristic, high-speed railway car. Their globes collapse into rings of ruby light and lie around their necks.

"Brilliant!" Kate runs her hands through her hair and tosses it about her shoulders. "We traveled like this in the Time of Ruberah. We could turn the ley line into airships that carried a thousand people at a time, and we controlled our speed and direction from an astral disk—a soft, razor-thin computer we stuck into the palms of our hands, which was programmed to the astral sphere of the Ruby Kingdom."

Miriam tunes her out. Please God, she won't have to use this astral disk thing—it's hard enough to keep up with the computers of this world, let alone deal with some intergalactic system. She wonders what's governing their speed now, but doesn't ask. It might be Kate, in which case she'd rather not know. *Foretune to travel well.* Watching the waters of the Atlantic splash by, she tells herself that gliding along beneath the sea—breathing air without knowing where it's coming from, losing complete control of her life—is a good thing. Panic beats beneath her every breath. They come to a swift, silent halt. "Where are we?"

"In Ruberah. Watch the ley line. It's changing again!

The red bullet expands and soars up, pushing back the ocean. Then its light falls back down, forming a pale pink dome over the ruins of Ruberah. Kate and Miriam gaze at great furrows of shattered crystal and clusters of marble and gold dredged this way and that by the tides of time. Still wet from the sea, the ruins of the once glorious city of Az'Rayelle glisten beneath shadows of the ocean waving against the dome.

"Look, Miriam, Mt. Rube!" Kate points to the towering jeweled mountain rising in the distance. "And there's *Mercy*, the golden galleon, just to the left of Rube."

The ship rests on her side with her masts splintered and broken on a coral reef. "Look at her sails," Kate says, "They're undamaged and still rigged to the masts. See, they're as bright in color as when Gold created them. One day, when there's enough love to ride on the wind—that's love from us, the human family—those sails will flutter back to life, and *Mercy* will rise and continue to help those in distress on the sea. My mother used to tell me stories about *Mercy* as she tucked me into bed at night. I'd puff up my cheeks and blow out huge breaths, sending love to *Mercy*, and then she'd begin."

A cast of sadness dulls the girl's eyes, and Miriam tries to cheer her up. "That will happen, Kate. Your mother wouldn't tell you that unless it were true."

Kate trudges forward, kicking rubble out of her way. As Miriam joins her, suddenly, without any effort on her part, she hears the Deva Chorus singing in some remote area of her brain—mellifluous and soothing.

Miriam Lewis, High Priestess of Sound!

Maybe it'll become second nature to hear the Devas. She chuckles to herself as she thinks of her girlfriends back in New York. What would they make of this whole thing? Not that she could ever tell them. They already think she should see a shrink, due to her relationship with Mitch.

"What's funny?" Kate asks.

"I'm wondering how I'll process all this when I return to New York."

"If you survive, you'll be happier. Everyone is happier when they return from a sacred future."

"If I survive? I'm not ready to die."

"Well … I am. I won't live very long … I never do."

"What kind of talk is that? You're a kid, you've—"

"I've lived many times, Miriam, but my life as Sol'aria was the longest I ever lived. I was sixteen at the time of *The Ending*."

Talk of death drags up Miriam's greatest fear, the thought of her daughter overdosing and lying comatose on the streets of New York. Here she is, stuck on the bottom of the Atlantic, paying for some dreadful deed she did in the past, when for all she knows Elaine might be … *No!* She forbids herself to go there. She'll look after Kate. She'll keep her alive at all costs. Perhaps then the great record keeper in the sky will look favorably on Elaine.

"No more talk of doom," Miriam says. "Foretune to travel well, huh? We'll find your mother and Mitch, and we'll all live long and happy lives. That's it. Don't give me any backtalk."

Kate shrugs. "Whatever."

If Miriam could strike one word from the English language, it would be "whatever," said with a shrug that implies, "I don't give a damn."

They walk in silence until they come to a set of solid gold gates standing about a hundred feet tall in front of Mt. Rube. A sun with diamond-crusted rays shimmers in their center. Kate places her palms on the gate. "I remember the last time I stood here. It was the day of *The Ending.*

"I was with our mother, Queen Leah. I held the Scrolls of Knowledge against my heart. Mother said the mountain would sink sooner than we had anticipated and we should leave for the harbor right away. I insisted I had time to enter Rube and hide the scrolls in the golden casket as planned. Mother forbade it. "It is as it is, Sol'aria," she said. "I watched flames of volcanic fire reflecting in her pale eyes—flames as fierce as her queenly will. She ordered me to flee to the harbor and join you on the *Silver Serpent.* She would wait by Mt. Rube, she said. The Royal Guard would arrive soon and escort her to the golden galleon. The last words she said to me were: "You are now the guardian of the Scrolls of Knowledge. They are the hope of the future. Guard them with your life."

Tears flood Kate's eyes. "I failed that task. I drowned and took the scrolls with me. Now Dark Master has them."

Miriam hugs the girl. "You couldn't help that."

"Yes, I could. I messed up the whole world."

"Hey, come on, kid, that's my stuff. I probably couldn't function without guilt, so just leave it all to me. Deal?"

The girl remains solemn. "Do you remember the day of *The Ending*?"

"Yeah, unfortunately I do."

"When you were on the *Silver Serpent,* you shouted at me to throw the scrolls into the fire. I meant to. I don't know why I didn't."

"It was chaotic, Kate. You were helping everyone around you."

"But I should have looked after the scrolls first. I ..." She stops, and with a huge sigh and snap of her fingers, reverts back to her old self. "Never mind. It is as it is. Once we've found my mother in the Black Heart, I'll find the scrolls."

"And after we've rescued Mitch," Miriam says.

"Yeah, yeah." Kate says, imitating Miriam's way of speaking.

Miriam grimaces. "The accent needs work, but you've got the attitude down pretty good."

"I should think so. I get lots of it."

"Okay. I deserve that, but you ... you run the gamut from being a great kid to full-fledged bitch."

Kate snorts a laugh. "I'm a teenager. I'm supposed to do that. Anyway, I know lots more American lingo, but I don't use it because it bugs Daddy, and I just haven't got the heart to aggravate him right now."

"There you go, being a great kid."

The girl skips her usual "I know," said with great aplomb, and looks back to the gates. "I have to ask how to open them."

Miriam gazes at Rube. With ocean flora growing all over it, it's hard to tell it's made of pure ruby. She narrows her eyes and studies it more intensely. The seaweed appears to be crawling over the mineral. *Oh, my God,* that's not seaweed. She elbows Kate in the ribs. "What the hell are those things crawling all over the mountain?"

CHAPTER THIRTY-FIVE

Dark Master's feelers

Kate rubs her side. "That hurt."

"Sorry, but look at Rube. It looks like worms crawling all over it."

"Oh, those. They're just the feelers. They come from the Black Heart. They're everywhere, sucking up energy for Dark Master. They feed off everything. Us too ... on our feelings, like fear, greed, anger ... stuff like that."

"There must be millions of them."

"Um ... gazillions, actually—at least one or two for every person on the planet. More, for some."

"I want to go home."

"Well, you can't. We're going to rescue my mother …
and Mitch. He needs you. Dark Master will torture him in ways
so terrible you can't imagine. He'll stick needles in his brain
and—"

"Stop it!"

"Sorry."

Kate continues to downplay the dangers of the feelers to
Miriam, and as she does, she misses something important about
them—but Tamara and her giants do not. Beneath their gulping
and guzzling, the feelers emit subtle noises like electronic beeps
that track back to the Black Heart and print images of Kate and
Miriam onto a screen in Mastermind Control. Dark Master then
forwards those pictures to a screen in Lara's cubicle—a prison
cell floating among millions of cells in the sprawling empire of
the underworld. Chained to a chair, Lara watches her daughter
while choking back fear. She knows the feelers live off the juices
of fright and distress, and she must gain control of her emotions.

Oxygen flows into Lara's nostrils through a thin tube
floating down from the ceiling. She does a breathing exercise,
inhaling and exhaling on the count of seven. Even so, the hairs
on her arms stand up. A feeler creeps into the cell, snakes up her
legs, and attaches itself to her hand. She freezes.

A tinny, nonhuman voice crackles through the speakers
at the base of the screen—the computerized voice of the

Mastermind.

"Lara Penrose, attach the feeler to your daughter's image on the screen."

The handcuffs of slime fall from Lara's wrists, and the voice continues, "Attach it now or watch your daughter die."

CHAPTER THIRTY-SIX

A pillar of sound

After a practice session of using their ruby intelligence together, Miriam's fear of the feelers drops away and she even feels a little excited about going inside the mountain.

"You're doing a brilliant job," Kate says. "Are you ready to work as a High Priestess of Sound?"

"Ready."

The Deva Chorus bursts into song inside Miriam's head as if on cue. They chant to the Goddess of the Ruby Sphere, and Miriam joins them, just as she did when she lived as Li'ram. Their voices reach a soaring crescendo in a glorious medley of interlacing harmonies, and the resonance of their sound shakes the sands beneath the ocean. A great swirling pillar of song spirals up around Miriam with the roar of *om* ringing at its bass.

"You did it, Miriam! You did it." Kate jumps up and down like a kid winning at her favorite sport. "You lit up the pillar of jeweled song. Utterly fab, isn't it?"

"I guess, but where did it go?"

"Oh, it's still here. It's just in the abstract. Sound is the cosmic language. The pillar of song will carry our message to Zan'drah, Goddess of Rube."

"What message?"

"That we want to get into Mt. Rube and speak with her." Kate studies Miriam, wondering why she doesn't remember that—maybe she's at the age where people start losing their memory.

"I asked for all that? I don't recall saying anything at all."

"You didn't. Sound doesn't carry words; it speaks of intention."

"You sure know a lot for a girl your age."

"I know." Kate grins and rolls her eyes.

Miriam rubs her temples. "My head feels as if everything inside it has been stretched out and hasn't quite fallen back into place."

"That's from the roar of *om,* the sound of the universe. You'll get used it. You can chant *om* and visit anyone who ever lived on the planet. You could talk to Buddha or Jesus or Elvis. He'd be fun and—"

"I'd keep that to myself, if I were you."

"Why?"

"People who talk to Elvis end up on the front page of the tabloids."

"So what?"

"So I sell apartments for a living. I can't act crazy."

Kate snorts a giggle. "You don't think you do?"

"You've got a point there. What now?"

"We bow to the sun in the gates and wait for them to open."

They stand side-by-side, hands in prayer, their heads bowed. The golden gates slide open, and they cheer and slap hands in a high five.

The tinny, nonhuman voice of the Dark Master speaks.

"You will restart Rube and deliver its power to me. You have fifteen minutes to do this. If you fail, torture worse than death shall befall the former Queen of Ruberah and the Prince of the Emerald Kingdom."

CHAPTER THIRTY-SEVEN

The path to Mt. Rube

The Prince of the Emerald Kingdom! Miriam's thoughts spin
out of control and she begins choking, as if water is seeping into
her lungs. Her world turns upside down, and she falls back
through time—all the way back to the pale pink light of Ruberah,
to *The Ending.*

Li'ram grips the railing of the Silver Serpent, *gazing back at the
flames engulfing the harbor of Az'Rayelle. A storm rages on the seas,
knocking the ship headfirst into a massive wave. She hears the hollow crack
of splitting wood—hard and final. The ship's hull fractures into two jagged
pieces. Da'krah floats away from Li'ram, calling her name as he tries to
swim back to her. "I will find you," he yells. A huge wave crests above
Li'ram. "Don't leave me," she cries out. The wave crashes down, driving*

Da'krah further from her. She strains her sight for one last glimpse of the man she loves, but a different man stands in his place. He lacks the commanding air of her beloved. He looks vague, like a man permanently stranded between his point of origin and his destination. Water blurs Li'ram's vision. Water gushes down her throat … into her lungs. Da'krah's spirit floats past her in a streak of emerald light. She walks into the future on the arm of the vague man with the close-set eyes.

"Miriam!" Kate shakes Miriam by the shoulders. "Come back. Come back."

Miriam coughs and gasps for breath, and then meets Kate's eyes—solemn and devoid of their usual sparkle. "I saw my death in Ruberah," Miriam says, her breath still faint from the ordeal.

"I'm sorry." Kate gathers Miriam in her arms. "I wish you had lived and shared the life you so longed for with Da'krah."

"Oh, honey, no … I wanted you to live. I could never have been happy without you." Much as Miriam wants to ask Kate if Mitch had been Da'krah in Ruberah, she doesn't. Her heart tells her that's true, and it also tells her it's time for her to shape up and look after Kate. "I'm okay now. In fact, I'm damn fighting mad. Dark Master, with his nasty little threat, has really pissed me off! Who does he think he's talking to? Huh? This is us—the most powerful sisters in the world. Wait 'til he tries to cross swords with us. He won't act so damned cocksure then. Huh? "

A slow smile crosses Kate's face. "You should get damned fighting mad more often, Miriam."

"Oh, I do. I do. I'm just off my game here. I'm a die-hard New Yorker, and you've got me running around beneath the sea."

"Me?" Kate shakes her head, "You wrote your sacred future."

"Yeah, well ... let's not go there again."

Kate taps her wristwatch, a man-sized Timex with a blue face and yellow rubber strap. "We've got to walk the maze in front of Rube. It's a meditative practice designed to calm the mind ... a necessary alignment to stand in the presence of the Goddess. I've set my watch alarm to go off every two minutes. We've already lost a minute, so we're down to fourteen before Dark Master—"

"Onward!" Miriam nudges the girl into the maze.

"Walk close to me, Miriam, and listen to the Devas. They will help us find our way."

"Got it."

They set foot on the golden pathways of the maze and whiz along side by side, treading on ground mined from the earth's heart. They clip from east to west, west to east, north to south, and back again, picking up speed. Unbeknownst to either, a feeler slunk through the golden gates before they closed. It flies behind Miriam, wriggling in a streak of slime, transmitting sounds to the Black Heart. Tamara observes another series of pictures streaming onto the screen in Lara's cell. Lara watches her daughter, her heart in her throat—her thoughts so keyed to Kate's safety that once again they pass through the underworld and into Tamara's light body.

"Tamara, don't let Kate out of your sight. Please."

"I will stay by her side. Rest assured of that, Lara."

"Thank you."

As Lara's voice fades, Tamara picks up on an unusual disturbance gathering off the Cornish coast. She wonders if she's remembering the feel of the atmosphere before Ruberah erupted or if she's intuiting a future disaster. She speaks into her direct ray to the earth's heart and asks Gold.

"They are one and the same storm, Tamara."

Tavy nudges Tamara. "What does that mean?"

"It means Kate's quest to use Rube has entered the Cycles of Time and opened the record of *The Ending,* and it's now flowing into the present. If the Goddess grants Kate and Miriam the use of Rube, they must remember its loving, creative nature and use it accordingly. If they do, the old causes that brought about *The Ending* can be forgiven. If they misuse Rube, volcanic fires from Ruberah will resurface and tear Cornwall from the face of the earth."

Tawridge scratches his brow. "If the Goddess should grant Kate and Miriam use of Rube, Kate will never just hand it over to Dark Master. There's bound to be a fight."

"True," Tavy says. "But it's all right for Kate to use Rube against Dark Master to free her mother. It can be used to right a wrong, but not just for the sake of vengeance."

"But that's the problem. Kate is young and revenge seems right to her," Tawridge says.

"I'm sure the Goddess will make all of that clear to Kate," Tavy retorts.

Tamara and the giants swerve around the twists and turns of the maze, keeping close to Kate and Miriam. The girl and the woman stride into a small golden square at the end of the maze. Tamara and her giants squeeze in after them, the glow of their light bodies floating up the walls and ceiling.

Kate checks her watch, now ignoring Tamara and the giants as if they truly did not exist. "We've got twelve minutes left to enter the mountain and meet the Goddess," she says to

Miriam.

This hard fact pulls Miriam down, and she ceases to hear the Deva Chorus. Her thoughts revert to the tragedy of *The Ending*. She had given up everything as Li'ram to be with Da'krah, and then they both drowned. No wonder she fears the sea, and yet here she is, fathoms beneath the ocean, hoping to rescue Mitch, the man she's now certain had lived as Da'krah. Will she ever stop loving him? Will he ever love her? Anxiety eats at her heart, and the feeler attaches itself to her spine, sucking at the energy of her misery.

This image of Miriam fills the screen in Lara's cell in the Black Heart, and in an adjacent cell, Mitch pricks his ears to the familiar frequency of Miriam's despair. He calls out, "Mir! Help me!"

His voice sounds in Miriam's ears as clearly as if he stood beside her. She clutches Kate's arm. "Mitch needs me. I can hear him."

Kate's mind moves quickly, like a computer, and she soon realizes they must somehow be connected to the Black Heart. She scours the area and spots the feeler clinging to Miriam's spine. "Stay where you are. Don't move."

"Why? What's going on? "

Kate rubs her hands in the ruby light of her aura and swipes the feeler off Miriam's back. It fizzles and splatters to the ground. "You attracted a feeler. It's gone, but if you get scared it will come back."

"Ohmigod!" Miriam leaps about, sweeping her hands over her back. "That hideous thing touched me?"

"Get a grip, Miriam. It's gone."

Kate's watch alarm goes off again. The loss of another two minutes jars Miriam back to her senses. "How do we get out of here and into the mountain?"

Kate scans the cube. "There's a secret door that leads into Rube. We have to speak a code to open it. Do you remember what it is?"

Unease knots in Miriam's chest. *You are not enough ... not enough ... not enough.* "I don't remember the code, but I know it was something our mother used to say a lot back in Ruberah—a saying that pissed me off, so much that I'm feeling that irritation now."

Kate sighs, "Who's the grownup here?"

"Oh, hey, hand me the magic wand, kid."

Kate closes her eyes and looks into the sun flame in her heart, asking for help. She recalls being Sol'aria and standing by Mt. Rube with her mother on the day of *The Ending.* Inner wisdom says her mother said the words to her on that day. She goes over their meeting, remembering everything that passed

310

between them.

It is as it is, Sol'aria.

"That's it!"

"What?" Miriam asks.

"It is as it is."

Miriam looks startled, and her heart hits her gut. "Yes, that's it."

"Great, so come on. Let's run our hands over the walls saying that until we find the secret door."

"I can't. Sorry, I just can't."

"*Really!*" Kate glowers at Miriam and then places her palms flat against the wall. She slides them slowly over the golden surface, whispering, "It is as it is." Her fingers caress a seam in the gold, and a panel falls down. She looks into a swamp of thick red mist swirling over a drawbridge—over the passage into Rube!

Kate swivels around to face Miriam. "Ta-da!" She snorts a giggle, "The mountain awaits the powerful sisters from Ruberah."

Miriam eases alongside Kate. Still preoccupied with emotions from long ago, she feels far from powerful. At least she can't see the awful feelers crawling over the mountain. Red mist seems to puff up from nowhere and shroud Rube from sight.

"I need to explain about that saying, it is as it is," Miriam says. "It upsets me because Queen Leah—our mother in Ruberah—said it a lot to me ... well to Li'ram. It remains indelible in my memory, because she said it in a tone of voice that implied I lacked the ability to see things as they really were."

"You did lack that ability, Miriam."

A startled expression crosses Miriam's face. "That may be true ... but it never helps to tell someone that."

"Oh, really?"

Kate raises a brow, and under her quizzical glance Miriam realizes she does exactly that to her daughter. *Straighten up, Elaine.* She gulps, feeling regretful, and vows never to say that again.

CHAPTER THIRTY-EIGHT

Ascending Mt. Rube

Inside Rube, a cavernous, carved-out passage opens all the way up to the peak. A white radiance spirals back down, filtering light over the seven layers of gemstones that comprise the massive jewel. The pungent fragrance of amber drifts on the air—oil that once floated on a pale pink sea—now made sweet and dry with time—lacing the silence that permeates the atmosphere.

Tamara and the giants rest their heads on Rube Stone, the great crusty jewel the Ruberians named the heart of the mountain, the first ruby to surface on Earth.

Kate's watch alarm sounds and she slaps her hand over her wrist, protecting the magical silence of the mountain. "Eight minutes," she whispers.

"Where's the Goddess?" Miriam glances about her.

"Probably in astral control—you know, in the Ruby Sphere."

"What? Out in space?"

"*Duh!*" Kate giggles.

"Okay. Stupid me. How do we get to her?"

Kate holds her hands in prayer mode. "We ask the Goddess to come and meet us."

"I thought we just did that."

"Yes, and now we have to let her know we made it through the maze and we're inside the mountain."

"She doesn't know that?"

"Miriam, the Ruby Sphere is decked from top to bottom with jeweled systems that govern the light and sound vibrations of rubies throughout the universe. The Goddess oversees that whole operation. She's busy. It's up to us to keep her informed."

"Okay, hold your fire. I'm praying already." Miriam closes her eyes and words begin to flow, but they come in song—the song of rubies—a language she spoke long ago.

A platform of diamonds suspended on ruby ropes sweeps down from the mountaintop like a craft from another galaxy. Kate climbs on and then helps Miriam. Tamara follows with her giants, squeezing their lights bodies into the small space. A cloud of pink light drifts above the lift, dropping ropes of rubies down to Kate and Miriam. The gems wrap around their foreheads—helping them tune up their jeweled intelligence. Two necklaces with large ruby pendants follow.

Kate caresses the jewel at the base of her throat and wrinkles her nose in delight. "Feel that vibration, Miriam."

Miriam fingers the pendant, and a wonderful happiness fills her heart. Love pours from her, love she wants to give to everyone, everywhere in the whole world. "I'd like to wear this jewel forever."

"Me too, but remember, we'll fall unconscious to the loving nature of rubies if we get scared or angry or flip into any negative emotions. We've got to dump all that stuff before we can meet the Goddess. That's the point of riding on the diamond lift."

Miriam wishes Kate hadn't told her that. Now she'll probably hold on to every misery that comes to mind.

The lift glides up through ruby rock—the first of the seven levels of the mountain. Light glistens from the gems, casting deep red shadows. Miriam feels like a child riding through a fairyland, until the shadows touch her and her mood changes. She glimpses images of herself fighting with Mitch, belittling him with harsh words. "Dear Goddess, give me another chance with Mitch, and I'll never be bitchy again." The Deva Chorus filters into Miriam's consciousness, and as the bass singers dominate the chant, more unpleasant aspects of her life come to mind. She sees herself rushing up Park Avenue to show an apartment, nitpicking her life. Why is she always so negative? Why is she always rushing everywhere?

Emerald light floods the lift, and contraltos fringe in on the chant. Mitch's affair with Gwenellen consumes Miriam. He probably landed in the Black Heart as a result of chasing after her, so it serves him right. He can damned well stay there. "Sorry about the damn word, Goddess, but actually, that's not considered a swear word, at least not in New York." Feeling absolved, Miriam reverts to denigrating Mitch. *Shit!* Where does it all come from?

The lift rises into the gold level of the mountain, and its soothing light softens Miriam's attitude. Mitch has the right to love someone else. Tension releases from her neck. The rich timbre of tenor voices blends into the chant, and the lift glides into a blue glow—mystical, like the center of a star sapphire. Miriam's inner chatter falls silent.

The purple beauty of the amethyst kingdom envelops her, and doubt and lack of self-esteem fade away. Her can-do spirit soars into life. She's a jewel in the crown of mankind: she'll get Lara Penrose out of the Black Heart, and she will see Kate and her mother safely home.

A melting vibrato of sopranos joins the chorus, and the jeweled platform soars into the diamond-bright light in the peak of the mountain. Kate and Miriam step from the lift and find themselves at the foot of a clear, rotating pyramid, which makes a soft whirring sound. The pyramid expands with every turn until it defies the dimensions of the mountain and speeds off into space. Kate and Miriam lose sight of the craft.

But Tamara doesn't. She watches it spin into space and hover alongside the Ruby Sphere. A panel slides open, and the Goddess alights from the orb in a sheath of red flames. She steps into the craft. Within seconds, it lands back inside Mt. Rube. The crystal rotates for a short while and comes to a complete stop.

Kate and Miriam shield their eyes against the brilliance, while Tamara sheds a tear over the two of them. Few have tackled such a journey as this. Love for each other has brought them here, love shown by the way Miriam clasps Kate's hand, so reminiscent of when she had been her older sister in Ruberah.

The light softens to a pearly luminescence, and with a flare of ruby flames, the Goddess steps from the pyramid. Tamara has often described the Goddess to Kate, but the girl's jaw drops upon sight of her.

Zan'drah, Goddess of Rube, stands eight feet tall, her bronze, muscular frame clad in a bodysuit of diamonds that clings to her like a second skin. She bears the sharp-chiseled features of a noblewoman carved on a sacred icon. Her eyes shine from the deepest depths of sapphires, and tiny rubies glitter in her brows. She wears her raven hair cropped short and slick against her head. The jewels of the seven kingdoms weave around an enormous pearl and cover her skull. Above her right shoulder, she holds a silver chalice smoldering with ruby flames.

The Goddess speaks to Kate first, her voice husky and haunting, like a low note on an oboe. "For what purpose do you seek the use of Rube Force?"

Kate rivets her eyes to the Goddess, exuding an aura of certainty and command, qualities valued by the Goddess, qualities she possesses herself. "To free my mother from the Black Heart."

"Tell me, my child, is wisdom yours?"

"I am aware in my jeweled intelligence."

The Goddess turns to Miriam. "And is your purpose the same?"

"It is. I am on my sacred future," Miriam manages, her voice jittery with nerves. "And also to rescue Mi ... er ..."

"The Prince of the Emerald Kingdom?" the Goddess prompts.

"Yes, him."

The Goddess lowers a bejeweled hand on Miriam's shoulder. "If I grant you the use of Rube, you must be the wise one. Do you accept that responsibility?"

The regal hand feels like an iron brick on Miriam's frame. The suffering she inflicted upon herself with this sacred future reverberates in her memory. *May I never do anything so stupid again.* Miriam nods to the Goddess. "I do."

The Goddess lowers her chalice and a wellspring of ruby flames flares up and forms a wall of fire that separates her from Kate and Miriam. Tamara and her giants remain behind the wall with the Goddess.

Tawridge whispers to Tamara, "Don't you think you should tell the Goddess that Miriam has been misled about you and our legend?"

Tamara shushes him, and the Goddess calls her to her side. "Beloved Zan'drah," Tamara says. "How may I serve you?"

Glancing into the Goddess's eyes is like reading history. Zan'drah holds all the circumstances surrounding Miriam's sacred future in her mind, every detail from the moment she and Mitch drove over the Tamar Bridge and into Cornwall.

"Just stay true to your legend, Tamara. The human family would be greatly diminished without you."

Tamara bows to the Goddess, assuring her she will do

that. "I wonder," she asks tentatively, "if you might remind Miriam that long ago she chose me to be her guide on her sacred future."

"This is a grand opportunity for you, Tamara."

The Goddess is a woman of few words, but what she does say comes loaded. Tamara knows it will take time to unfold the full measure of her statement. Meanwhile, she'd better remember that with grand opportunities comes the chance to make grand mistakes.

The wall of fire burns out, and the Goddess addresses Kate and Miriam.

CHAPTER THIRTY-NINE

Riding on the fire of rubies

"I grant you Rube for the mission you have spoken of. You must return it to me by the turn of the next tide on the Cornish coast."

The Goddess departs in a burst of red fire. Still dazed by her presence, Kate and Miriam step back onto the diamond lift. Tavy, Tawridge, and Tamara join them, the radiance of their light bodies melting into the afterglow of the Goddess. No one speaks as they ride down the mountain. The magnetism of the Goddess lingers and holds them captive.

The lift stops, and as Kate and Miriam get off, the fire and beauty of the Goddess grows dim in their memories. Standing on the cool, jewel-crusted floor of the mountain, Kate looks at her watch—four minutes until Dark Master carries out his threat.

"Where did the Goddess go?" Miriam asks, feeling disoriented.

"Back to the Ruby Sphere," Kate says. "Do you remember what she said?"

Miriam rubs her eyes, adjusting to the darker atmosphere. "Yeah, we can use Rube until the turn of the tide in Cornwall. When's that?"

"Thirty minutes from now."

"What? That's not enough time."

"Yes, it is. Rube will get us to the Black Heart within seconds. We'll beat Dark Master's deadline."

Miriam thinks of Dark Master's threat against Lara and the Prince of the Emerald Kingdom. She massages a knot of tension at the base of her neck. Will she ever get used to knowing that Mitch had once been an ambitious and commanding prince? "Where is the force?"

"It will be here soon. We have to wait for a while. It's a test of trust. Don't you remember?"

"Another damn test! Haven't we passed enough?"

"It is as it is, Miriam."

"Don't say that to me."

"The mountain is a hallowed place, Miriam. Why are you angry?"

"I feel as if I've lost control of my life, and that scares me."

Kate slips her hand into Miriam's, "Don't worry. I'll look after you."

"Aw, honey, I'm sorry. I'm such a pain in the ass."

The Deva Chorus falls silent, and the white radiance ceases to stream down the hollowed passage. A rich ruby darkness settles over Kate and Miriam, blocking them from the worries of their lives. This gives them time to reflect on the gift granted them by the Goddess.

Tavy and Tawridge talk between themselves, parsing Zan'drah's words, noting the Goddess said Kate and Miriam could use Rube *for the mission they spoke of.* No mention was made of the Scrolls of Knowledge, and that could lead to trouble, as Kate would not consider leaving the Black Heart without them.

Tamara contemplates the grand opportunity coming her way. Kate's mother spoke correctly. We do all belong to the Black Heart in one way or another. As an immortal she should be above this, but she is not. The loss of her father remains lodged in her heart. Back in her nymph life, when she defied his order to leave Tavy and Tawridge, she lost her connection to him for a few moments. It happened when the winds rushed in, her world spun around, and the moors collided with the heavens. The wind whispered something to her father, but she could not hear its message. After that, he seemed to struggle with himself for a while, as if resisting an order. Then he ripped the land apart, and she could no longer see the light of his love for her in his eyes. She's not been able to fathom why or what changed him so drastically, and therefore, unable to dissolve her grief. This attachment forms her tie to the Black Heart. Given the least opportunity, Dark Master will try to probe her sorrow and knock her off center so he can draw energy from her river. She's become skilled in dodging these attempts, but he is about to gain a new advantage over her. Kate, whom she has guarded since birth, will soon enter his domain without her protection.

As each ponders his fate, the rich ruby darkness begins to swirl, and the roar of *om* fills the mountain. The sound amplifies as it passes through the jeweled interior, picking up the voices of all who have chanted it throughout time, all who chant it at this moment, and all who will ever sing its song. The voices layer one on top of another—one tongue—one sound for all mankind: one call for Rube.

Then it comes—the force that has slept for millions of years. The great river made of cosmic fire, sound, and the brilliance of rubies hurtles down from the mountaintop and laps around Kate and Miriam's feet. Its flames feel warm and gentle against the skin, like being kissed by a summer breeze. Miriam and Kate laugh and splash fire at each other like children playing in the ocean.

"I'm so happy," Miriam says. "I don't need anything or anyone. I'm just plain happy. It's wonderful. I never want it to go away."

Kate douses her cheeks with flames, uttering squeals of joy. "This feeling comes from the heart of the Ruby Kingdom, but we can't hold onto it. We have to let it go and become one with the power behind it, the cosmic fire of Rube. Do you remember that?"

Miriam nods and recalls how, as Li'ram, she had always resented having to give up this happiness to work with the force. The old resentment rises again.

You must be the wise one.

Why had she agreed to that? A primordial memory zips open, and she remembers meeting the Goddess on the golden sands of the primordial just before her birth as Li'ram. Zan'drah had invited her to become a High Priestess of Sound. Li'ram had hesitated, sensing she might long for a love that would come between her and that job. But under the spin of Zan'drah's aura, the lure of her beauty, and the awe of her power, she had accepted.

"I'll steer Rube." Kate marches to the front of the

flames, her hair fanning out on a draft of the fire, making her almost indiscernible from Rube. Miriam imagines Kate would like nothing more than to actually vanish into the fire. The sooner they rescue Lara Penrose, the better. Kate really needs her mother. Who else could understand her? And who but Miriam could understand Elaine? Miriam's heart skips a beat—Mitch.

Miriam wades through the flames and stands behind Kate. "I surrender happiness. I take on the full power of Rube."

"Wow! You remembered the exact words. That's impressive, Miriam."

"Damned right. Now you do the same."

Kate repeats the words, and a wheel of flames forms in front of her. She grips it like the steering wheel of a car, looks over her shoulder at Miriam, and holds up her left hand, palm forward. A disk of light glows against her skin. "We're connected to Astral Command!"

Rube can expand to circumnavigate the planet or contract to a few feet in length. Rube can streak into space or inch over the earth at a snail's pace. The Goddess will have modified its range before handing it over to Kate and Miriam, narrowing it down to suit their mission. But still, it's a mighty power and an even mightier act of trust.

Locked into her jeweled intelligence, Kate studies her astral disk, seeking the code for Rube to find the Black Heart.

Five symbols appear on the silvery screen. She taps them, and Rube blasts forth from the mountain.

Tamara and her giants cling to the underside of the flames, their light bodies flowing through the ocean as the sacred fire careens toward the Black Heart. With Rube alive on the planet, people everywhere enjoy a charge of happiness. Most accept it as just one of those moments that sometimes happens for no apparent reason. Others, those who once lived in the Time of Ruberah, recognize it as the loving nature of rubies coming back into the world. Whatever they're doing, be it the most menial of tasks or a coveted pleasure, they do it with joy—a feeling that was once second nature to them.

Rube slows down as it nears the blue-black waters of the underworld. Tamara and her giants slip from its power and stream backward, directing their light bodies away from the raging whirlpools that form the entrance to the Black Heart.

Kate reels Rube in to a few feet in length and coasts in the dark, slimy waters, studying her astral disk. Miriam stands at the rear of the flames, her eyes closed, singing with the Deva Chorus.

In her role of silent watchdog, Tamara spots a wisp of emerald light trapped in the raging whirlpools: the Soul Flame of the Emerald Sphere! Dark Master must have followed her dream travel with Mitch to the spheres of the Jewel Kingdom. The ruler probably caused the hairline fracture in the Emerald Sphere to crack open, and when the flame slipped into the cosmos, he drew it down here. But how?

Tavy and Tawridge catch sight of the green flame and gasp in horror, "Let us get it and take it back to the jeweled spheres," Tawridge says.

"Not yet," Tamara says. "Neither Kate nor Miriam has noticed it, and neither knows it's missing from its jeweled orb. Let's not draw their attention to it now."

"But Kate should know Dark Master stole—"

"We've lost Kate … at least for the moment. We will gain nothing by telling her."

"I agree with Tamara," Tavy says. "This is why Dark Master captured Mitch. He probably detected a green glow in his aura on the day Mitch drove into Cornwall. He must have immediately identified him as having once been the Prince of the Emerald Kingdom. Remember how Dark Master shadowed the prince's life back in the Time of Ruberah? He stalked Da'krah day and night, urging him to ignite the sleeping force of the Emerald Mountain. He insisted the prince owed this to his people. Da'krah banished him over and over from his thoughts, so then Dark Master created unrest among the people."

"I remember," Tawridge says. "The ruler made them envious of the Ruberians. He raved about the riches of the Ruby Kingdom, and then told them the Emerald Force would be far greater. They would all have bigger and grander homes than the citizens of Az'Rayelle. Oh … my goodness. The people stormed the gates of the palace. They camped there for days demanding Da'krah bring the force to life."

"The ruler never gives up," Tavy says. "Look at what he's done in a day. He smote Mitch with love for Gwenellen so he could control him through her. He set up a fight between Kate and Gwenellen, which awakened Kate to her spirit power, knowing full well that then nothing could stop her from coming for her mother and the Scrolls of Knowledge."

Tavy raises a fist. "He's lured us all here. Mark my words, he wants to take another shot at igniting the Emerald Force."

Tawridge punches his hand into the ocean, expressing his disgust with the wily ruler. "So why didn't he take the flame inside the Black Heart?"

Both giants rest their eyes on Tamara. "Because it is an unborn source of energy," Tamara says. "It's as fragile as a premature baby, more so, as it is not of this world. Dark Master cannot touch that flame. It will die unless handled with love."

"Then how did he it get down here?" Tavy asks.

Tamara thinks back to when Mitch and Miriam crossed her river. Dark Master had surfaced from the underworld, caused a tremendous storm, and beaten back the golden sail that appeared as Mitch looked into her river. "I think the ruler stole a piece of light from Mitch's aura, a trace of his ancient memory, as he drove into Cornwall. He probably transported it onto one of his screens in Mastermind Control and then used it to lure the Emerald Flame all the way to the door of his kingdom."

Tavy tosses in his waters. "Maybe we should at least try to warn Kate and Miriam about this before they enter the Black Heart."

Tamara is about to agree with him, but she's too late. Kate stabs a code into the astral disk, and Rube shoots through the raging whirlpools and into the Black Heart.

CHAPTER FORTY

Dark Master's kingdom

Backfire from Rube creates a cavity of downward spiraling waters, and Tavy and Tawridge use their might to bend their light forms against its pull, keeping them from being sucked into the hole. They cling to each other, wavering dangerously close to the rim. The spiral hits the ocean bed, wells back up, and surges across the sea. Massive tidal waves roll toward the shorelines of the world. Winds of hurricane force thrash against the raging waters at the entrance to the Black eart, and the fledgling green flame falls and flutters close to the mouth of the underworld.

Tavy and Tawridge plunge their arms into the cavernous darkness. White-hot lasers, thin as needles, pelt into them. Tamara draws light from the sun and tosses it over the lasers, lessening their sting. The giants pull the flame to safety and place it in Tamara's hands. The oceans calm, and people terrified by the sudden storm stop running from the beaches and gaze back at the shore, wondering if they had imagined the massive waves only a moment ago.

"We'd better get that flame back to its sphere right away. It's upsetting the balance of the planet," Tavy says. "I'll take it. I can be there and back within seconds."

Tamara opens her hand, and they marvel at the beauty of the soul flame—a fleck of glitter, seeded with billions of patterns for creation—not yet ready to be known by the human family. Light showers down from the Emerald Sphere, calling its beloved home. They ooh and aah as lime-tinted stars shine in the sky, but their moment of wonder comes at great cost. More lasers escape from the mouth of the underworld and slice into Tamara's light body. She loses her balance, and the tiny flame flies from her hand into the Black Heart.

Tavy and Tawridge begin to race after it, but Tamara pulls them back. "That flame can only blossom in an atmosphere of love as strong as ours. Dark Master knows that. He wants us to enter his kingdom together so he can capture us and use us. We must not give him that chance. I will go in, and you will wait here. I'll call if I need you."

"No!" the giants shout in unison, but while they kick and spin and voice their objections, Tamara slips past them and into the underworld.

Tamara holds her hands to her heart, protecting the wound her father inflicted on her. She draws the power of her river into her being and nurtures every drop that has flowed through her since her birth as the Tamar. Loving every aspect of herself gives rise to her vibration, hopefully to a level beyond detection by Dark Master's tracking devices. She proceeds, resolving not to slip from this guardianship of herself.

Tamara travels slowly, weaving through the passageways of the kingdom, her eyes pinned to the glow of Rube in the distance. As wet as it is, the Black Heart smells like dry rot and feels as bleak and soulless as Dark Master's intent to control the world. The waters run frigid, but a filtering system pulls in warmth from the sun—enough to sustain those imprisoned here. These unfortunate souls reside in cells made of a gel-like substance, hundreds upon hundreds of them, bound together by nettings of seaweed. Narrow canals flow between them, their borders defined by petrified wood. Uneaten remains of fish litter the waterways, heads and backbones tossed out by the prisoners. Everything creaks and drifts with the motion of the sea.

Tamara moves close to Mastermind Control—an area filled with screens much like those in modern movie theaters, monitoring different areas of the world. The red fire of Rube dominates those in the innermost circle. Dark Master stands huddled within his army of black-caped warriors, his shoulders hunched and his hooded head thrust forward. Tamara scans the displays and detects a green glow on one of them. Easing a little closer to it, she determines it to be a reflection from a human aura—Mitch's, no doubt.

She speeds away from Mastermind Control. The dreaded ruler must be waiting for something specific to happen. Otherwise Kate and Miriam would not be whizzing through the underworld unhindered. She catches up with Kate and Miriam as they cruise down the canal where Kate's mother is held captive. Ruby light falls on the prisoners as Kate passes by each cell.

"Help, please!" One prisoner cries.

"Don't leave us!" another shouts.

"I will send help for everyone as soon as I can," Kate says.

Making eye contact with one of the prisoners, Miriam releases a little yelping sound. She quickly closes her eyes and returns her focus to the Devas.

A mass of darkness forms beneath Tamara. She looks down. The folds of Dark Master's cape spread over the rim of the planet, touching the restless dead. Ghosts flock into the cape. Dark Master promises to return them to their earthly lives and lavish them with riches, if they will pledge their souls to his purpose. They pledge. Dark Master sucks in their energy, and the screens of the Mastermind grow brighter.

In search of Mitch, Tamara dives beneath the flames of Rube and skims ahead of Kate and Miriam. She finds Mitch in a cell a short distance from Lara's. He sits chained to a chair. The tiny soul flame floats above his head, imprisoned by a swarm of lasers that send messages back to Mastermind Control. They splash onto a screen and project images of Mitch's brain. Emerald fire runs through his limbic system and settles in the temporal region, where his jeweled memory rests. Dark Master transports a flicker of Rube from another screen and uses it to probe Mitch's ancient knowledge. Mitch sits taut on his chair with his hands balled into fists, unaware of the ruler's tyranny.

Two thin, clear tubes fall from the ceiling of Mitch's cell. One feeds oxygen into his nostrils. The other carries his daily supply of fresh water. Mitch raises a shaky hand, releases a clip from the water tube and swigs a gulp. He keeps his eyes on the ceiling. A short while ago, a streak of ruby light shot across it. It came and went in a second, but that second was like no other. He thought of Miriam. He sensed her presence so strongly that he called out for her help.

"Da'krah, Prince of the Emerald Kingdom." The tinny voice of the Mastermind crackles through the air. "You were once a brilliant man of science … a prince of great fortune, but look at you now. You're a man of no regard, a failure. I can change that. I can return your power as Prince of the Emerald

Kingdom."

Mitch cowers. The same voice spoke to him when he arrived, saying if he cooperated he would not be harmed. Mitch thinks of Jed Flyer, who would demand to know where he was and why he was here. Jed would also know who this prince guy was by now. Mitch struggles to emulate him, but the steely-edged detective's persona eludes him. He recalls Tom Reilly's book about metaphysical adventures. "I think you've got the wrong person," he says. "I think you want Tom Reilly. He's sick. I'm in Cornwall covering a story for him."

"I don't make mistakes."

Tamara senses a shift in the Mastermind's focus, and she scoots down beneath the floor of Lara's cell. She tries to gain Lara's attention by swirling back and forth beneath her, but makes no impression on her. Lara leans forward on her chair, the weight of her willowy body resting on her feet as if at sprint point. She stares at the screen where, earlier, Dark Master threatened to show her Kate's death.

The shadows of Rube fall on Lara's cell, and her heart nearly bursts from her chest as she senses her daughter drawing near. "Kate! Don't come in." Lara wrings her hands. "You've got to leave. Go at once or you may be captured too."

"We're coming to get you, Mummy." Kate thrusts Rube into reverse, gathers speed, then plunges the flames through the bars of Lara's cell, burning them to oblivion.

"Fucking hurry up!" Miriam shouts at Kate, holding onto the girl to keep her balance as the flames twist and turn in the tiny space.

Kate steers Rube through the chains binding her mother to the chair. They melt, and Lara leaps inside the river of fire. Emotion engulfs mother and daughter, too much to express. They fall into each other's arms at once, weeping and laughing. Miriam looks on, longing for such a reunion with her daughter. Picking up on her despair, Lara draws Miriam into their hug.

"For how long do we have use of Rube?" Lara asks, assuming control.

"Until we rescue you and Mitch," Kate replies. "He's in here too. Then we've got to get the Scrolls of Knowledge."

Mitch? For a moment Lara draws a blank on that name, but then she recalls Tamara showing her images of Miriam's arrival in Cornwall. Mitch must be the man who came with Miriam. She glances at Miriam, understanding the angst burning in her eyes, but Lara must not be swayed by emotion. "Did the Goddess sanction both the rescue of Mitch and a search for the scrolls?"

Miriam hesitates under a thunderous look from Kate. "She said we had use of Rube until the turn of the tide in Cornwall." Miriam swallows hard and averts her eyes from Lara.

"You're the adult, Miriam. You must have agreed to be the wise one. We can only do what the Goddess agreed to. Did she mention Mitch? Did she mention the scrolls?"

Miriam wrestles with herself, hating to let Kate down. "She said we should rescue you and Mitch, but I guess we forget to ask her about the scrolls."

"But you and I made an agreement." Kate scowls at Miriam and then pleads with her mother. "I've got to get the scrolls back. I lost them when I was Sol'aria, and it's up to me to make that right."

"I've had several communications with Tamara, Kate. I know you turned your back on her, and that you talked Miriam into traveling into her sacred future without her guardianship. Because of that, your first duty is to look after Miriam, to see that she gets home safely." Lara holds up a hand, forbidding any back talk from Kate.

"But Kate only meant to help me," Miriam says, defending the girl. "Tamara tried to kill me. She pushed me over the cliffs because—"

"Kate!" Lara locks her eyes on her daughter. The whole vigor of her being demands an explanation.

Kate squirms and bites her lip. "I didn't say Tamara tried to kill Miriam. Gwenellen said that, and Miriam believed her."

Lara looks at her daughter out of incredulous eyes. Kate, trying to duck a confrontation with her mother, glances to the floor. She catches sight of Tamara, waving at her from the beneath the cell.

"Go on, Kate." Tamara speaks telepathically to the girl. "I heard you promise to tell Miriam the truth about me. Do it now. Get it over with and then tell your mother I'm here."

The girl pouts and twists her mouth from side to side, an expression she assumes when contemplating an apology. She huffs a breath. "I'm sorry, Miriam. I should have made it clear that Tamara would never harm you or anyone."

Miriam lets out an anguished cry. "That means Mitch tried to kill me."

"Oh my goodness!" Lara embraces Miriam and calms her down. "Let's complete our mission and sort this out later."

"Yes, come on," Kate insists, forgetting all about Tamara. "Time is running out."

Kate resumes her place at the front of Rube, and Lara smiles at Miriam. "We can take up the rear and work together as High Priestesses."

Miriam recalls the day of *The Ending*. She had allowed Lara—then Queen Leah, her mother—to take her place as High Priestess and go with Sol'aria to save Mt. Rube. She had stayed in the palace gardens, waiting for Da'krah—waiting to stand in the ruby rings with him. If she had gone with Sol'aria, they could have run to the mountain. Sol'aria would have had time to place the scrolls in the golden casket inside Mt. Rube before it sank. Kate wouldn't bear the awful sadness she carries today. "No," Miriam says. "I'll do the High Priestess job. You stay with Kate."

Lara kisses Miriam on the cheek, strides to the helm of the river, and stands beside her daughter. Miriam sinks into old hurt feelings about Mitch and falls silent to the Deva Chorus. Feelers swarm into the cell, slithering through the walls and the ceiling, feasting on her misery.

Lara flies back to her side, fighting her way through the slimy creatures with the strength of her will. "Miriam." She lays her hands on the woman's shoulders. "Rube may be the strongest force on the planet, but it will not protect you against yourself. If you can't focus on the Deva Chorus, tell me, and I'll take over."

Memories from *The Ending* haunt Miriam again. She determines to settle the score once and for all. "I can do it. You go back to Kate." Miriam clenches her jaw, blinds herself to the feelers, and opens her mind to the angelic chorus.

Mother and daughter kneel together at the helm of Rube. Lara directs Kate to create a vision of them returning safely to Cornwall. "See each one of us walking onto the beach of Trellan Bay. Create the future we want."

Kate follows her mother's instructions and selects a series of numbers on the astral disk. Rube speeds forward, but black-hooded warriors slam laser-like swords across the entrance to Lara's cell, creating a shield as formidable as a medieval portcullis.

"We can pass through them," Lara says to Kate. "Bring in the power of the sun beyond our sun: the White Sun."

"I don't think I know the code for that."

"Yes, you do. You are a Sun Master. Only you can do it. Calm your mind and listen. It will come." Lara grabs the wheel. "I'll steer. Go to work."

A terrifying moment of doubt settles on Kate. She thinks of her life at boarding school, playing field hockey and jumping rope with friends. She's just a kid, isn't she? Feelers slither toward her. Tamara pushes the boundaries of her guardianship rules and invades Kate's thoughts. "Ask for my help, Kate."

Kate's heart thunders in her chest, and she gulps a breath of relief. "Tamara … what should I do?"

"Press the diamond on your astral disk and hold it for three seconds. The pearl symbol will appear, and then follow the prompts."

The girl programs her disk, and the pearl shimmers

before her, soft and luminous and almost unbearably familiar. An ache rips through her soul, and her eyes mist over. She gulps and trembles but keeps working.

Forks of blue-white lightning pelt down from the White Sun and infuse the flames of Rube. The feelers fizzle and die. Kate snatches the wheel from her mother and rams the river of fire through the shield of swords. Explosions flare through the passages of the underworld as Dark Master's warriors flop one on top of the other like robots on a broken assembly line.

Kate swings Rube into Mitch's cell, only to meet with the huge and menacing form of Dark Master himself.

CHAPTER FORTY-ONE

Fighting Dark Master

The ruler swivels his diaphanous cape about him, and Kate clings to her mother. The closeness of the black-hooded monster confounds Lara for a moment. She draws a quick breath and begins whispering to Kate and Miriam.

An intense energy spins off Dark Master, making it impossible for Tamara to eavesdrop on the women. Kate has obviously forgotten her again, but Tamara hopes Lara will think to call for her help. As she wonders how she might get their attention without being detected by the Mastermind, a forewarning of danger taps Tamara on the shoulder. Much as she tries to escape it, she cannot.

A voluminous, blue-black cloud descends over her, and she finds herself looking into her father's angry face. Sorrow floods her whole being, and she feels her energies depleting. She raises a weakened hand to the sun, but the Mastermind slashes it down.

You have no choice!

Her father's words pound on her thoughts, and she struggles to claim her resolve to live in joy and not sorrow. She thinks of Tavy and Tawridge, and she concentrates with all her might until she glimpses a memory of them dancing beneath the oceans of the world, spreading love over the planet. She clings to the vision, pressing its image against her heart until her innermost being begins to well with happiness. The shadows of the Mastermind evaporate. She is herself again, but she has been detected.

Still hiding beneath Mitch's cell, she glances up to find Kate, Lara, and Miriam huddled together just as they were a moment ago. Dark Master hasn't moved either. He looms behind Mitch larger than before, his ego boosted by his recent manipulation of Tamara's grief. His inner voice assaults her ear.

I am impassable ... everyone belongs to me. Their weakness is but a second from my command. Even yours, Tamara. I am impassable ... everyone belongs to me...

Tamara tunes him out and looks back to Mastermind Control. She is still in its eye, but she is not at its center. Far worse—an image of the Emerald Soul Flame flickers on the main screen.

Tamara has no time to consider how the ruler managed that feat. She forms a plan of action. She envisions the crystal waters at the far end of her river, bows deeply into them, and gathers the faces of all her former charges into her mind's eye. She pulls up rays from the earth's heart and sends one to each person—to the many who live on this planet and the multitudes who now inhabit other galaxies. Each returns a love ray to her, and the mighty power floods her river. Tamara forwards it to Mastermind Control. The alien nature of this energy scrambles the vast network of its tracking systems. The screens go blank.

Chaos follows: Dark Master swivels his head around barking out orders, the women break from their huddle, and Lara waves her arms frantically at Mitch. "Hurry, jump on board."

Rube melts the chains locking Mitch to the chair. Mitch hesitates, and Miriam leaps from the flames of Rube, drags him off his chair, and throws him into the river of fire.

"T A M A R A!" Miriam yells, "Where the hell are you?"

CHAPTER FORTY-TWO

Gold's one rule

Miriam's confidence soars, and she beams with pride at having been the one to remember to call for Tamara. "You are now my guide," she says to Tamara. "I'm sorry I doubted you."

Tamara slips into the helm of Rube to work with Kate. "I'm sorry too," the girl says, sweeping her eyes up into her favored pleading pose.

"I accept your apologies."

Tamara leans in close, studying Kate's astral disk. Lara takes up the rear of Rube assuming the duties of High Priestess of Sound, and Miriam ministers to Mitch, who passed out upon landing in Rube.

Contacting Astral Command, Tamara asks the Goddess for full use of Rube. The Goddess grants her that power but insists Rube be returned to her by the turn of the tide in Cornwall. This gives them less than two minutes to exit the Black Heart and get home. They speed from Mitch's cell into the passages of the underworld.

Dark Master soon regains control of his forces and chases after them, the sweep of his cape fanning far and wide through the ocean. Tamara sends a message to Tavy and Tawridge, telling them they should pass through the mouth of the Black Heart at any moment. She keeps the bad news to herself. The giants will see it soon enough.

When the Mastermind trapped Tamara in the painful memory of her father, Dark Master siphoned enough energy from her river to ignite the Soul Flame of the Emerald Kingdom. Now it skims across the ocean heading toward Trellan Bay, no doubt programmed to tear Cornwall from the earth.

Rube exits the Underworld, and the giants climb into its flames. Tamara taps the earth-imaging icon on Kate's astral disk and narrows the view down to Trellan Bay. Emerald-tinted waves smash against the cliffs, ripping off clusters of rock and hurling them into the air. Winds uproot a bank of young fir trees in the kitchen gardens of *Penrose Hall*, and they soar into the sky, their branches peeling back with the speed of their flight.

The lights go on at the hall, and guests file onto the Atlantic Terrace. Huddled in bathrobes and blankets, they stare at the debris riding on the wind.

Tamara adjusts the imaging device back to the Emerald Flame, watching it surface from the sea and float onto the sands of Trellan Bay. She looks at Tavy and Tawridge, meeting the sadness reflected in their eyes. They do not have time to retrieve the Soul Flame. The decision Tamara hoped never to face has arrived. If she uses her power to prevent the disaster about to befall Cornwall, she will do the one thing Gold warned her not to do: She will interfere with a fate decided by Kate and Miriam back in the Time of Ruberah. She will alter their destinies. As a result, she will die, as will her giants.

Lara moves to the front of Rube and folds her arms around Kate, fully understanding the situation. She looks at Tamara and musters a brave smile. "We are ready. Do what you must, Tamara."

Tamara glances at Kate, the darling of her heart. Can she let the girl die? How can she not? Tamara's job is to guide the whole human family. The ache of the loss of her father cuts through Tamara's heart. This grief keeps her susceptible to human emotion. This grief clouds her vision.

"Tamara," Tavy whispers, picking up on her dilemma. "We can't let this disaster happen. Taw and I have talked about it, and we're willing to die to save the multitudes who would otherwise perish."

"Oh, beloved friends," Tamara's voice quavers with emotion. "I am in agreement with you, but remember, as a result

348

of breaking Gold's rule, we will die to our immortal lives. We will be reborn in the human race—into bondage, and our struggle to break free would be long and arduous."

"We know that," Taw says, "but we will die as an act of love. Love will be our last thought, and so it shall be our first when we are reborn. We will find each other and begin again."

Tamara looks at Kate, and her whole being floods with relief. Then she meets Lara's eyes and communicates with her telepathically, informing Lara of her decision. "I hope you and Kate and the many Ruberians who have completed a sacred future, will become leaders and teachers."

"I will keep Kate on track with her life's purpose," Lara says. "And I will always be at Penrose Hall, ready to help anyone who needs me."

Tamara turns to her giants. "Are you ready?"

They smile and open their arms to her. "We are."

"I have but one condition," Tamara says, "and I am resolute on the matter."

"What is it?" Tawridge asks.

"I will destroy Dark Master. That must be upon my soul, and mine alone."

"No!"

"I will hear no argument on this."

"Why?" Tavy asks.

"I am able to draw upon the energy of our sun and the White Sun. I will eradicate the ruler, but of course his death cannot be permanent."

Why not?"

"The Black Heart embodies the deeds committed by mankind's lower nature. Everybody deserves the chance to meet the consequences of those actions. That's how people learn and grow. We'd never work our way out of bondage if we deprived them of that. Let's hope I can deliver the right amount of power from the White Sun to erase the ruler for as long as it takes to save the Emerald Soul Flame and Cornwall. After that, I will fall back to Earth, and we will die together."

The giants knit their brows in pain. "If you insist," Tavy whispers. Tawridge gives a limp nod of his head.

Tamara reaches back to her river, hauling its waters to trail behind her. The giants do likewise with their rivers and they blend them together for the last time. The story of their legend flashes before Tamara. She hears their laughter as they dance across the moors. She sees the countless faces of those who have been guided by her. She rises up through the flames of Rube in her light body. Lara waves farewell, while Kate keeps her head buried against her mother's chest. Miriam remains bent over

Mitch as she tries to bring him back to consciousness, unaware of the danger at hand. The events of Tamara's eternity stream behind her in a flow of crystal clear waters. She soars higher and higher, keeping one hand aimed at the sun while positioning herself over Dark Master. As she prepares to draw energy from the sun, a burst of white light unfolds in the sky. She looks into her father's face, into the light of his love for her. Tamara blinks, wondering if her age-old longing for him has caused an illusion.

"Father," she narrows her gaze. "Are you real?"

"I am. Come, beloved child, step out of time for a few moments." He opens his hand to Tamara, and she clasps it and rises into the white light beside him. A thousand thoughts cross her mind, but one question prevails above all others: "Why, Father?"

"After the end of Ruberah, you died to your life as River Spirit to be born again into the human family. You lived many lives to gain the understanding and compassion you would need to one day form a new river for a new people. When that time came, Gold asked if I would be your father, the one who would turn you back into a river. Few on the planet would be able to muster the love and the power to do that. I could, because you were my daughter in an earlier round of time on planet Miron. Back then, we had acquired awareness in the seven jewel kingdoms. We loved one another with all the capacities and graces of these dominions. Those virtues awakened in me again, and I commanded their forces and agreed to deliver you to the destiny of your choosing.

"I viewed the lives you lived during the Age of Raging Storm, when Tavy and Tawridge ruled the moors. The giants taught you of kindness and compassion for all creatures and all people, and you developed a deep love and respect for them. If I forbade you to mingle with them, your memory of their true nature would return and you would seek justice for them. Thus, I set the cause for your rebellion and your transformation.

"When we stood upon the moors that last time and the winds blew in, the earth's heart spoke to me again and showed me this moment in time, when you would choose to break Gold's one rule. I asked to take your place. Gold granted me that right. I claim that right now. I will destroy the program Dark Master has designed to rip Cornwall from the earth, and you will continue your work."

Tamara gazes at her father, her heart in her throat. The beauty of his spirit holds her spellbound. She thinks of the long years of agony, of wondering why her father stopped loving her. Why had she not even pondered the possibility that he'd acted out of benevolence?

Tamara holds her gaze steady on the soft light of love in her father's eyes. She longs to live in the embrace of his wisdom for all time. Every particle of her being falls into harmony with his great soul. This is her grand opportunity. This is why the

Goddess insisted that Rube be returned to her on the turn of the tide. Now Tamara must act as befits Zan'drah's expectations and as befits being her father's daughter. She pushes aside her yearning to hold onto her father. "It is as you desire, beloved father."

"You are the light in my eyes and the love in my heart. You are the daughter I raised, and I am proud of you. Do not mourn me, beloved child. Rejoice in who I am."

Tamara gulps a breath, willing herself to steady her emotions. "I rejoice in you."

Her father draws the power of the solar wind into his great warrior body. "Grant me the wisdom of your feminine forces, Tamara."

Tamara bows in response, as she always did when they rode into battle together, her soul soaring with joy. Her father touches his hand to her heart, thanking her. His cheeks puff out and his chest expands. He stands tall, his back ramrod straight.

"Foretune to travel well, beloved daughter."

He dives from the sky and plunges his body into Dark Master. The ruler's black-hooded head snaps off of his body. Her father tucks it under his arm, gathers the fathoms of the ruler's cape, and drags it down to the bottom of the Underworld. He storms through Mastermind Control, slashing the screens and freeing all the prisoners from their cells. The dark empire goes up in flames and showers the planet with black confetti.

The winds die down. The seas grow calm. Tamara's father scoops the soul flame of the Emerald Kingdom from the sands of Trellan Bay, bathes it in the light of the White Sun, and slips it back through the crack in the Emerald Sphere. He runs a finger over the fracture in the globe and seals it. He strides across the night sky into the brilliance of the orbits.

He wades through the billions of tiny lights, stops at one, and taps on its side. The dot expands and fills out, like a big, silver globe. A door opens, and her father steps into his orbit.

PART THREE
WHERE HAPPINESS LIES

CHAPTER FORTY-THREE

On Trellan Bay

The tide changes, and Rube evaporates without a trace. No one panics. Tavy and Tawridge sweep Kate, Lara, Miriam, and Mitch into their rivers and float in a holding pattern a few feet from the headlands of Trellan Bay.

Free from the ties of the underworld, peace reigns over the planet, and everyone feels uplifted and happy. Soldiers in the midst of battles lay down their weapons, wondering what possessed them to want to kill one another. People engaged in the simple routines of their lives stop and smile at each other in recognition of their beauty—their sameness.

It doesn't last, as Tamara knew it would not. Her father's destruction of the Mastermind allows everyone a brief reprieve from their ties to the Underworld, and forms a reference point that will shine through in times when they come close to acting against their true nature. Within minutes, ghost forms peer over the rim of the globe, looking to reincarnate and reap the riches promised to them by Dark Master. Their desire whips up a strong wind that rips across the oceans, gathering the remnants of the ruler's cape. The ghosts chant for the return of Dark Master, and a black-hooded head pops up and sits on top of the newly formed cape. The head spins in a complete circle, then stops and faces Tamara. The tinny voice of the Mastermind drones:

Time is no more my enemy than yours, Tamara. You guide but a handful of pitiful souls, but the world at large belongs to me. In the end, I will control all the jewel kingdoms. I will control you too. Your light will die in my shadow.

Tamara turns her back on the ruler, biting back the desire to laud her recent victory over him. She swims toward Kate, Lara, Mitch and Miriam, huddled together in Tavy and Tawridge's rivers. The next part of the journey might be the hardest for Kate and Miriam. Both wrote emotion-driven sacred futures, and those original feelings will erupt again. The problem is, they can be erased only in the light of their jeweled intelligence, which, without their ruby globes, can be hard to remember.

Tamara draws up rays from the earth's heart and splashes them over herself, preparing to deal with her charges.

Kate leaves the group and swims off alone. Tamara eases alongside her.

The girl snatches up shreds of burnt parchment floating on the waves. "They're from the Scrolls of Knowledge," she says, looking up at Tamara. "The symbols are all blurred. The scrolls are gone ... blown to bits ... lost forever."

"The knowledge is not lost, Kate. It's alive in you, as it—"

"But I was the guardian of the scrolls, and I let them fall into Dark Master's hands. I wrote a sacred future as Sol'aria, promising to get them back, vowing that would be my foremost purpose until it was done. You know that. I threw that future into your river."

"Against my advice and against my willingness to receive it."

"I don't care. I promised anyway."

"That doesn't make it valid, Kate. If you remember, the knowledge in the scrolls came directly from the Goddess. She placed it in the pink stars of the Ruby Sphere, which then fell and splashed onto the scrolls, appearing in the language of rubies. When the right person looked at those symbols, they opened and shone in living images."

"Of course I remember. I dream about that at night.

So?"

"So," Tamara says, smiling kindly at Kate, "rubies embody a living, vibrant consciousness. Their force has been ever expanding throughout the universe since the day of *The Ending.* What was written in the Scrolls of Knowledge would be obsolete today. You didn't need any written instructions to operate Rube. Once the Goddess granted you use of its force, that knowledge came alive in you."

"But my mother, the Queen of Ruberah, appointed me guardian of the scrolls. She said to guard them with my life—that they would be of the utmost importance to generations to come."

"Your mother was not wrong. The Scrolls of Knowledge would have borne witness to a time in our evolution that few know about. If they were meant to be discovered now, my father would have saved them."

The girl's bottom lip trembles. "What are you saying?"

"Don't hold onto the past. Everything you need is with you right now." Tamara spots the sliver of blue-black energy in Kate's aura—Dark Master's deadly vapor. She attempts to yank it out, but Kate smacks her hand away and pulls her mouth back hard over her teeth. The muscles at her throat twitch, and her eyes darken to deep jade as she fights to hold onto the excitement of her cherished cause for living.

Tamara rivets a loving gaze on Kate, hoping she will remember her jeweled intelligence and use it to heal herself. Waves lap around them, their sound filling the silence as Kate stares straight past Tamara into the emptiness of the ocean. "I could use my earthly helper to assist me with Miriam," Tamara says, offering her hand to the girl.

"Don't touch me. Don't say anything, and don't give me any more advice. I am a Sun Master of Rube, and I can look after myself."

The girl swims to shore in a fast crawl, crashing her arms into the sea and kicking her feet with the full force of her young, strong body. Picking up on her daughter's distress, Lara swims after her.

Tamara douses herself with more rays of golden light from the earth's heart, and swims to Miriam.

Miriam kneels in the rear of Tavy and Tawridge's rivers cradling Mitch's head on her lap. She strokes his forehead, trying to help him recover from his torturous time in the Black Heart. Looking in her aura, Tamara traces the emotional fallout from her sacred future, forming a graph of sharp twists and turns. Tamara vows to stay true to the guidelines of her job, no matter how tempted she might be to bend them on Miriam's behalf. She joins Tavy and Tawridge at the helm of their rivers. "We can go to shore now."

"What about that vapor from Dark Master in Kate's aura? When did that surface?" Tavy asks.

"Just recently. The ruler has upped his effort to maintain some control over Kate, so that will keep the vapor visible. I'll find an opportunity to get it out of her."

Tawridge speaks to Tamara, keeping his voice low so Miriam can't hear. "I'm sensing Dark Master will not give up on the Prince of the Emerald Kingdom so easily."

"I suspect you're right, but we mustn't let that influence us. Miriam can use her jeweled intelligence now. She can—"

"Oh!" Tavy shakes his head. "I don't think she's given that a thought since Mitch came on board. Look at her. The pink glow in her aura is barely visible."

"Yes," Tawridge says. "She seems more in love with Mitch now than when she arrived here."

"I think it's just that her feelings for him were covered up to some extent by her attitude back then. Now they're exposed and raw. The best thing we can do to help Miriam is to believe in her. Imagine her using her jeweled intelligence to heal herself and solve the problems that may come her way."

"You're reminding us not to interfere," Tavy says.

"I am." Tamara smiles at her beloved friends, and they flow together into Trellen Bay.

Tamara spots Gwenellen right away, standing at the top of the cliffs, looking down at them. Clouds of blue-black vapors billow around her. Gwenellen preens her neck and caresses her throat, reveling in Dark Master's attention. She cups her hands and shouts down to Mitch. The sea swallows her voice, but her electric presence charges the atmosphere and drifts over Mitch as he staggers onto the sands with his arm draped over Miriam's shoulders. He begins to recall his dream of balmy seas and an island floating in a place beyond time. Someone calls his name, a woman ... young ... golden hair ... beautiful.

"Gwenellen!" His head clears and his strength returns. He shakes himself free from Miriam and heads toward the cliffs.

CHAPTER FORTY-FOUR

Mercy rising

Her masts tower into the sky and graze the stars, and sheets of dark, greasy waters spill from her stern. Those who were once imprisoned in the Black Heart crowd onto her decks and hoist her sails. *Mercy* glides toward Trellan Bay, her golden silks billowing against the night sky, her passengers cheering and embracing one another.

The freed prisoners swing their arms above their heads and chant for joy, and the young chorister leans into the prow of the galleon and sings his song. His sweet, clear voice echoes over the land. The galleon noses into Trellan Bay, and her glow radiates into the harbor of Port Issey. The villagers, already awakened by green fire and angry waves, flock to the cliffs to see the legendary ship. Phones ring around the peninsula, and local media blasts the airwaves with BREAKING NEWS.

Guests at the *Penrose* speak excitedly about the phantom ship, and the news that Lara Penrose has been seen alive on the beach. The walking ladies lace up their hiking boots and trudge through the soggy grounds toward the sea. The young honeymooners dawdle behind, and the older guests sink into chairs on the Atlantic Terrace, rocking and gazing into the glow of the galleon.

Tamara feels the spit and fire of another psychic battle brewing between Kate and Gwenellen, which tells her Lara made no headway in helping her daughter remember her jeweled intelligence. Tamara flies low over the coastal path in her body of light, scanning the area from *Penrose Hall* to Devil's Neck.

Gwenellen remains on the cliff path at the bottom of the rose arches, her gaze glued to Mitch as he climbs up the cliffs to meet her. Firebrand stands a few feet away from Gwenellen, swinging his head toward Devil's Neck and then back to Gwenellen. As Mitch nears the top of the cliffs, the stallion snorts trails of ruby light. Tamara watches them flow toward Devil's Neck, then drop beneath the cliffs and land on Kate, who lies in hiding on the ledge beside the gorse bushes.

Tamara looks quickly back to *Penrose Hall*. The walking ladies stalk up to Gwenellen. "See here, young lady," one says. "We think you're up to no good. You're a bad penny. You'd best leave people alone."

Gwenellen laughs. "Mind your own business, you old busybodies." She skips along the cliff path, pushing the villagers aside until Firebrand blocks her way. The stallion kicks his hooves into the earth and snorts as if inviting her to ride him. Gwenellen surveys the throngs of people on the path ahead staring at the golden galleon. She can't fight them all, but she could gallop through them on the horse. She prepares to draw more energy from the Black Heart, enough to obliterate the beast, if necessary, but the old biddies get in her way.

They close in on her and goad her to get on the horse. They sneer and accuse her of being frightened of him. "Scaredy-cat," they all shout. "Coward!"

The voices, thinned and raspy with age, infuriate Gwenellen. "Get away from me." She shoves the women aside and mounts the stallion.

Just then Mitch heaves himself up from the cliffs and onto the path. He dusts off his hands and dashes to Gwenellen. "My darling, I'm here!"

"Not now, Mitch." Gwenellen presses her thighs against the restless horse. "Hike back down the cliffs and go to the rocks at the foot of Devil's Neck. I'll see you there in a few minutes."

Confused but afraid of upsetting his darling, Mitch obeys and begins trekking down to the beach. The walking ladies gasp and nudge each other, giggling at the sight of his bare bottom.

Gwenellen digs her heels into Firebrand's belly, and the stallion gallops down the cliff path, forcing the villagers to move back onto the fields. The crowd thins out as Firebrand nears Devil's Neck, as few will get close to the craggy strip of land with the raging seas beneath. The stallion comes to a sudden halt, and Kate climbs up from beneath the cliffs and swaggers onto the path.

"This a warning, Gwenellen. Mitch is with Miriam. Leave him alone."

"Get out of my way, you silly little girl."

"Hurt Mitch, and you'll regret it."

"The Prince of the Emerald Kingdom belongs to Dark Master. He has ever since he was born in Ruberah and he always will. You can't do anything about it. Now move before I run you down."

"Get off my horse."

"Or what?"

"Or I'll force you off."

Gwenellen cracks her knuckles, pulling might into her hands. "Go on, then. Give it a try."

Kate nods to Firebrand and he rears onto his hind legs.

Gwenellen tries to dig her fists into his head to bring him under her control, but Firebrand crashes back down on all fours and bucks his head low, tossing her forward. He then rises onto his hind legs, throwing her back, and he repeats this over and over like a rodeo pony. Gwenellen flops back and forth clinging to his mane, afraid to let go, lest he trample her to death. Slippery with sweat, the stallion bends low on his front legs and dips his head beneath the edge of the cliffs. Gwenellen flies off the horse and plummets toward the sea.

Kate yells after her, "Got it now? Leave Mitch alone."

Gwenellen's body descends with the stiffness of a corpse, but before she hits the sea, a geyser of blue-black energy gushes up and surrounds her. She bounces on the vapors, just as Miriam had bounced on the golden light sent to her by Tavy and Tawridge. It doesn't take long before she regains control of herself. She waves up at Kate. "You'll never defeat me."

Kate stomps her foot and rubs her face against Firebrand. She's got to get Mitch back with Miriam. But for that love spell, they might still be together.

Mitch sprints across the sands of Trellan Bay, his eyes riveted to Gwenellen. Tears stream down his face—tears of relief that she seems unharmed by the fall. Even the sight of her plunging into the ocean did not awaken his memory of Miriam hurtling off the cliffs a short while ago. Mitch wades into the sea and swims out to Gwenellen, so besotted by love that he pays no heed to the golden galleon or the chill of the cool night air.

"Oh, my darling, my darling, I thought I'd lost you." He climbs onto the rocks beneath the headland and clutches at the woman of his dreams.

Gwenellen pushes him away. "We've no time for this now."

"But I've waited so long."

"Wait a little longer." She bats her eyes and softens her tone. "Please."

Mitch slicks his wet hair back from his face. "Of course, my darling."

The golden galleon edges closer to the land, her sails aflutter with the winds of love sent by those lined up along the cliff path.

Mitch drops his jaw at the sight of the vessel pulling alongside the rocks. "Where the heck did that come from?"

"You'll see." Gwenellen waves at the passengers and shouts, "Throw me the ropes and I'll secure the ship."

Mitch scans the decks, shocked by the crowds with their

long, unkempt hair and scraggly beards. "Who are all those people?"

"Be a sweetheart, Mitch. Just stand back and let them get off. Then we can be alone." Gwenellen nudges him aside, catches a rope and ties it to a boulder.

A gangplank swings down from the galleon and people begin to shuffle off the ship. Some jump into the sea and swim to shore. Others climb over the rocks at the base of the cliffs. Gwenellen's eyes devour each passing person, seeking one in particular—the one who belongs to her.

Oblivious of her quest and longing to kiss her, Mitch holds her by the waist and swings her around to face him. "I love—"

"Stop it!" Gwenellen knocks his hands off her and looks back to the gangplank. It's empty. The prisoners have all disembarked. Her eyes scour the sea, searching for the one she must find. The rejoicing crowds swim in close clusters and splash so much that she can't tell one from another.

Mitch swallows his hurt feelings and looks back to shore. Hundreds file down the cliffs. As they reach the beach, they wave and cheer at those swimming to shore. The freed prisoners surge onto the sands, and as they meet the villagers, they cheer and hug each other like victorious warriors in an epic movie.

From the corner of his eye, Mitch spots a woman who

seems vaguely familiar. She stands alone on the beach, not too far from him. She smiles and raises a brow, as if asking him if he remembers her. Her short hair falls slick against her cheekbones. He knows her, but just can't place her. He closes his eyes, thinking hard. The woman's face shimmers on the inside of his eyelids, but she's not smiling—pain clouds her eyes.

Mitch shivers and opens his eyes. A girl with flaming red hair joins the woman on the beach. Pink light glows around them both. He feels dizzy, and senses himself being dragged backward through time. The dizziness fades. He's in another world.

A woman stands at the bow of a ship called the Silver Serpent. *Her honey-colored hair flows long and sparkles with rubies. She looks like a princess from a fairy tale. A man approaches her. He wears a band of emeralds around his head. Malcontent broods in his eyes. Mitch senses the woman loves the man but that he's using her.*

Another wave of dizziness hits him, and he's standing beside Gwenellen again. His stomach knots and he feels guilty, as if he'd been the man in the emerald headdress. As if he had wounded the beautiful princess.

His past begins to crowd in on him, and he pushes it back and tries to connect with Jed Flyer. The detective eludes him, but the woman on the beach draws his eyes back to her. The girl next to her cups a handful of pink light, whispers something into it, and tosses the light to him. Her voice falls on Mitch's ear.

"That was you, Mitch, on the *Silver Serpent*. You, when you were Da'krah, Prince of the Emerald Kingdom. And that was Miriam when she was Li'ram, Princess of the Ruby Kingdom. You loved her, but you manipulated her to gain use of Rube. She's been angry with you all these years, but she's not—"

"Mitch, darling." Gwenellen swipes her hand back and forth around his ear, breaking up Kate's voice. "I think the gnats are biting you." She smiles but seethes inside. The one prisoner she needed to catch got away. Mitch will not. "It's a perfect night for a sail. The seas are calm and the air is balmy. Come. This is the ship that will take us to our tropical island." She links her arm through Mitch's.

Mitch dissolves like sugar in simmering water, as does his memory of the woman on the beach. Gwenellen hugs his arm against her breast and kisses his cheek. "Later tonight we'll sleep in a hammock beneath the stars on our own island." She drops her voice to a husky, sexy tone. "I'll make you so happy."

Gwenellen's words have their desired effect. Mitch swoons, as the dream of his own Shangri-La lies within reach. But even the promise of Gwenellen grows dim in the light of the gifts offered Mitch as he boards *Mercy*. Having left his shoes in the mine, Mitch walks barefoot. As his feet touch the golden deck, a sunburst of light from the earth's heart sweeps through his aura and wipes away the blue-black webbing of his ties to the underworld. At once, he realizes the woman on the beach is

Miriam—the woman he needs. Fond memories of being with her and her daughter fill his mind. Elaine needs him, and he can help her. His life's highest calling is to help Elaine. Nothing feels better than that. He tugs his arm, trying to pull away from the voluptuous young woman beside him. Who is she? Why does she smile at him? What is he doing with her? "Listen … I don't know …"

"Shush!" Gwenellen licks her forefinger and places it on Mitch's lips.

Words back up in his throat, and he cannot complete his sentence. Waves of blue-black mist seep into his brain, trapping him back in the paradise of his desires. Gwenellen sinks her mouth onto his. The fire in his groin leaps to life. He longs to lose himself in the luscious secrets of her body.

Gwenellen withdraws from the kiss. "We'll make love as soon as we're on the open seas." She picks up an oar and pushes the ship away from the cliffs.

"Oh, my darling." Mitch fawns at her side, "Let me do that."

"No. I can manage. This is a ship of dreams, Mitch. It will bring the dreamer whatever he wants. So close your eyes and think of our island … of soft, sandy beaches … a place where time does not exist … the eternal place between places."

"You will be there with me, won't you?"

"I will." Gwenellen runs the tip of her tongue over her lips. Mitch leans against the railing of the vessel and drifts into his fantasy life.

Gwenellen hoists the sails and takes command of the ship's wheel. The galleon heads out to sea.

CHAPTER FORTY-FIVE

On Trellan Beach

In the few moments when Mitch stepped onto Mercy's decks and realized who Miriam was and what she meant to him, a possible new future flowed into Tamara's river for him. It shimmers there now, reflecting his truest desire, which matches the life Miriam longs to share with him. Tamara reaches into the deep waters of her river and pulls the images onto the sands of Trellan Bay. Sighting the new future, Tavy and Tawridge ask if there's any chance Mitch could know about it.

"Not now. Gwenellen took care of that, but Miriam could help him. She could contact him through her ruby vision and help him to see it. Her jeweled intelligence is far stronger than Gwenellen's psychic abilities."

Tawridge strokes his chin. "Miriam hasn't said a word

since Mitch left her for Gwenellen. She just digs her feet into the sand and stares at the galleon as if longing will bring Mitch back."

"She's forgotten all about her sacred future, and she's forgotten about being a High Priestess of Sound," Tavy says.

"Perhaps we could remind her," Tawridge says, laying his biggest smile on Tamara. "Perhaps nudge her memory a teeny-weeny bit."

"No, we can't, Taw. Miriam must remember her jeweled mind by herself, and that's not very likely at the moment." Tamara points into the Black Heart. "The feelers are sucking up her angst and depleting her volition."

"What about Kate?" Tavy asks. "Maybe she could remind her."

"She could, but Kate would have to access her own jeweled intelligence first, and right now she's locked into her willful self."

"I'd never have guessed Kate would forget her ruby mind so quickly," Tawridge says. "She's talked about it incessantly since she was a small child, longing for the day when she could use it."

They watch the girl wading into the ocean, yelling at Mitch at the top of her lungs. "Gwenellen is not as she seems!

Take control of the ship and come back to Miriam."

The galleon passes the great headlands of Trellan Bay and sails into the English Channel. Tamara flows the crystal waters of her river around Miriam and magnifies the images of her and Mitch in the life that could be theirs. She highlights scenes of them traveling to exotic places, taking Elaine with them, talking and laughing, being a happy family. But Miriam remains captive to her thoughts of losing Mitch and blind to what could be.

Kate trudges in from the sea and stands beside Miriam. "We could ask Tamara to let us look through her spirit vision into the galleon. Then we could try to get Mitch away from Gwenellen."

It's not the solution Tamara had hoped for from Kate, but she's willing to give it a chance, if that's what Miriam's wants.

"I don't know, Kate. I think I'll just go home."

"You can't, Miriam. You have to finish what you came to do."

"Yeah? I came here to make things work with Mitch. He's sailing off with another woman. What about that don't you understand?"

"It's what you don't understand about it that matters. You don't know the whole story. If you leave without finding that out, you'll be unhappy for the rest of your life."

"So what else is new?"

"Come on, Miriam, don't be a loser. Tamara is right here. Ask to have a look into the galleon. See what's going on between Mitch and Gwenellen. It might not be what you think."

Miriam tosses the idea around and decides that seeing Mitch with Gwenellen might help her let go of him. "Okay. What do I have to do?"

"Ask," Kate says. "You always have to ask Tamara for what you want."

Miriam takes a deep breath and asks Tamara if she may look through her eyes into the galleon. Tamara ushers her into her arms. Kate leans in too, insisting Miriam needs her. Tamara draws them both close to her heart, which offers them a good view of the new future for Mitch shining in her crystal waters. Both look straight past it and into the golden galleon. While Kate rests in her embrace, Tamara swipes Dark Master's blue-black vapor from Kate's aura and tosses it high into space, directing it into the White Sun. The vapor sparks and sizzles, then flows into the universe in a stream of raw, clean energy.

CHAPTER FORTY-SIX

Onboard *Mercy*

Gwenellen leans against the railing of the galleon with her arms around Mitch's neck, brushing her lips over his in a teasing kiss. She draws away, hauls herself up, and sits on the ship's rail.

"Be careful!" Mitch holds her steady. "I don't want you to fall overboard."

"If your next words were the last you would ever say to me, what would they be?"

"Gwen—"

"Shush!" She stops his shocked utterance. "It's not a game. I need to know."

Mitch kisses her forehead. "I love you."

"Ooooh!" Gwenellen wriggles her shoulders. "Would you like to add a little something to that? Would you like to say, I love you and I'm yours forever?"

Mitch strokes her hair. "I love you and I'm yours forever."

Gwenellen's eyes deepen to blue-black and her hair begins to lengthen and trail down to her feet in long silky skeins. Her legs soften, turn silver and meld together into a tail. She trills a laugh. "I am a shape-shifter, Mitch. I can be many different people, but this is the real me. I am the Mermaid of Zennor, and you belong to me forever."

His eyes glaze over, and his heart sinks into the familiar emptiness of his old self, as Gwenellen flips over backward, splashes into the ocean and shakes her fist at him. "Welcome to your own Shangri-La, Mitch. You are forever in the place between places."

Tamara closes her spirit vision, but keeps Miriam close to her heart, giving her a chance to process what's happened. Gwenellen's true identity has little impact on Miriam. She thinks only of Mitch. Will he return to her?

While Miriam remains subdued, Kate leaps up and

down, squealing with delight. "I knew it!" she says. "I knew Gwenellen was the Mermaid of Zennor." The girl's pleasure ends abruptly as she suddenly glimpses the fading images of Mitch and Miriam's once new and vibrant possible future.

"Oh!" Kate slaps her hand over her mouth as the scenes of the happy family sink to the bottom of Tamara's river and fall asleep. She looks at Tamara out of soft, remorseful eyes. "I could have helped Miriam. We could have worked together as High Priestess and Sun Master. We could have freed Mitch from Gwenellen's spell. Why didn't you remind me of these things?"

"You told me not to do that anymore."

"Don't be beastly, Tamara. You could have reminded me just this once."

"You know that once a person returns from their sacred future, they are responsible to remember their jeweled intelligence. If I had prompted your memory this time, you might rely on me again under circumstances even more perilous than this one, and I wouldn't be able to help you."

"What could be worse than this? You know Miriam wanted that future more than anything in the whole world."

"But not enough to remember how to own it."

"Then save Mitch. Get him off that ship, and I'll never forget my jeweled intelligence again. I promise. Please, *please* wake up that future. Please, give Miriam another chance."

"I cannot wake up that future … it's already in the past."

The agony of Kate's mistake marks her countenance, revealing the regret she feels for having let Miriam down. "Mitch could still choose to come back to Miriam, couldn't he?" she asks.

"He's on the golden galleon, Kate. It is as Gwenellen said … a ship of dreams. Will Mitch dream of being with Miriam?"

Kate looks to the night sky, feeling it clamp over her like a spangled lid. She heaves a mighty sigh and moves closer to Miriam, who has not heard a word of her telepathic conversation with Tamara. She slips her arm around Miriam. "You're very quiet. Are you all right?"

"I don't know. I guess I'm afraid to know what happens next with Mitch."

"Let's go to my room and smoke. I'll give you back your Virginia Slims."

"No, I'd better look through Tamara's eyes again and see what Mitch is going to do. He surely won't want—"

"Don't do that, Miriam. When I first met you, I said you could do better than Mitch, and that's true. You're a super person. You can get—"

"Hey, kiddo, don't worry about me. Run along and—"

"I'm not leaving you."

Miriam tussles Kate's hair and turns to Tamara. "May I look through your vision into the galleon one more time?"

Tamara waits a moment before answering—waiting for Kate to suggest to Miriam that she look through her jeweled vision, but she can tell from Kate's expression this is not to be. She draws Miriam into her river. "Yes, you may."

"I want to see, too." Kate presses her eye to Tamara's.

"Kate!" Lara strides down the beach with Lance. "Kate … come with us, darling." Lara holds her arms out. "We're going into the house now."

"Go and be with your family," Miriam says.

"But I want to stay with you. You're my family too."

Miriam tears up. "True, but your mom and dad really need you right now."

Kate glances at her parents, standing with their heads bent together, smiling at her. "I'm so sorry I failed to get Mitch back for you, Miriam. I did lots of things I'm sorry for." Tears begin to flow down her cheeks. "I asked Tavy and Taw to cast a love spell on you and Harry, 'cause I wanted to keep you in Cornwall." She sinks her face into her hands and sobs.

"Hey ... come on." Miriam takes Kate's hands off her face and holds them in her own. "I did something much worse than that to you. I don't care what you say about this, because I know I'm to blame for getting you involved in the experiment that destroyed Ruberah. I've caused you much more unhappiness—"

"No, Miriam— "

"Yes, so what do you say we just forgive each other and move on? We're the royal sisters from Ruberah. We can do anything we set our minds to. Right?"

Kate smiles. "Right ... and I'll be a better friend in the future. I promise."

"You're great just the way you are. Now go on, go be with your parents. Scoot!"

Kate starts to protest, but Lara calls her daughter again. Miriam gives Kate a light swat on the butt. "Go on. Do as your mother says."

"Can I come to New York and visit you?"

"If your parents say so." Miriam hugs the girl and rests her cheek on her head. Their auras interlace and glow with the pale pink light of Ruberah, but still, neither thinks of blending with their ruby intelligence.

Lara smiles at Miriam and taps Kate on the shoulder.

"Come on, darling."

"Can I visit Miriam in New York?" Kate asks, looking from one parent to the other. "Miriam says I can, if it's all right with you."

Lara glances at Miriam. "I hope Kate didn't invite herself."

"Nah. She's welcome any time."

Miriam hugs Kate and her parents, and watches the three of them walk away, their arms linked around each other.

Tamara draws Miriam into her arms, and they look again into the golden galleon.

Mitch leans over the railing of the ship watching the after ripples of Gwenellen's dive. He feels empty like he did when he was a boy. Empty when his house burned to the ground down and his mother died. Alone.

He steps back from the railing. Foolish as he's been, he misses the wild ride of being so in love that nothing else mattered. What a relief from the arid landscape of his aloneness—never daring to let anyone get really close because there's nothing to know about him except shame and failure. Failure will mark his epitaph.

He paces the decks and rolls his shoulders, shedding the weight of dread—dread that Gwenellen did not really love him—dread that proved true. His heart feels crushed as if squelched against his back by some medieval torture device.

He strolls into the captain's quarters where large, slanted windows offer expansive views of sea and sky. Wide planks of golden wood cover the floors, and painted signs of the zodiac decorate the vaulted ceiling. But the room is naked of furnishings—naked like the page of a new novel. An image of Jed Flyer with his skin-tight jeans and sleek, blond hair nudges into his thoughts. Mitch suddenly becomes aware of the tear in the back of his jeans. He slaps his hand over his butt. He needs to fix that. He spots a door in a built-in compartment.

This is a ship of dreams, Mitch.

Jed tells him to think Lucky jeans, black T-shirt, and black loafers. Prada shoes. Prada is his footprint.

Mitch gulps a breath, and his heart throbs in his chest. He tugs on the door to the built-in closet. A slow grin spreads over his lips. There they are—the jeans and shoes he's just imagined. He rips off his old clothes and climbs into the new.

This is a ship of dreams. It will bring the dreamer whatever he wants.

He glances around the cabin and thinks of Jed Flyer's loft. Like magic, Jed's furniture fills the room—low-slung, black leather couches and large, metal tables stacked with books; a brown suede recliner and a side table with a gooseneck reading lamp; a state-of-the-art music system and a sleek, ebony desk; a MacBook Pro.

He sits before the computer, smacking his knuckles against the palm of his hand. Characters and plots spin in his head like apples and oranges in a slot machine. He crooks his fingers over the keyboard. Words fill the screen.

Jed Flyer rode his Harley onto the Sunset Strip, his blonde hair tucked beneath his black helmet. His muscles rippled beneath his T-shirt, and a woody, resinous fragrance wafted off his cheeks—mysterious, like the smell of a French cathedral ...

CHAPTER FORTY-SEVEN

Tuesday morning at Penrose Hall

Miriam crosses the reception hall and follows Lara outside onto the circular driveway. The women embrace, saying their farewells. Their ancient ancestry tells them they will meet again—many times. Miriam catches Lara's spirit of happiness, which helps to alleviate the sadness growing in the pit of her stomach. She hated this place when she arrived, but Lara and Kate have made it feel like home.

A plump, middle-aged woman with short, stringy brown hair walks up to Lara, a slight stiffness to her stride. An ugly dark mole sits above her top lip sprouting black hairs. "That be some climb up 'ere from the village. Are 'e Mrs. Penrose?"

"I am."

"I'm Mabel Trecarne and I'm 'ere about the job as maid, and 'e won't be sorry if 'e gives it to me." She taps the side of a large, black handbag. "I've got me references."

Lara smiles, noticing something familiar in the way she walks, dragging one leg slightly behind the other. "Your references?"

"Aye, two of 'em, just as 'e wanted."

"Right. Go on in." Lara points to the kitchen door at the side of the house. "I'll be with you in a moment."

"Gwenellen's replacement?" Miriam asks.

"She may be Gwenellen herself. A shape-shifter uses many different forms."

"Oh, my God! You're not suggesting that woman could be the Mermaid of Zennor!"

"Maybe. Before Dark Master lured her with promises of wealth, beauty, and power that might tempt even the best of us, she was a rather pleasant mermaid. She had a bit of a jealous streak, but nothing out of the normal."

"And Dark Master played on that weakness in her?"

"Yes, just as he played on your desire for love."

"Is that a weakness?"

"A desire that drives us to behave in a way that's not in harmony with our true nature can be destructive. Did you love Mitch with an open and honest heart when you came here with him?"

"Well … not exactly open and honest. I loved him, but I also wanted to punish him. I didn't understand why that feeling festered in me, but now I know. I guess it came from our lives in Ruberah."

"Yes, most likely, and that opened an avenue for Dark Master to pursue you. Gwenellen played a major role in his plan, and Dark Master probably upped the ante on her reward if she helped catch Mitch too. After all, he expected to gain the bounty of the Emerald Kingdom. The ruler likes to lay blame, and no doubt he dumped a lot of it on Gwenellen. As punishment, he took away her youth and beauty."

"He sure did a good job of that." Miriam observes the hefty, middle-aged woman as she lumbers around the house. "You won't hire her, will you?"

"Yes, I expect I will. She might change. I have to give her that chance."

"You're crazy, Lara. Dark Master could win her back at any time. Come on, tell me you're kidding."

"I may be a little crazy, but I like it that way." Lara wrinkles her nose and laughs. "Besides, without Gwenellen you might not have awakened to your jeweled intelligence—maybe not for ages to come. I'm grateful for that, aren't you?"

"My … what did you say?"

"Ah … you've temporarily forgotten." Lara laughs lightly. "That often happens to people when they return from a sacred future. You had all sorts of help while you were on that mission—your ruby globe and then, for you and Kate, Rube itself. Don't feel badly. Kate forgets hers too, but when she does and she catches herself, she just giggles and lets it go. That's such a big difference in Kate. I couldn't be happier! Still, I'm sure she'll give me plenty of opportunities to remember my jeweled mind."

Lara's mention of Rube reminds Miriam of the wonderful happiness she felt when she first bathed in its great river of fire. "How will you do that?"

"What?"

"Remember your ruby mind."

"Oh, it's easy. You just step away from your thoughts for a moment. You know … make a little space … and the Devas will come to you. You'll hear them singing just like you did on your sacred future. They'll have a message for you, but it won't come in words. You'll just know what it is."

"Really? It's that simple?"

"Yes."

"Why didn't Tamara tell me?"

"Did you ask her?"

"How could I ask about something I had no memory of?"

"Your jeweled mind is always with you, Miriam. The trick is not to let your emotions dominate you. You'll get the hang of it." Lara kisses Miriam on the cheek. "Kate put some sandwiches in the car for you. Drive carefully. We love you. Come back soon and bring Elaine."

Miriam watches Lara hurry toward the house, wondering if she could ever become as kind and fearless as she. She looks up to the small, round tower where Mitch stayed. Sunlight glitters on the crystals in the granite, and pigeons squat in the turrets, warbling. Gulls wing over them, wailing. The sea pounds against the land, drumming its eternal beat. Miriam recalls her last sight of Mitch on the golden galleon—the way he sat at his computer. The way the whole force of him seemed to run through his hands and turn into words on the screen. The way he wriggled in his chair as he conjured the story. The way his face broke into a smile when he paused to read what he'd written.

Mitch chose to live in a world of make-believe rather than share a life with her. Elaine had not even crossed his thoughts. Elaine thought Mitch loved her. In the end, it seemed he cared little for either of them.

She climbs into the small red hatchback and rests her hands on the steering wheel. She's not driven a manual shift since the VW bug she owned in college, let alone driven on the wrong side of the road. She sighs and inserts the key in the ignition.

She notices a brown bag on the passenger seat and peers inside at the lunch Kate made for her. She salivates at the sight of chicken folded between the crusts of home-baked bread. She ate a full English breakfast a couple of hours ago, but she could use a nibble. She pauses, waiting for her inner insatiable beast to rear up and demand the food. It doesn't. Miriam rests her forehead on the steering wheel, letting tears of gratitude stream down her cheeks. She wipes them away and sits back in her seat. A Mars Bar rests alongside the brown bag. She laughs, remembering Kate telling her about the Cornish Piskies—naughty little faerie folk who like to play tricks on people. Thoughts of Kate fill her heart to overflowing with love. She fondles the candy bar. Her mouth waters at the thought of the sumptuous tastes of chocolate and caramel, but she suffers no hunger pangs.

Dear God, thank you.

CHAPTER FORTY-EIGHT

Gifts from Gold

Tamara receives a message from Gold instructing her to visit Mitch on the golden galleon. "I grant you full rein with him. Help him as you deem right."

"I will do my best," Tamara says, appreciative of the trust placed in her.

"Take the crystal waters of your river with you. Everything will unfold as it is meant to be. Protect the Prince of the Emerald Kingdom, if you can. Foretune to travel well."

Tamara gathers the sparkling waters of her river and flies in her light body to the galleon. She finds Mitch still hunched over his computer, his eyes glued to the screen. She swirls around him, covering his body with her river. Her presence distracts him a little as she waves around his head, and his thoughts scatter. He writes about Jed Flyer straddling his Harley, weaving in and out of traffic on the Sunset Strip, but he loses control of the detective and the story. Jed picks up speed. Mitch tries to slow him down, but different words fly onto the screen. The speedometer on Jed's Harley hits a hundred miles per hour. "Stop, Jed, *please!*" Mitch yells at the top of his voice, but his fingers keep pounding on the keys.

His face creased in his daredevil smile, Jed upped his speed another notch. Horns blasted and tires screeched as motorists swerved to avoid the detective. The silk of his paisley scarf whipped in front of his eyes and blinded him to a red light. Jed shot through the intersection and plunged headlong into a tractor-trailer.

Jed's body lay mangled beneath the bike. Blood seeped from his head and pooled on the tarmac. A rueful expression crossed the detective's eyes.

Death leaned in. "Time to leave, Jed Flyer."

"No!" Mitch pounds his fists on the desk and lets out an earsplitting scream. The agonized sound bounces off the gold-vaulted ceiling of the captain's quarters and echoes back through his life. As it meets the anguish of his boyhood, years of unshed tears break loose and stream from his eyes. He gulps and sobs, his body shaking with pain.

Tamara lays her hands on his shoulders and directs love

from the earth's heart into his own. His tears begin to subside. He heaves a steadying breath and looks up at the computer screen. He rests his fingers back on the keyboard, highlights the description of Jed's death, and hits the DELETE key. The words remain on the screen. Mitch sinks his face into his hands. He's on the highway with no stop signs and no exits—going nowhere. Alone.

Leaning over Mitch, Tamara touches the computer screen. A golden sail floats into view. Mitch looks up, and a new vibrancy shines in his eyes. He senses Tamara nearby. "What's that?" he asks, pointing to the sail.

"Click on ACCEPT at the bottom of the screen."

He clicks without hesitation, and the golden sail falls away. A green button lights up on the task bar.

"Click on that?" he asks.

"If you wish to know the truth about yourself."

He swallows hard, moves the cursor to the button, and clicks.

A green-tinted document appears on the screen. Mitch leans in close and studies a crest at the top of the page. He touches an emerald sphere about one inch in diameter. Light radiates from its center, light so green it's almost blue. Stars, suns, dots, and waves shimmer before him.

"What does this mean?" Mitch asks.

Tamara taps the screen, and the symbols translate into English.

> *Beloved River,*
>
> *It is the night prior to my meeting with the High Priestess Li'ram and Sun Master Sol'aria of the Ruby Kingdom. Tomorrow, with their help, the human race should be the beneficiary of a force of power from our sacred Emerald Mountain, an energy that will afford our civilization a tremendous leap forward in evolution.*
>
> *The greatest scholars of our time and my people have expressed an overwhelming enthusiasm for me to ignite the Emerald Force. There was but one voice of dissention—that of Li'ram's father, the late king of the Ruby Kingdom. However, when I discussed this with him, I found him failing in health and in cognitive thought. Therefore, I remain assured of my decision to proceed.*
>
> *I have not sought your advice on this matter, as I am not able to believe in you to the extent that I would follow your guidance, should you even answer me. In the sadness of my childhood, you remained hidden to me. Why, when other children claimed you appeared to them and helped them? I am deeply wounded by this, and yet I write this letter as I might call out to you with my*

dying breath. But I write for a reason more terrifying
than death. Should my effort to ignite the Emerald
Force prove catastrophic, I do, for lack of knowing what
else to do, cast my fate into your hands.

I commit these words into the Cycles of Time to follow
me through my eternity. If one day we read them
together, then I will have wrought a great calamity upon
the human race and you will find me the most desolate
and wretched of men. If mercy be your nature, as so
many believe, I would ask one thing of you. Let me do
no further harm. Destroy me for all time to be.
I am in truth,
Da'krah, Prince of The Emerald Kingdom.

Mitch looks from the computer screen directly into
Tamara's eyes. His shoulders drop from the pent-up perch of an
engrossed reader, and his spirit vision opens. The pink glow of
Ruberah shades his sight. He reflects on the horrors of *The
Ending* and gasps out loud at the sight of the sinking *Silver Serpent*.
He hears the hard and final crack of her wooden hull splitting in
half. Li'ram's screams pound in his ears as the seas thrash
between them, separating them in the final moments of their
lives. He feels his transition from commanding prince to lost
man—the man who inhabits him today.

Mitch tugs on the ends of his hair at the back of his neck

and reviews all that's happened to him since he crossed the Tamar. He watches blue-black waves of energy rise up from the Black Heart and swirl around him on the day of his arrival at *Penrose Hall*. He cringes at the sight of himself mooning over Gwenellen like a schoolboy with a crush. He witnesses his fall into the Black Heart and his rescue by Kate, Miriam, and Lara. He's saddened by the way he's treated Miriam, but his spirits rise when he sees that she completed the sacred future she wrote for herself on the day of *The Ending*. Mortified, he watches Gwenellen lead him onto the golden galleon.

"Why didn't I turn away from Gwenellen when I realized I didn't even know her?"

"That time came and went in a heartbeat. Gwenellen was prepared for it, and she lured you right back to her."

"Why did I stay here on the galleon after I found out who she was? Why didn't I go back to Miriam?"

"Habit. When life becomes difficult, you turn to your fictional detective."

Mitch looks around the captain's quarters. "I'm finished with everything Jed Flyer," he says.

At once, the furnishings vanish, and Mitch finds himself barefoot and back in his old jeans, but he no longer cares about his appearance. He hardly recalls the detective who once inhabited his psyche more fully than himself. His thoughts come from a solid new center—a place of common sense and ease.

"I love Miriam, but I guess it's too late for that. She'll never forgive me for Gwenellen."

"She might. She's had a firsthand look at how Dark Master works."

A smile flickers over Mitch's expression. "I wonder … you know … I've always felt a deep connection to Miriam's daughter. Can you explain that?"

"Yes, I can. In a different round of time, you lived on Miron, a planet similar to Earth, but which came and went long before Earth was formed. Elaine was your daughter there. The Mironese had developed a high command of jeweled intelligence, but they miscalculated the life span of their sun, and it expired before expected. The great star exploded, turned into a red giant, and burned the planet to cinders. You and Elaine escaped in one of the many space ships that had been designed for such a purpose. Sadly, most people died before they reached the ships. You had use of your diamond intelligence, and so you charted a course for the Diamond Sphere. The Goddess of Diamonds transformed you and your daughter into light beings, and you became stars in the galaxy of White Suns."

"That's some story, and yet somehow, it feels true. So then what happened?"

"With the birth of planet Earth came another chance for

mankind."

"Yeah, I remember … Gold sent a message into the universe asking for help to begin a new age of jeweled intelligence. Elaine and I decided to go. We met lots of light beings from different stars and planets along the way." He laughs. "I recall one woman who alighted from a ruby star. I felt my human nature right then. I was bowled over by her."

"Indeed you were, and that woman would become Li'ram, and much later, Miriam."

"I hurt Li'ram when we lived in Ruberah. Why? What happened to me? Why did I fail so miserably as Prince of the Emerald Kingdom?"

"As a White Sun you had become a pure being of love— you lived in harmony with the whole universe. You faced no opposing forces within yourself, and you forgot about the nature of duality that prevails in the physical world. All desires bear the seeds of their opposites. You acted with great courage when you agreed to be born Prince of the Emerald Kingdom. You embodied a seed of light from that sphere, which allowed the Emerald Mountain to begin to rise up from the ocean. This was your purpose, and you knew full well it would take mankind many centuries to acquire the wisdom and stability to use the power of emeralds. Dark Master knew that too, but the ruler had other plans. He shadowed you from the moment you were born, and he created the desire within you to ignite and develop the

Emerald Force in the name of serving your people."

"Why didn't you intercede and help me? My mother died giving birth to me, and my father, King of the Emerald Kingdom, was away most of the time."

"Dark Master stalked you day and night. I could not reach you. He overwhelmed you then just as he did when you set eyes on Gwenellen. A while ago, as he held you prisoner in the Black Heart, he siphoned knowledge from your ancient knowing and tried to ignite the Emerald Force again. He succeeded to some extent and planned to rip Cornwall from the earth."

The color drains from Mitch's face. "I knew nothing about that. I felt nothing but fear while I was in the Black Heart. But why, of all the things Dark Master could do with that power, would he destroy Cornwall?"

"To disrupt my river and gain greater control over people. The mind of man is a mighty force."

Mitch rubs his eyes. "I'm sorry to have been so useless to you."

"You have been most useful, Mitch. You brought Miriam to Cornwall."

"Yeah, but I didn't know about her sacred future."

"You could have refused the assignment to write about Cornwall. You could have refused to bring Miriam. You didn't, because deep in your subconscious you knew she should come."

"That's amazing. Can you tell me more about Elaine? What happened to her in Ruberah?"

"Elaine never lived during that time. You both decided she should wait in the primordial until you grew up and married. Then she would be born as your daughter."

"Well, that's a blessing, I guess, but I'm angry with myself for having failed everyone so badly. I don't know how I'll live with myself."

"No child could resist the ruler of the underworld. The memory of your life back then eats at your soul; you even devised a fictional character to escape the misery. Now that you know the whole story, you can have compassion for yourself. When feelings of guilt or shame arise, remember they are distortions of your true nature. Look them in the eye and you'll see that. If you deny these feelings, they will fester and create a field of energy—the kind that opens you to the Black Heart."

Mitch runs his hands through his hair. "That makes sense. I just hope I can remember to do it."

"The future is made of shadows from the past, shadows waiting to gain your attention. You will meet them. Train yourself to take a moment before you react to troubled thoughts. Embrace the man you are now and the man you want to become. Then decide how you will proceed."

"I get it." Mitch smiles. "I really get it, but is there anything specific I can do to make up for the terrible mistakes I've made?"

"Lead a happy life. You will transmit that happiness to others, and it will affect them. This is your debt to the human family."

"But I'm laden with guilt. I can't just will myself to be happy."

"Indeed you can. Use your jeweled intelligence. Think of your Diamond Mind and let it guide you."

Mitch wants to protest, saying he has no idea how to do that, but an energy rises within him, fluttering like the wings of a butterfly. Diamond-bright light radiates in his aura, and command crackles off him. He stretches himself, assuming his full height, which seems taller than before. "I'll do my best."

CHAPTER FORTY-NINE

New endings

In her apartment in New York, Miriam looks at her daughter slumping on the sofa, her lips sealed in an angry line. Hostility palpitates off her. She's not uttered a word to Miriam since her outraged response to the news that Miriam had broken up with Mitch. Elaine's bitter accusation that Miriam had left Mitch to spite her sliced into Miriam's heart, more deadly than any weapon from Dark Master's kingdom.

The TV blares but Elaine is not watching it. She lays a hand on the place where Mitch used to sit, and tilts her head back, staring at the ceiling. Tears stain her cheeks. By the way she misses Mitch, you'd think he had been a life-long doting father instead of a sometimes TV-watching buddy.

Miriam pauses, noticing how quickly she falls into her

old habit of belittling Mitch. Elaine is far from stupid. She has a high IQ. Maybe Miriam has blinded herself to some quality in Mitch that Elaine sees—something that for her outshines all else about him.

The Ending pounds on her memory, and she recalls the hard, clear break of the *Silver Serpent* splitting in half. The compelling presence of Da'krah had slipped away, leaving a vague and seemingly lost man in his place—Mitch. Waves of compassion roll over her, softening her feelings. Mitch must carry a terrible agony over the loss of Ruberah. Da'krah had no faith in River Spirit, and so he would not have written a sacred future.

She closes her eyes, feeling grateful that she found Tamara, and that she helped free Lara from the Black Heart. Also to be reunited with Kate, her darling sister from Ruberah. Lara's advice about finding her ruby mind comes back to her. Miriam slows her thoughts and listens behind the rhetoric of her mind. Pink light shades her vision, and the gentle chanting of the Deva Chorus rings through her consciousness. It is as it is, they tell her.

"Ah," she releases a long sigh, letting herself experience the possibilities of that reality. She can do nothing for Elaine except love her and be here for her. Elaine is on her own journey, and she will change when she's ready to. When Miriam aches for Mitch or falls into want, she can tune into the Devas. Miriam breathes deeply and evenly, listening as ten thousand voices rise in song. Happiness envelops her—the happiness of great comfort and no reason.

CHAPTER FIFTY

New beginnings

Tamara drifts in her river in her glittering body of astral light, waiting for the next person ready to meet his sacred future. As she muses on who that might be, an arrow of diamond-bright light slices into her waters and lands on the stilled images of the once possible new future for Mitch and Miriam. Tamara tracks the diamond glow back to Mitch in New York. The dazzling light beam streams forth from his mind as he mounts the stairs of the subway at Columbus Circle.

Tamara watches Mitch dash across the busy intersection, heading west, darting through the crowds. The light of his aura sweeps over those around him and lifts them into a moment of hope and happiness. "Who is *he*?" people whisper, standing aside and smiling at the man with the fast, purposeful stride.

Mitch pauses outside the door to Miriam's apartment and gathers energy from the gold flame in his heart. He cups the light in his hands, gazes into it and envisions Miriam and Elaine and himself living happily together. He directs those images into the arrow of his Diamond Mind. They land in Tamara's river, and the stilled pictures of his dream life with Miriam spring into action.

"Thank you, Tamara."

Tamara bows into Mitch's Diamond Mind. "Foretune to travel well."

Mitch pats his jacket pockets. Three tickets to Tahiti lie in his left pocket. His mother's engagement ring rests in the other—a ruby surrounded by a circle of diamonds. He blinks back tears. His mother had slipped the jewel off her finger just before she died. "Give it to the woman you love, Mitch."

Tamara looks toward the boggy scrap of land from whence her tears first flowed into a river. A new soul pillar for the human family—a gift from her father in his orbit—glows above it.

The innermost waters of Tamara's heart swell with love as she recalls her recent moments with her father. With one glance into his eyes, their entire history flashed upon her spirit vision. Now she can remember their lives in another round of time, when they lived as father and daughter in the Sun Kingdom, a realm beyond jeweled awareness. Gold had asked them to return to the human family to help them evolve. Tamara smiles. She'll be close to her father from now on, as close as the moment at hand.

Soft pink light flickers at the base of the new soul pillar. Each time someone acts with the love of his true nature, the pink light increases. When the pillar is full, Mt. Rube will be raised back to Earth and the Age of Jeweled Intelligence will begin anew.

It is written on her river—written in Ruberah on the day of *The Ending*

ACKNOWLEDMENTS

Special thanks to my friend Jana Lamb for her editorial input and support through the evolution of this novel. To Scott Hale for the book cover design, and for his ever generous creative spirit. To Kathryne Squilla of LWS Literary Services for editing. To mega reader Gale Mcnish for her insightful suggestions. To Julie Blackstone for proofreading.

To Gary, thank you for your love.